Innocent Betrayal

Anthony's Story

2nd Edition

A Novel by

Cynthia Valentine

Library of Congress Cataloging-in-Publication Data

ISBN # 978-1-7371445-0-2

Valentine, Cynthia

Innocent Betrayal Anthony's Story

2nd Edition

Front Cover Design: Destiny Publishings'

Graphic Artist: Safeer Ahmed

Cover Model: Felix Mata Guerra

Editor: Destiny Publishings'

This book is dedicated to the loving memory of my #1 supporter, cheerleader, and fan...

My sister

Anita Marie Peters-Lane

Nov 12, 1957- Oct 25, 2013

*This book is also dedicated to the
loving memory of
my supportive, sweet friend and
sister in Christ for over 40 years.*

Sheila Smith Turnipseed

June 18, 1959 - Nov. 19, 2023

Preface

You say you can't believe I'm as good of a man as people say I am? It's interesting that whenever we hear about a black man, he's portrayed as a trifling dog. Brother-man is either in jail, cheats on his woman, doesn't take care of his kids, or is seen as weak if he says yes to most of his wife's desires. That doesn't make you soft; It makes you wise. Real men know when to hold and when to fold. He doesn't have to prove or say he's a man. He just is.

How about the narcissistic brother that is so self-loathing and in pain that he hates women? He lives to clip her wings. Bruh disgraces her by calling her every name except the one she owns, wounding her spirit. Dude defaces the beautiful woman he says he loves with his fist. Man, what's wrong with you? Before you attempt to answer, that question was rhetorical.

Oh yeah, the man that doesn't respect himself. This dude exhibits no self-esteem. He intentionally wears his pants, exposing his boxers as if he's locked up. To further depict prison mentality, dude unintelligently spends the day holding them up.

My Brothers, have you surrendered to the stereotype? You've been called a dog for so long; you find yourself barking at your girl. Have the lustful desires of your family jewels taken the place of you being a good father? Did you succumb to sexual favors instead of honoring the gift of God's favor? Have you forgotten or taken for granted the jewel that has always had your back amid adversity? Then somehow you have the nerve to be surprised when you come home and learn that she's left you and taken all the furniture too. Yet, when you hear that I am a good man, you don't want to believe it.

My brothers, my sisters, what that tells me is you should check yourselves. Have you considered I'm not the one with the problem? Is your world so dysfunctional that abnormal has become normal?

Sisters, what kind of men are you allowing to step to you? Perhaps you've been casting your pearls before swine. Bruh, man up! Stop being so selfish. Be the husband and father your family needs—they desire. You might end up being the happiest man in the world.

I wasn't always a good man. Sit back, turn these pages, and learn how an Innocent Betrayal almost wrecked Anthony's story.

Chapter 1

Break Up to Make Up

As far back as I can remember, my family made memories in our two-story home in Baldwin Hills, California. A breathtaking view through our den's large plate glass windows peered over Los Angeles. It also captivated and played into my boyhood imagination. I pretended to be "Nero the Superhero" on assignment to fight the forces of evil throughout the city. I went from being a superhero to a famous guitar player on my fifth birthday. Dad took me to the music store to purchase a brown Yamaha acoustic guitar with nylon strings.

Despite adverse reports from the doctors, my mom gave birth to my baby sister three days after my sixth birthday. Feelings of happiness filled the air in our home when they brought Sheila home, all wrapped in pink. Dad told me to look out for my sister and never let harm come her way. He proclaimed that she was a miracle from God that made our family even closer.

In contrast, when my baby brother Howard was born five years later, I thought my family would surely break up. There were three elements present. My mom was pregnant, my dad was working a lot, and my mom had befriended our neighbor, Miss Josie. They didn't mix well like oil, sand, and water.

My friends and I called her Nosey Josie. I wasn't very fond of her either. Anytime my mom sent me to her house for something, she would ask me probing questions or gossip about my parents on the phone.

Things got worse when my baby brother Howard was born two weeks early, and Dad came home two days later from his business trip. I had never heard my parents so mad at each other. Loud voices coming from downstairs awakened and frightened me that awful night. I crept down the wooden stairs of the kitchen when I heard my mom yelling, "Who were you with, Ray Bradford?"

Dad pleaded, "Baby, let's not do this. I wasn't with anyone."

Her voice grew even louder, "Don't insult me by lying. I can tell the two of you have something going on. Every time I turn around, she's in your face."

Dad responded agitatedly, "She's not in my face. And keep your voice down. My children are sleeping."

"You weren't concerned about your children when you were with her."

"Woman, I told you nothing is going on. I was working hard, so that you and my children can have a better life."

"I'm not a fool. I want you and your stuff out of my house tomorrow. I'm getting a…"

Dad cut her off, "That's enough, Loretta. We agreed not to say that in this house. Enough is enough! You are taking this too far now."

"No, Ray, you took it too far, and I want you out of here tomorrow."

"I'm not going anywhere. You're out of your mind if you think I'm leaving my kids, especially with you like this."

"Like what? What are you trying to say?"

"Nothing."

"No, go ahead and say it."

"We've been down this road before."

"Say it, Ray!"

"I'm not."

"I know what's going on. You're cheating, and now you're trying to make me think I'm crazy."

"Keep Josie out of my house, Loretta. She's filling your head with foolishness and tearing up your home. You are so blind you can't even see it."

"She saw you. Now you want to bad-mouth her to get out of it. I'm not playing with you, Ray. I want you out of here tomorrow, or else."

"Or else, what?"

"Don't try me, Ray."

Dad's voice grew louder, "Or else, what? Loretta! Are you threatening me now? What are you going to do?"

I heard a slapping sound, so I ran downstairs by the kitchen door and peeked around the corner. My dad was holding my mom's wrist. She was grappling, trying to get loose. Dad said, "You tried to hurt me."

Mom just started crying, "Let me go!"

Dad let her wrist go and offered, "I'm so sorry I hurt you. I know I wasn't here."

Mom yelled again, "Just tell the truth; stop lying, Ray!" She slapped him in the face.

My dad attempted to grab her wrist again, but she was swinging her arms all over. Confusion and fear provoked me to run over to my dad. I started hitting him in the legs, hollering, "Stop it! Leave my mommy alone!"

Dad turned around, grabbed my arms, and said, "Stop, Anthony"! Pulling me behind him, he made his way to the dining table. He sat down and pulled me close to him. "Son, I'm not doing anything to your mom."

"Why is she crying?"

Dad looked up at Mom standing in the archway, "Lorretta, do you see it now? Talk to your son."

She indicated yes by nodding her head. Dad invited her to sit on his lap. He held her tight and kissed her on the cheek. She sat with her head down for a moment. Then wiped the tears from her eyes.

"You okay, Mom?"

She rubbed my head, "Mommy doesn't feel well. I need to get some rest. Why don't we go upstairs and check on your brother and sister? After that, I'll lay down with you until you fall asleep."

By morning, there was a quiet shift in the atmosphere. After breakfast, Dad took Sheila and me over to my grandparent's house. We visited them for about two weeks.

Our parents acted like they loved each other again when we came home. Deep down inside, I was angry at my dad. He had hurt my mom and made her cry.

By the age of twelve, I emerged into the studio culture. I earned money by emptying trash, running errands, and completing other duties. Folks at the job would whisper that I was a carbon copy of my dad. I was exposed to all different genres of music. Neo-soul, oldies, R and B, and gospel were my favorites. I would often be found in the halls bobbing my head to oldies.

Ricky and Daniel were brothers who were about eight years older than me. They were also the nephews of Jack Housen, the top music executive at the studio. After finishing my duties around the studio for the day, I sometimes sat in with them in the Artist and Repertoire department.

By the time I got to college, I had transitioned from errands and trash into A and R. That's when Ricky and Daniel taught me other fringe benefits of the industry. While on music tours, we would party, drink, and dip in the pools of many women.

At 20 years old, I had a job that paid good money. I was on the Dean's List in school and had pledged Kappa Alpha Psi.

Not only that, but I had also gotten my own apartment near the college, my first BMW, and I had a smorgasbord of women. That is until Tangi literally stopped me dead in my tracks.

She was a backup singer who worked for the studio. Initially, I was attracted to her because she loved sports and had a charismatic personality. We'd watch the game together on the road and talk all night like she was one of the fellows.

Tangi and I started playing around and flirting during rehearsals or on the tour bus. After a while, I struggled to get past the curves that defined her sexy body. Her high yellow skin tone illuminated her brown eyes, dimpled cheeks, and alluring smile.

It was a natural transition from flirting on the tour bus to fooling around just short of going all the way. The transaction was completed once we checked into the next hotel.

Our supposed one-time thing turned into a fling that neither she nor I allowed to end. Like two infatuated children, keeping it on the low, she and I worked at the studio by day and played the part of lovers a few nights a week.

However, our secret was exposed when Daniel brought in a beautiful new talent named Shante'. She was assigned to me, so I spent lots of time working with her on development. This cut into the time I was spending with Tangi.

One evening, I was in the booth with my eyes closed, singing a love ballad with Shante'. My eyes opened, and I encountered Tangi's disgruntled face through the pane of glass. She was standing behind Daniel and Ricky, who were on the mixing boards.

Daniel offered, "Man, that was smooth when I came out of the booth. I could feel the passion." Noticing Tangi standing behind him, he said, "Hey, I didn't know you were here. Are you singing back up for Shante?"

"No, I came to see Anthony."

I asked, "Can I call you in a couple of hours, Tangi? I need to focus on my artist right now."

She sat down and folded her arms, "You have no trust credit, Anthony, since you don't know how to return texts or phone calls."

Daniel interjected, "Do we have a business situation here, or is this personal?"

"Oh, it's very personal." She glared at me, "You didn't tell them, Anthony? While spending late nights focusing on Miss Shante', did you tell her you are sleeping with me? Could it be you are sleeping with her, too?"

Embarrassment, coupled with anger, invaded my soul. Shaking my head, I asserted, "You can sit in the lobby or go home and wait until I call. Either way, this is not going down. I don't need this kind of energy while I'm trying to work."

With a wrinkled forehead, Ricky cut in, "This seems like a good time to take a break." As he walked past, he offered, "Handle your business. We'll be back in fifteen."

As soon as they walked out, I went in on Tangi, "What was that? I thought we would keep our business out of the studio?"

"Maybe they should know."

"Know what? I thought it was about hanging out and having good sex. I don't recall a commitment."

"Do you hear yourself, Anthony? You make me sound like a tramp."

"It's what we agreed on."

"I didn't agree to be a tramp."

I'm not saying you're a tramp, but I wasn't aware that we had an exclusive relationship that required us to check in, either."

After a brief moment of silence, she walked in front of me and delicately expressed, "I haven't heard from you in two days. You haven't called, sent, or even returned my text?"

Her tender tone obscured my anger. I drew her close, "I wasn't trying to put you off. When I'm working, Baby, I get in a zone. I've been focused day and night on Shante's showcase."

I paused before I kissed her lips and asked, "Where is this going, Tangi?"

She rubbed my chest, looking into my eyes, "It didn't feel good not hearing from you."

"It seems like you want more than a bed buddy."

"Maybe so," She poked me in the chest, "But I do know I didn't like how you and Shante' were feeling each other in that booth."

"She's my artist, and that's it." The Stylistics, Makeup to Break Up, was dancing in my head when I reached into my pocket and handed her my house key. "Why don't you wait for me at my place? I think we have a lot to talk about. Just promise me you won't do anything like this again."

That evening, after a long conversation, we agreed we would date exclusively. We also reaffirmed our commitment to keeping our relationship professional at work.

Although Tangi and I reached a resolution, the fellows and I did not. The next afternoon, I couldn't get in the studio well before Daniel started his rant, "Man, what was that last night? Please tell me you didn't slip up and sleep with Tangi."

"I did."

"What were you thinking? You don't play where you work."

"She's not like the rest of them. I like her."

Daniel forged, "Hear me loud and clear. Last night was just a precursor of what your world will be like if you don't end it."

"It was just a misunderstanding. No harm."

She messed with my money, and I'm not feeling it when my money is involved."

"I feel you, but it's all good now. Tangi was feeling a little insecure. We discussed it and agreed to keep things professional at work. It won't happen again."

"I have a question." Daniel said, "Was that the agreement when you slept with her the first time?"

"Yeah."

9

"And yet she was here clowning last night."

"Trust me. I have it handled. I gave Tangi a key to my place. She can see me there."

Ricky entered the room, "What's up, fellows?"

Daniel snickered, "My man is not only sleeping with Tangi. She's his girl. And check this; he gave her a key to his place."

"Anthony, say it ain't so. Haven't we taught you anything?"

"What, Rick?"

"Man, you know the rules. Never mess around with women you work with. Jump-off women are met, messed around with, and left jumped off. They never come to your house. Now you've given her a key. Rules are not meant to be broken. She showed you who she was last night."

Daniel cut in, "That's what I told him."

I rebutted, "Nah, we're good. Besides, Tangi is not a jump-off chick."

Rick said, "I heard she was a crackhead."

"Nah, that's foolishness. She drinks a little wine, but that's it."

"I thought for sure I saw her drinking some Hennessey," said Rick.

"Quit playin', man. She's not doing all that. It's just talk. You know the rumor mill around here."

"Okay, but what if it's true? What happens if it doesn't work?"

"It's not true, and it will work."

Advice taken: Innocent.
Advice ignored: I'm betraying myself.

Chapter 2

It Takes a Fool to Learn

Things were pretty smooth with Tangi and me for about two months. We didn't have any issues at work because we never crossed each other's paths. She had no reason to be insecure because she and I spent almost every night together at her place or mine.

On her birthday, I showed up at her place unannounced. She opened the door and smiled, "What are you doing here? I thought you told me you would be tied up at the studio all night."

"I wanted to surprise you. I got box seats for the Lakers game and thought you might want to go to celebrate your birthday."

"Come on in, you."

As soon as I entered, I noticed that the place smelled like weed. I asked, "Is that you smoking?"

She countered in an aggressive tone, "Why are you questioning me? That's probably why you showed up unannounced."

"Woe, slow your road! Unannounced? Is there such a thing as unannounced? We have keys to each other's place. You are at my place more than you are at your own. I told you I wanted to surprise you for your birthday. The essence of a surprise is to show up unannounced."

"You don't have to come in here questioning me."

"I'm not questioning you, Tangi. I'm just stating the obvious. This place reeks of weed."

"And that's a problem because?"

"Your defensive because? Tangi, it's a problem because you are being defensive. I think I have the right to know what you are into if we are in a relationship."

"Fine! I smoke at home sometimes."

"Why all the attitude?"

"I don't have an attitude."

"If you say so. Is there anything else I need to know?"

"Like what?"

"Is this it, or are you doing anything else?"

"Yes, this is it. It relaxes me after I get off work. You know how tense it is in the studio."

"I know there's tension, but what's wrong with unwinding with a book, a hot bath, or a glass of wine."

"A book or wine might be your thing, but weed relaxes me." She came close to me, whining, "Are you mad?"

"Nah, I don't understand all the attitude, and I don't know how I feel about my girl smoking weed."

"What if I told you it gets me turned on?"

I pulled her around the waist and kissed her on the lips. "I'd ask what you were doing before I got here, and where can I get some of what you had?"

"I can show you better than I can tell you."

After Tangi and I finished fooling around, she fired up a blunt and offered to share it. I was reluctant at first, but then I went all in. I have to admit, that was some good stuff. We got so high we forgot all about the Lakers game. Our time was spent sexing, smoking, and drinking.

The tone was not only set for the evening, but it was also set for the next four months. I was drinking and smoking weed so much that I even started doing it by myself. Alcohol and weed aided in my diminishing performance at work. I was showing up late and missing appointments. I even missed my flight for a critical engagement out of town once. Needless to say, Jack was livid.

My parents were unhappy with me because they felt I was starting to make wrong turns. I stopped attending church because I didn't want to be a hypocrite.

Sunday dinner with my folks wasn't an option. I discerned I was embarrassing my dad at work because he barely talked to me while we were there. Judgment and disappointment on my parent's faces weren't something I was looking forward to.

Daniel, Ricky, and I started butting heads at the studio. They did a lot of things, but they were vehemently opposed to drugs. When they discovered what I was doing, we no longer partied together.

My drinking and experimenting with drugs finally reached a sobering reality. This A-student received a D in History and was in jeopardy of failing three other classes. My frat brothers got on my case because of my behavior. Humiliation occupied me when they had an intervention, and I was the special guest. That was my bottom.

Since I cared a lot for Tangi, I wanted her to get sober too. One evening I expressed my feelings to her concerning the matter. Collectively she and I both agreed to stop getting high and drinking.

I am reminiscent of a time when I had not used it for a couple of weeks. The old me was coming back, and I was feeling great. I got there due to many prayers, a made-up mind, and determination.

Concern interrupted my victorious season while I was on a business trip. My telephone calls to Tangi were unanswered for at least two days. Positivity tried to keep the upper hand, but my imagination got the best of me and started spinning "It Takes a Fool to Learn" in my head. Who or what she was doing became a mainstay in my thoughts. Going over to her place moved to the first spot on my "to-do" list.

Once my flight landed in LA, I learned "what" she was doing was the clear winner. A knot of disappointment jumped in my throat when she answered the door with glassy eyes and every word slurred. This ex-dope comrade knew she, indeed, was high.

I came inside, closed the door, and probed, "I've been calling you, and you didn't answer. What's going on?"

"Nothing, I'm just relaxing."

She walked toward her living room, and I followed. "I thought we weren't going to do this anymore."

"Do what, Anthony?"

I rubbed her face softly, "Get high."

"So now you're checking up on me?"

"I came by because I was concerned. I've called you for two days, and you didn't answer."

She sat on the couch, "I didn't feel like talking to anyone."

"I'm not anyone, Tangi. I thought we were supposed to be in a relationship."

"We are."

I sat beside her. A stabbing pain of hurt joined the knot of disappointment in my throat when I noted a line of cocaine on the table. Gesturing toward the Coke, I asked, "What's this? Is this you?"

I rather a man would have come out of the room whom she was cheating with and announced it was his. But she said, "I told you I was relaxing."

"With cocaine?"

"It's been a rough week. I needed something more."

"You told me you only smoked weed and had stopped."

"I did stop." She moved closer to me and whined, "I just needed a little something while you were gone. I missed you so much."

"Weed is one thing, but when did you start using cocaine?"

"I told you I could stop any time."

"That's what you said about weed. We both agreed we would stop and get our lives together."

"I'm trying to stop."

I got up and started pacing the room with reality. "No, you can't stop. You can't stop weed or cocaine. Tangi, you're an addict. We need to get you some professional help."

She raised her voice, "No! I told you I don't have a problem!"

"That's the first sign that you have a problem. You deceive yourself into thinking you don't."

She stood, "I'm not deceiving myself."

I started for the door, "I have to go."

"Don't you want me? Don't you care about me?"

"Yes, that's why I want you to get some help. I don't want you like this. It's a turn-off."

"I promise you I'll stop. I don't want to lose you."

"You can't do it for me. You have got to do it for yourself."

"It is for me." She started crying, "Just don't leave me."

I covered my forehead with my hand, "I'm going home, Babe. Why don't you get some sleep? We can talk in the morning."

She pleaded, "Take me with you. That's the reason why I got high. You left me all alone."

I put my head down. At that moment, I realized this was a bigger problem than I had initially thought. I felt like an idiot for getting involved. And like a jerk for going down the wrong path with her instead of leading her to righteousness. I kissed her on the forehead, and offered, "I will take you somewhere this weekend when you're doing better."

"That's cold."

"Tangi, you're slurring, your eyes are glassy, and you can barely walk."

"Why don't you stay here with me at least until I fall asleep?"

I lay in bed next to this stranger who was once my friend. The beauty I used to see in her face, and the curves of her body I used to love were marred by a sour taste in my mouth. My eyes were now opening. I no longer recognized her as I thought I knew her. I felt Tangi had faded, and I was involved with an addict. Once she'd fallen asleep, I put the set of keys I had to her place on the side table near the door and let myself out.

I didn't feel like going home, so I went to my parent's house. I sat outside for a moment, pondering what I'd done to my life. Guilt gripped me by the neck every time I thought of Tangi. My dad always told me to care for, love, and cherish women.

Humility convinced me to swallow my pride, go inside, and ask my dad for help. I really needed his support, wisdom, and guidance. Finally working up my nerves, I got out of the car and went inside. I greeted my mom briefly in the kitchen and went into the den, where my dad was watching TV. I asked, "What's going on, Pops?"

Barely looking up at me, he responded, "Hey, Son, I wasn't expecting to see you back until tomorrow."

"We got finished early, so I got a flight out."

"It's good that you weren't around the studio yesterday."

"What happened?"

"That backup singer named Tangi got fired. Jack said she had been missing gigs or showing up late. To top it off, she came up to the studio drunk, high, and talking loudly. He fired her on the spot. From what I hear, she's an addict."

I was so embarrassed. This definitely wasn't the best time to talk to my dad. I skipped the subject, "Jack left me a message on my cell. He wants to meet with me on Monday. Do you know what that's about?"

"He says he's cleaning house."

"That doesn't sound encouraging."

"I'm not trying to encourage you. You need to expect the worst. The way you have been carrying on is ridiculous."

"I know I haven't done everything right, but I wouldn't say it's ridiculous, and I would expect my father to support me."

"You created your current situation. Therefore, you must suffer the consequences. You've got to fight this battle on your own."

"I don't expect you to fight for me. Just believe in me. You act as if you've never made a mistake."

"What do you mean by that?"

"You've made mistakes, Dad." I sighed, "Never mind, it doesn't even matter. I'm out."

My stomach was in knots when I got to the studio on Monday. It began to rumble as I pondered if Jack would fire me. I went by his office. His assistant Patsy told me Jack had a family emergency and would be late. I sighed with relief.

Later that day, he came in briefly, but I was in the sound booth with my artist. He didn't want to disturb me, so I dodged the bullet that day.

It had been a few days since I had last spoken to Tangi. The idea that she was using crack cocaine and wouldn't get help was a turn-off. Clearing my head was a priority. That meant I ignored her texts and phone calls. I didn't even go to my apartment because I feared Tangi might drop by. My frat brother Craig let me hang out at his place.

The next day when I went into the studio, Jack still wasn't there. Sheena, my new artist, and I were in my office when Tangi came in. I could tell she was high, and her breath reeked of alcohol.

With slurred speech, she inquired, "Why haven't you called me?" She gazed and gestured towards Sheena, "Who is this trick?"

Not wanting a scene, rubbing her face, I inclined her, "Baby, you know how I get when I'm working. Why don't you go to my place? I'll meet you there in a couple of hours."

Her voice escalated, "I'm not going anywhere! I've been at your place for two days, and you haven't come home! You think I don't know what's going on! I know you're sleeping with someone else!"

Still trying to quiet her, I indulged, "You are the only woman for me. Baby, I need you to quiet down. I just got back in town yesterday and came straight to the studio. I promise I will come right home, and we can talk about it." I took her by the hand, "Let me walk you to the car."

Sheena interposed, "She doesn't look like she is in any condition to drive."

Tangi whirled around, "Who do you think you are? Don't judge me!"

"I'm not judging you. It's obvious to the eye that you cannot drive."

"I was trying to calm her down, Sheena. Can you give me a couple of hours? I need to take care of this."

"Clearly." She got up and started moving towards the door. "Hit me on my cell."

Tangi motioned towards Sheena, "You low-life trick! You better stay away from my man!"

"Chick, you are a non-factor. Get out of my way while I still feel sorry for you. Clearly, you are a drunken, insecure addict who needs help."

I shook my head, "Sheena, this is not helping."

"Is this your girl, Anthony?"

I just stood there like a deer in headlights. I was too embarrassed to say yes. But I knew if I said no, Tangi would cause a mess. So, I said, "It's complicated."

"Well, handle your little complication. This is too much drama for me."

Tangi got even louder, "So it is what I thought. You think you will get rid of me and hook up with her later." She grabbed the back of Sheena's shirt, and asserted, "Stay away from my man!"

I snatched Tangi and loosened her grip. Sheena stated, "I can't believe you grabbed me. Anthony, I didn't sign up for this drama."

"I'm so sorry. I'll handle it."

"Handle it, Anthony or Jack will hear about this."

Ricky came to the door, "What is going on in here? I can hear yawl down the hall."

Sheena held, "Anthony's little drug-addicted complication is out of control. I'm done!" She walked out. Ricky exited behind her.

I turned to Tangi, "Do you realize what you've done? You're going to make me lose my job."

"What I've done? You are the one sleeping around."

I yelled, "I'm not sleeping around, Tangi! I'm just turned off by you. I don't know what's worse, your insane jealousy or your addiction. Here's the truth. I haven't been out of town. I didn't want to go to my house because you might be there."

"Oh, is that how you really feel." Tears started coming from her eyes. She leaned back on the edge of the desk, "So, are you saying it's over?"

"Tangi, I can't do this anymore. You come to my job clowning and refuse to get help for your addiction. So yes, it's over."

"What about your baby?"

"What baby?"

"That's what I came by to tell you. I'm pregnant."

I was overcome by emotions, and my heart dropped to the floor. I leaned on the desk next to Tangi and softly inquired, "Are you sure?"

"Yes, I took a test."

"How far along are you?"

"Six weeks."

"Why didn't you tell me?"

"I just found out myself."

"Tangi, you have really got to get some help. You don't want the baby to be affected by the drugs, do you?"

"Why do you care? You said you didn't want me anymore."

"I'll always care about you and be there for the baby."

"What about me?"

"I told you. I will always care about you and be there for the baby."

"You sound like a broken record. Let me get this straight. You want the baby but not me."

"It doesn't matter whether I want a child or not. What real man doesn't want to take care of his children?"

"And me?"

"I will always care about you, respect you, and support you as my child's mother. But I can't pretend. I am not doing this anymore. I'm done."

"Fine, I will get my things from your apartment. I'll leave the keys on the kitchen counter, and you won't hear from me anymore."

"What about the baby and getting some help."

"We're not your concern."

"Let me take you home. We need to discuss getting some help. We need the baby to be healthy."

"No. I don't need a ride. My sister is waiting for me outside."

"Tangi, what about getting help?"

"You said you don't want me. I'll let you know if I'm keeping the baby."

"Please don't do that."

"My baby, my body. I'll let you know." She walked out.

I sat at my desk in disbelief until Ricky came in and asked, "What the heck happened? Sheena is furious. How are we going to handle this? If Jack finds out, he is going to hit the ceiling."

"I messed up. I'll fix it. I guess this is when you say, I told you so."

"No, man, this is when a true friend shows compassion. Why don't you go home and pull yourself together? Your dad just got here. You are in no condition to deal with him right now. I got you covered. I'll come by your place later, and we'll figure this out."

"My head is all jacked up. Tangi just told me she's six weeks pregnant. She's a drug addict, Man. What kind of chance does the child have? I know I don't need to be here. And the last thing I need is my dad's judgment. But I can't go home. Can I kick it at your place? Tangi is supposed to be getting her things from my spot. I can't deal with her right now."

"Yes, you can go over and chill."

"I was hoping you would say that. Thanks, Man. I know I messed up, and you have every reason not to deal with me."

"We all make mistakes. You will always be my boy."

"Thanks."

As I was gathering my things, my dad came into my office. "What's going on, Son?"

"I'm not feeling well. I'm on my way home."

"I just got a call from Sheena." The rhythm of my heart sped up as my dad continued. "She said there was an altercation between her and Tangi. That was disturbing because, first, this is a place of business. Second, I know Tangi to be a drug addict who no longer works here. Third, somehow Sheena was under the impression you were in a relationship with Tangi. Explain that to me, Son."

"We were in a brief relationship."

"You didn't think it was important enough to tell me that the other day when I brought her name up?"

"That wasn't a good day to tell you anything. You were too busy sitting in a seat of judgment."

"I wasn't judging. We only exchanged a few words before you stormed out."

21

"You act like you never made mistakes."

"I have made mistakes. That's why I am trying to prevent you from making some of the same foolish ones. Son, why do I feel you are speaking about something specific? What's on your mind? Talk to me."

"I'm referring to the time you cheated on Mom."

"I have never cheated on your mother. Where did you get that foolishness from?"

"I heard you and Mom arguing. She was mad because you were with a woman when you were supposed to be out of town on business."

"When was this?"

"Around the time Howard was born. You guys argued about it. I heard the two of you fighting in the kitchen. Mom slapped you, and then I came in. The next day you and Mom sent Sheila and me to Granny's house until yawl made up. I've never forgotten about that. You hurt my mother by cheating on her. So how can you judge me?"

"Is that what all this is about?"

"All what?"

"The nasty disposition you display towards me from time to time."

"Call it what you want."

"I know how things appeared that night, but your mother…."

I raised my voice and stepped towards my dad, "Don't start in on my mom! You were the blame! You were the one having an affair, not her!"

Dad countered and said, "Step back and bring your voice down before I knock you out. I don't care how mad you think you are. I am still your father. Lorretta was my wife before she was your mother. I wasn't about to speak ill about my wife. I wasn't having an affair."

"Then what was that about?"

"Ask your mother. I would rather she tell you. I wish you had come to me sooner. It upsets me that my son thought terribly about me for many years. The one thing I have always tried to keep is your respect. I don't ever want you to be ashamed of me."

"Like you're ashamed of me?"

"I'm not ashamed. I am disappointed. You have so much going for you. You are intelligent and a master at your craft. I don't understand why you're running around with a young lady like that and doing God knows what else."

"I didn't know she was like that. Things just got out of hand."

"Well, it's over now, right?"

"No, it's not. Tangi says she's having my baby."

"Do you believe her?"

"Why wouldn't I?"

"Did you wrap it up?"

"It didn't get there a few times."

"What were you thinking? Are you out of your mind? We've been over this."

"Clearly, I wasn't thinking. I did a whole lot of things that weren't smart. If I could take them back, I would. I'm in trouble, Dad."

"What do you mean?"

"My grades are slipping. I didn't know how heavy Tangi was into drugs. As many drugs, as she uses, something could be wrong with the baby. My child can come out all jacked up. After what happened today, I know Jack is going to fire me. I messed up, and I've been trying to straighten it out, but I don't know what to do. I need you, Dad."

"It sounds like it's time to turn it over to Jesus."

"I haven't been to church in a month of Sundays. I'm sure I'm the last person God wants to hear from."

"That's not true. Every day there are new mercies."

"I need all the mercy I can get."

My dad came over and wrapped his arms around me. I cried on his shoulder as he took my burdens to the Lord in prayer. Then he took me to lunch, and we had a heart-to-heart talk. I told him everything about me, Tangi, the alcohol, and the drugs.

As we were going to the car, my cell rang. It was my neighbor. He said water was leaking from my apartment to his unit beneath me. My dad volunteered to go over to my place with me.

I entered my apartment and could hear water running in the bathroom. I figured Tangi had been there and spitefully left the water running. Moving towards the bathroom, I noticed that the water had even saturated the carpets in the hallway.

I turned the water off, then went into my bedroom to see if she had done any damage there. I was caught off guard when I saw Tangi lying across my bed, face down, with my robe on.

I called out to her, "Tangi!" She didn't respond, so I shook her to wake her up. She still didn't move. Noticing a pill container on my nightstand, I called out, "Dad, call 911!" He quickly entered the room and picked up the phone on the nightstand.

I checked her pulse, and there was none. I called her name repeatedly as if she was going to answer. Finally, the shock subsided, and reality set in. I grabbed her in my arms and held her close to my heart. I knew she was gone. I cried out, "Why, Tangi!" and then wept like a baby until the paramedics came. They pronounced her dead at the scene.

Advice taken: I would have been innocent:
Advice ignored: I betrayed myself...

Now: Look at what has happened.

Chapter 3

Misguided Ghost

The police were all over my apartment. Barrages of questions were thrown at me while Tangi's body lay thirty feet away in my bedroom for hours. Once the coroner took her remains, a police officer named Raymond presented me with a bag of cocaine, meth, and some other drug paraphernalia and asked, "Does this belong to you?"

I sighed, "No. It must have been hers."

"How do I know that?"

"Because it's not mine. Tangi is the only other person it could belong to."

"Isn't this your place?"

"Yes, but I haven't been here for a few days."

"Why was she here?"

I covered my face with my hand, "I've already been over this with the other officers."

"Humor me, and let's go over it again."

Dad intervened, "His girlfriend just died. Can't you see he's upset? He's been over and over this. I don't see why this can't wait until tomorrow?"

The officer closed his book, "Alright, but be at the station tomorrow at noon. This place needs to be processed. He's going to need to stay somewhere else until it is released. It might be wise to get an attorney."

"What are you saying?"

"This is his place. There were drugs found on his premises. He says they are not his. If there's no evidence to prove otherwise, he might spend some time in prison."

When Dad and I arrived, Jack and our corporate attorney, Joshua Rodgers, were at my folk's house. My emotions were all over the place. I was upset because I still loved Tangi despite not wanting to date her anymore. Fear was lurking, taunting me with the possibility of prison. Shame now owned me, claiming I allowed myself to sink so low. However, there was a light of encouragement. Even though I made many mistakes, Jack and my dad were still there for me.

Joshua had me rehash the day's events and my back story with Tangi. After they left, I didn't feel like going downstairs to dinner. My mom sent me a plate up by Howard. At the time, he was ten or eleven, curious and full of probing questions. "What's going on? Why were Jack and all of them here? Mom won't tell me anything."

I sat him beside me and explained, "Your brother did some stupid things that I never want you to do. I might be going away for a while."

"Where too?"

"We will talk about it later. I want you to remember that whatever dad tells you, do it." I hugged him, "You know I love you, right?"

With a look of ambivalence, he nodded, "Yes."

"There is nothing I wouldn't do for you in this world, Howard."

"I know, but what's happening to you?"

"I made some bad choices. Now I'm trying to figure out how to fix them."

He leaned forward and rested his elbows on his legs, "You have Dad helping you. He won't let anything bad happen."

I stood up and started for the door, "I love you, Dude. I'm going to go to my room."

I went to bed that night heavy and barely able to sleep. When I did drift off, I kept waking up and discovering that my reality was an endless nightmare.

Mom made me my favorite omelet in the morning, but it didn't soothe me like it usually did. Afterward, Dad drove me to the police station, where we met up with Joshua. My thoughts traveled back to a few days prior. At that time, I dreaded the meeting I was supposed to have with Jack. Anxiety caused my stomach to rumble. That day, I would have instead been facing the loss of a job. Now, it is the loss of Tangi's life and possibly my personal freedom.

Officer Raymond asked me a few more questions. Then, I was placed under arrest. Joshua pleaded for me to be released on my own recognizance. We were told I had to be booked. Since it was Friday, I would have to wait to see the judge on Monday.

I was searched, fingerprinted, and stripped of my clothes. I took a mug shot and went from being Anthony Bradford to inmate number 5554. Jail was an awful experience. No, I wasn't raped or beaten up. It's just an experience that I don't care to talk about. I will share that I was left with myself to think and pray. Self-reflection brought on revelation, which revealed how I'd been acting like a follower and not a leader, a boy and not a man, a rebel and not a respectable citizen, and a heathen and not a saint.

I thought about Tangi taking her own life along with a child I will never get to meet. I'm not ashamed to say I fell asleep with tears of tremendous remorse on the first night.

Saturday, I prayed to God for forgiveness. I also made Him a vow that I would never drink or do drugs again. That night, when I went to sleep, I had a dream. I was in a green pasture following a rainbow. I ran and ran and ran, trying to get to the end. When it seemed like I got there, a beautiful young lady with a red sweater turned around. She was smiling, and she offered me a can of Iced Tea. I opened my eyes from dream to reality when I heard the cell door open. Hallelujah rang in my soul when the guard said, "Bradford, you're being released."

I said, "I thought I had to see the judge."

"Your attorney is waiting. I'm sure he'll explain."

Joshua informed me I was released because my account of the event was confirmed. My fingerprints were not found on any evidence. I couldn't wait to get out of that place.

Mom had a big breakfast waiting, including my favorite Ultimate omelet. This tradition started when I was in middle school. I was bringing home my base guitar. Mom was supposed to pick me up after band practice.

I was excited to see her because I had just made First Chair. She forgot and left me at school. I stood, waiting until all the other students were gone. It was late, and the school office was closed, so telephoning my mom was not an option. A long night of studying for an exam was waiting for me to get home. My backpack was super heavy, and we lived about 10 miles away.

It was a stupid option to think I could walk. Three blocks into my long journey, my friend and his mom saw me struggling and gave me a ride. I was happy to get a lift but still angry at my mom.

Upon entering the house, I dropped my stuff inside the front door. Mom entered the vestibule and immediately started, "Anthony Bradford, where have you been? You know you have to be out there on time if you are going to be a part of the carpool. School was out hours ago. I called Rosetta, and she said you weren't in front of the school. She waited for 10 minutes. And why did you drop your stuff in the entryway? Take them to your room."

I was already angry about her forgetting me. Now she was yelling. I let her have it, "Did you think about coming to the school to find me?!"

"Young man, don't take that tone with me. I'm not having it. Go to your room and wait until your father gets home."

I snatched my backpack up, stormed down the hallway, went to my room, and started studying for my test. Mom came to my bedroom door about two hours later, "Anthony, dinner is ready. You can come to have your dinner and return to your room."

I was too angry to eat, so I pouted, "I'm not hungry."

"Have it your way, but it will be too late if you decide to come to your senses later."

My dad got in at about 8 PM. He came to my room. By this time, I was lying on my bed, starving. My anger had subsided, and now I was just hurt. He sat at the foot of my bed, "Son, what' is this I hear about you disrespecting your mother?"

"She left me at the school today after band practice. I couldn't wait to see her because I made First Chair today. Mom didn't even remember that she was supposed to pick me up. When I entered the house, she yelled at me for missing the carpool. Tears fell from my eyes. I got mad, and I did talk smart. I wasn't trying to."

My dad summons me, "Come here, Son." He held me for a minute. Then he said, "I won't punish you this time. I can see that you are sorry. You need to apologize and not talk to your mother or any woman in that manner again. Women are to be valued.

"Yes, Dad."

"I'm going to go talk to your mother. I love you, Son." He smiled, "First Chair?"

I returned the smile, "Yep."

"High fives, you are the man."

About fifteen minutes later, my mom came into my room. I was sitting on my bed. She sat beside me, "Anthony, I am so sorry. Your dad told me what happened. I had so much on my mind, and I forgot. How did you get home?"

"EJ and his mom, Miss Lorie, saw me walking a few blocks from the school and gave me a ride."

She hugged me, "Oh, my poor baby. Had you started trying to walk home? You would never have made it. I'm going to have to call Lorie and thank her. So, what's this, I hear? You got First Chair?"

I blushed, "Yep."

"Well, that's cause for a celebration. Tomorrow, for breakfast, you can have anything you want."

"Thanks, Mom, and I'm sorry for being rude to you."

She said, "I know. Why don't you take your shower, and I will warm you up a little something to eat?"

The following morning, Anthony's ultimate omelet was born: two eggs, three kinds of cheese, mushrooms, chicken, and red salsa. Any time after that, when I needed comforting, Mom would make me an ultimate omelet. Clearly, I needed an ultimate omelet, and this time, it tasted like freedom.

After breakfast, I went upstairs to my room. Although I was free from jail, my mind was still bound in grief, guilt, and shame. I only came out for the next two days to go to the bathroom. I found myself slipping into a depression.

My dad came in Wednesday morning and sat beside me on the bed, "Son, we need to talk. I know this was challenging, and no one can tell you how to feel.

But your world will fall apart if you don't start making some moves. They've released your apartment."

"I'll stay with one of my frat brothers until I get a new place, but I can't go back there."

"Son, this is always your home, especially in a crisis. I'm not putting you out. But we need to make some decisions. The property manager called and said they would give you another apartment, but you have to pay for the water damage. Do you need help with that?"

"I have rental insurance. It will cover the damages. I have no plans on going back there. I can't go to my place or the building. There are too many memories that I'm not ready to relive right now."

"What do you want to do? You can't just leave it."

"Give me a minute to think. I'll figure something out."

"You've got to go back to school and work eventually."

"I will. I just need a little more time."

"Tangi's funeral is on Saturday. Do you plan on going?"

I put my head down. My father touched me on the back, "You don't have to decide now. Think about it. Whatever you want, I'm here for you."

The following day, I called my frat brother Craig. He, Carey, Richard, and Paul came over that afternoon to get my keys. They and my other frat brothers collected my clothes and valuables and bought them to my parent's house. They donated the furnishings and the rest of my things to the Salvation Army, as I'd requested.

That night, when I went to sleep, I had another dream. I was in the middle of the desert. There was nothing as far as I could see. I was hollering repeatedly at the top of my lungs, "Help me!"

A phoenix bird appeared and lifted me by the back of my shirt. It carried me over the city and placed me in the beautiful meadow's grass. It was so beautiful all around me. From nowhere, the same lovely lady I'd seen in my last dream ran by. She was holding the hand of a little boy. When I woke up, I believed she must have been an angel telling me the baby Tangi was carrying a boy, and he was okay.

Later that day, I shared my dreams with my mom. After I finished telling her, she shared, "Dreams are foretelling. They can be a window to the past, present, or future."

"What do you mean?"

"You can be repressing an experience, and it will manifest in a dream. In the present, a desire could be played out in a dream. Then, there are times when the dream is prophetic. We know and prophesy in part. It could be revealing what is to come."

"What do you think my recurring dream with the lady means?"

"I don't know. God will give you a revelation if there is a meaning behind it."

"I think it has something to do with the baby Tangi was carrying."

"How are you feeling about all of this?"

"She was a hellion, but I miss her."

"Were you in love with her?"

"No, Mom, I've never been in love. I know she was not who I was supposed to be with, but I still loved her. The fact that she was carrying my baby intensified everything. Did she kill herself because of me?"

"Listen to me. Don't put that on yourself or in your spirit. Suicide is a cowardly act. It's a permanent, selfish solution for a temporary problem. Tangi was a misguided ghost who didn't know her way. She had a lot going on and needed some help." Mom sat beside me on the bed, "Your dad told me about the discussion the two of you had the other day." She rubbed my face, "He never cheated on me, Anthony."

"I remember the argument so clearly."

"You did hear the argument. I do not deny that. Let me explain what was going on. When your sister was born, I had a difficult season of postpartum depression. I was relentless to live with. I didn't think your father and I would make it. Your grandma recognized what I was going through because she also struggled with postpartum. I got help, and I was okay. When your brother was born, I immediately started in on your dad. That's what you saw." She rubbed my face, "Dear heart, when I saw your troubled face that night in the kitchen, it got my attention. I realized I was going through it again. Your dad and I thought it best for you and your sister to go to your grandparents while I was getting treatment. You see, Son, you actually helped me."

"So, he wasn't cheating?"

"No, and it pains your father and me to know you've been living with this anger for so long. I praise God your dad is the man he is. After I took him through that season, I'm surprised he didn't leave."

That conversation with my mom brought clarity and revelation. I spent the rest of the week trying to make amends and putting my life back together. After all I'd been through and lost, getting fired seemed inconsequential.

I went to the studio to sit down with Jack, ready for him to lower the hatchet and cut me off. I began, "I'm not coming back to ask for my job. I came to say I'm sorry for disappointing you and my dad. You gave me a chance, and I blew it."

Jack leaned back in his chair, "Anthony, you are like a son to me. As much as I love you, I'd planned to fire you so you could learn your lesson. I thought you acted unprofessional, used bad judgment several times, and jeopardized my business. However, your dad and I had a conversation and collectively decided to give you another shot."

"Why? After all, I did."

"Simply put. You deserve to get fired, but you are family and exceptional at your job. You've had to grow up tremendously in the last few weeks. If I thought taking your lively hood would help you be a better man, I'd kick your legs right from under you. I know it won't. I believe you've learned your lesson and need to start over. Understand this, though: if you ever get out of line again, I won't hesitate to fire you, no matter how much I love you."

"Thanks, I won't disappoint."

"I know. I have put some things in place to make sure you succeed. You have a new personal assistant, an older lady named Anita. I'm also giving you an intern. Her name is Tyra."

"Wow!"

"Don't celebrate yet. We had to pay a lot to get you out of your dilemma. You will work longer and harder for a few months to pay retribution. I want you to take the next two weeks off and clear your head. You are expected to hit the ground running after that. Listen, son, we all made mistakes when we were young. The key is to learn from them. Let's not make the same ones again. Enough said. Let's move forward."

Friday night, my parents, Sheila, and I went to the mortuary to view Tangi's body. I was a little uneasy about it. When we got to the room, no one was there. Tangi looked so beautiful. I stroked her hair and kissed her on the lips. Someone came into the room as I stood up, "Hello, I'm Angie, Tangi's sister. I turned around. You would have thought it was a ghost or Tangi was standing there. They look so much alike.

My dad responded, "I'm Ray Bradford. This is my family: my wife Loretta, daughter Sheila, and son Anthony."

She said, "Nice to meet you all."

"Tangi worked at the studio with my son and me."

She looked at me, "Oh, you are Anthony Bradford. You and Tangi were seeing one another, and she was found in your apartment?"

"Yes, my father and I found her."

"Now it makes sense. You are the one who sent the check to the funeral home for three thousand dollars."

"Yes, we were pretty close. I thought it would help."

"You did, huh? Was the three thousand to clear your conscious, or was that how much she was worth when you finished with her?"

My dad cut in, "That's enough. We just came to pay our respects."

"I know your kind. You do your dirt and then think a check will cover the damages." She started crying, "My sister is dead because of you. You drug her through the mud and then dumped her like garbage."

34

My mom offered, "With all due respect. I know you are grieving, and I'll give you that, but you will not do this to my son. She took those pills, and he was not there."

I said, "Mom let it go. It's okay. Let's just go."

"Don't bother showing up at the funeral. You are not welcome. I will have you removed if you set foot on the grounds."

"That won't be necessary, Ma'am. I've said my goodbyes."

"When we got in the car Sheila held, "How dare she try and blame you. I just wanted to slap her or punch her in the face."

I replied, "I'm sure she's just grieving."

Mom chimed in, "I think that was very generous of you to send the money."

"It's the least I could do for Tangi."

That Sunday, my family and I attended church. Pastor took his text from the book of Job. Job lost everything, but God restored him. I sat thinking, "Job was a just and upright man, but I am not. Pastor also shared the same scripture as my dad had the other day about new mercies, and I had another chance. I went up as soon as it was time for the alter call. I reaffirmed that I would not do drugs or alcohol again. I also took a vow of celibacy and promised God if he put the right woman in my life, I would do right by her.

I had a lot of mountains to climb, and I knew it was not going to be easy. Returning to school was inevitable, but my fraternity brothers made the transition easy. They showed me the meaning of true brotherhood the day I returned. I thought it would be awkward, and I would have a barrage of questions firing at me. On the contrary, they acted as though nothing had ever even happened. After I left school that day, I went to the bank. In honor of my unborn son, I opened an account for my future children. I also started some investment accounts and secured pre-approval on a home loan to buy a condo.

Advice taken: Innocent, and I get a new start.
Advice ignored: I can end up in a bad situation again.

Chapter 4

Starting All Over Again

For the next three years, my life was void of dates. Socializing with others was limited and becoming obsolete. I preferred spending my free time at home writing music. My life was dedicated to finishing school, working hard, and having a solid spiritual life. My dad often told me I lacked balance and wondered if my experience with Tangi had left me jaded.

All my hard work paid off. I graduated with honors. I advanced in the company and received several awards for writing and producing hit songs. Although I had all these significant accomplishments, my days were becoming shorter than my lonely nights. I yearned for someone to spend my life with.

I suppose anyone would be happy when they have been given a few days off work and they're still getting paid. For me, it was the precursor to the overwhelming loneliness I had been feeling. Religiously, I would rehearse the same mundane routine. I would be summoned to Jack's office. On the way, I would rehearse a familiar bible verse I'd remixed in my mind, "Yeah, though I walk down this short hallway, I won't fear where I'll be. Only you know where Jack is sending me. I'll carry your rod and staff to glorify thee. Lord, please send a wife to comfort Anthony." I'd facetiously smile inside myself, put on my game face, go inside his office, and have a seat.

Jack will tell me about this unbelievable talent that I must see. We will listen or look at the person on tape while bobbing our heads instinctively in sync. This will signal that this singer warrants a personal visit. He will stick to the usual script and explain how there are other talents in the area I should also visit. I will give the scripted answer, "You got it, Boss." As I leave, he will remind me to enjoy a few days off before leaving for my trip.

I will visit my expensively decorated office and meet with my highly paid personal assistant, Anita. I will tell her where I am going and what I need. I won't have to do anything for the trip because either she or my intern Tyra will make the arrangements for my flight, car service to and from the airport, car rental, and suite at the best hotels, and set my appointments on the other end. I will quickly gather my things.

On the way out, I will stop by the receptionist, who will give me envelopes. These envelopes she hands me will be checks and bonuses directly deposited in my various accounts.

I will head for my fully loaded BMW and rush to my tri-level condo with amenities any brother would drool over. I will go to church, or I may go to my parent's house for a home-cooked meal. I might also stay home for those two days, longing for a wife and kids to share my life with.

The car service will pick me up from my home, the studio, or parent's house. I will board the flight before everyone else and sit in first class, where I can stretch my legs and get plenty to eat or drink. Once I get to the opposing airport, the car service will be standing with a sign prominently displaying my name or a luxury rental vehicle will be waiting.

My next stop will be at the hotel, where I will stay in a luxurious suite. I will see new talent through concerts, showcases, and personal visits. Sometimes, I'm away for up to two weeks, and that's okay. I am so busy I don't have to think about the loneliness waiting for me at home.

After being out of town on business for two weeks, I arrived at Los Angeles International Airport. The car service took me to the studio to get my BMW. I was putting my bags in my trunk when Daniel came out of the studio to my vehicle and asked, "What's up, Man?"

Pulling my keys out of my pocket, I said, "I just got off the plane."

Daniel inquired, "What are you getting into tonight?"

We shook hands and bumped shoulders and I replied, "Nothing. I'm just going home to relax."

"Man, I knew you would forget about my gig." Said Daniel "Is that tonight?"

"It's tonight."

"I don't know. I should go home and relax. I'm a little tired."

Daniel encouraged, "Come on, Man. Relax tomorrow. It's going to be low-key. You can see some beautiful women—And they will be there."

"No doubt, but I'm not feeling that right now."

"You are over the top with the whole hermit behavior and this celibacy thing. You don't have to take anyone home. Looking is not going to hurt."

"Nah, man, it's not that. I am ready to settle down with the right one. I've just had enough with the petty women."

"I feel you. You don't even have to get in the mix. Just come by for a little while, speak to a few people, get yourself something to eat, and make it an early night."

"Alright, I can do that. Let me get to the house, and I'll come through later."

On the way home, the idea of going out for the evening grew on me. That night, I felt unusually lonely and didn't have anyone to spend time with. Daniel's invitation was exactly what I needed.

I arrived at the mixer at 10 PM. and stood at the front door, casing the room. It was the usual crowd with a couple of new faces. After a few minutes, I was approached by my assistant Anita, "Hey Anthony, how was your trip?"

"It wasn't what I expected. I'll talk to you about it Monday. I want to relax tonight and get my head off the job."

"Let me get you something to drink, cranberry juice, right?"

"You don't have to do that."

"I know, but I don't mind."

As she walked away, I continued to case the room. It was plenty of beautiful women, as I knew it would be, but none got my attention. I saw some of the brothers gathered near the bar. I figured I'd speak, get a plate, and then go home.

Anita returned and handed me my drink, "I couldn't believe it when Daniel told me you were coming."

"I felt like getting out tonight. What are you doing here? This isn't usually your scene."

"My friend wanted me to come with her. Tanya, the one I was telling you about."

I got a little disturbed, "Seriously, Anita? I told you I wasn't interested."

"I know. Calm down. I wasn't trying to hook you up. Tanya is in the industry."

I heard a voice behind me, "Why are you giving him an explanation, Anita?"

I turned around. Wow! This female was drop-dead gorgeous. She would put you in the mind of that actress, Denise Vasi. She had smooth caramel brown skin and light brown eyes, and her brown hair lay on her shoulders. Her red stretched lace dress accentuated her figure. She looked at Anita, "I'm ready to go." Then, glaring at me, she asserted, "I don't like being in the company of such arrogance."

Anita interrupted, "Tanya, this is my boss, Anthony."

"He's your boss, not mine. You have to put up with him." She stated as she began walking away.

This female captured my attention because she was so fine and held it with her feisty attitude. Before I knew it, I gently grabbed her hand to prevent her from walking away.

Miss Lady turned and gave me a stern look, "Excuse you."

I stepped close to her. "Look, I don't blame you for all that attitude. What I said was insensitive. Don't go. Let me make it up to you."

"Why should I?"

"Because what I said wasn't about you. I don't want you to take it personally."

"Mr. Bradford, perhaps you are used to having needy women throw themselves at you. I have my MBA in business, in which I graduated in the top ten of my class. I am currently working on my Doctrine. I am very stable in my career and have a six-figure income. I drive a Benz and own my home. These are my real fingernails; every strand of this hair is mine. None of it was purchased. So, no, I don't take it personally. Why should I? The way I see it, you would be lucky if I let you be in my company. Massa Bradford, may your servant Anita be dismissed? I want to cut my evening short, and she and I rode together."

Anita exclaimed, "Tanya! I'm sorry, Anthony."

"That's alright, Anita. Let the pretty lady speak her mind."

Tanya stood silently, looking towards the bar. I knew I had offended her, and I wanted to make amends. However, she didn't appear to be able to receive it. Although I initially did not want to meet her, I was glad the meeting happened. Not only was she beautiful, but her ambition was attractive as well.

Over the weekend, I thought of ways to get to know Miss Tanya. Monday morning, I went to work. Before I could get settled, Anita came into my office very apologetic. "Anthony, I am so sorry about the other night."

"Not a problem, have a seat. I need you to do something for me."

"Sure, what do you need?"

I reclined, "Before you get started on the promotion calendar, I need you to send Miss Tanya two dozen pink roses."

"Not red?"

"No, red roses are reserved for "the one.""

Using air quote gestures, "The one?" She asked.

"Yes, the one I plan on spending the rest of my life with. Pink roses say I'm sorry."

"Got it."

"I want the card to read. If I'm lucky enough to be in your company, I want to take you to dinner sometime."

"How does that sound?"

"It sounds good. Tanya appears to be hard, but she's not."

I said, I figured that was the case. I'm assuming you have the address?"

"Yes, Sir, I do."

"I want them sent to her job."

She blushed, "Oh. I get it.

I'll make that happen."

"Can you get me that address as well?"

"No problem. I'll take care of that right away." She got to the door, came back, and stood in front of my desk, "I promise I'm not trying to pry, but I just wanted to give you a heads up."

"What's going on?"

"Tanya and I have dinner plans for tonight at The Automne Brise. I might not make it, and it would be a shame if she ate alone."

I blushed, "I feel you."

"Our reservations are for 6:30 PM."

"Thanks for not prying, Anita."

"No problem. I know how private you are."

That evening, I showed up at the restaurant at about 6:35 PM. Tanya stood in the lobby wearing a white pantsuit, and her hair was up in the back. I walked up behind her, "Hello, Miss Tanya." It was utterly a bold move, but I didn't care.

She turned around, "Mr. Bradford. What are you doing here?"

"A brother has got to get some dinner."

"Okay, Brother, enjoy your meal."

I blushed, "Did you get the flowers I sent?"

With a slight smile, she answered, "Yes, I did. They are very lovely. Thank you."

The hostess stepped up and announced, "Tanya Cartwright."

"That's me," Tanya replied as she approached the hostess counter.

"Anita called and said to start without her. She may not make it."

"Oh wow, that's too bad," I snickered, "Am I lucky enough to be in your presence long enough to buy you dinner?"

"Somehow, I don't believe it's a coincidence that you are here and Anita isn't. Since you went through the trouble, we can have dinner. There is only one condition."

"I'm listening."

"I pay for my dinner, and you pay for yours."

"That's fair."

Then she asked the waitress, "Can you show us to our table?"

Dinner with Tanya was delightful. She was extremely passionate about her job, school, and career goals. While she was talking about them, there was excitement in her voice. It was so attractive. I was looking forward to another date. Perhaps I could get to know her softer side. What was her favorite flower? What was her relationship with God? What did she like to do on a rainy day when she had the day off?"

After dinner, I walked Tanya to her car. Just as she said, she drove a white Mercedes-Benz. She pulled her keys from her handbag, and I reached for them. This woman barked, "What are you doing?"

"Well, I thought I would unlock the door."

"I think I can pull that off, and I thought we'd agreed to split the bill."

Crossing my arms, I tried her, "Are you seriously getting an attitude because I got the check?"

"I didn't need you to buy my dinner. I told you the other night I'm not some needy chick."

I felt myself getting upset. "Who said you were? I just paid for dinner. I didn't think you were needy until now."

"What is that supposed to mean?"

"You are so busy trying to prove how you don't." Using air quotes, "need a man." You're showing that you need more than a man. You need God, counseling, or whatever it will take to make you complete."

"I don't need your validation."

"Apparently, you do."

"And what makes you think so?"

"It's apparent that you have to floss your education, the car, the house, the job, or whatever else. Then there's your tuff-as-nails persona. It isn't attractive at all. Any real man can see right through it."

"So, you're one of those brothers uncomfortable or intimidated by a woman with a career?"

"No, I'm a brother who finds a confident, ambitious woman attractive. But there needs to be some balance. I hoped to get to know the woman apart from her stuff."

"Insulting me is not the way to get to know me."

"Insulting you? Wow! That's what you got out of what I just said?" I ran my hand down my face, "I'm going to say good night." I touched her car door handle, "I would get your door, but you know. You got this, right?" Then, I walked away.

On the way home, I thought about how much this woman frustrated me. It didn't make sense that she could be so beautiful and intelligent yet nasty, insecure, controlling, and bitter. Blasting on my car radio on the oldies station was, "Starting All Over Again is Going to Be Ruff." And how.

Dad invited me into his office to watch a recording of a new group the following day. After viewing the recording, he said, "I want you to see this other young lady we are thinking about signing." He put in a new tape. When it was over, I offered, "She's fire. What's the holdup?"

"She wants to use all of her people."

"Wow! She sounds like a Diva."

"Yep, she might be a handful. But look at her."

"She's a beast. Her runs are sick."

"Definitely. I will send this over to Jack and see what he says. How was your trip?"

"It was a bust."

"No new talent, huh?"

"There might be one. The one I thought I was going to sign was great on tape. He had major pitch issues during the live performance, and he was singing off-key. Dude was more concerned with trying to dance. To add to the madness, I went to Daniel's party when I came home."

Dad sat back in his chair, "That doesn't sound like a bad thing. You need to get out of the house."

"I met this drop-dead gorgeous lady."

He grinned, "Still doesn't sound like a bad thing."

I sat down, "She's ambitious, and this woman was so pretty. She even has her own hair and fingernails. To top it off, she wore a red stretch lace dress on her perfectly curvy body."

Dad grinned, "I'm still trying to figure out how this is bad."

"Her attitude was foul, and she's insecure."

"Deal breaker. You found all that out at a party."

"No, I met her at the party. She bit my head off. I figured it was because I had offended her. I gave it another try, and we went to dinner. The dinner was wonderful. I was looking forward to getting to know her. Check this out, though. I walked her to her car. I reached for her keys to unlock her door. She went sideways."

"Because you were going to open her car door?"

"That and because I paid for dinner."

"Yeah, it does seem like a lot is going on there. You know what to do."

"I know. Ask myself if she's the one. If not, I need to move on. I haven't talked to her, but I often think about her."

"Uh-huh, when?"

"What do you mean, when?"

"What time of day?"

I smiled, "At night, that red stretch dress speaks to me."

"Man, you said you want a wife. Then, get your mind out of the gutter. Don't even play. You know what that's about. The next thing you know, you will be caught up. If she's not the one, move on. You don't need space fillers or a temporary fix for your loneliness."

"You're right, but Man."

"But get out of my office so I can get some work done."

"I'm out."

Advice taken: Innocent.

Advice ignored: I'm betraying myself.

Chapter 5

Just My Way

Daniel and I were scheduled to go to a dinner meeting with "the Diva" we were considering signing. To my surprise, Tanya was a part of her team.

During the meeting, Tanya was energetic and knew her stuff. Once the meeting portion was over, she ordered a glass of wine.

Everyone laughed and talked until the only two remaining were her and me. I enjoyed her company. When I walked her to her car this time, she pulled the keys from her purse and handed them to me. I asked, "Are you sure?"

Tanya blushed, hunched her shoulders like a schoolgirl, and said, "Yes, I'm sure."

I put the key in the door and opened it. Then, I handed it to Tanya. She solicited, "No hug?"

I agreed, "Alright." She and I hugged until she pulled back and blushed.

"What?" I questioned.

She asked, "Can I call you sometime?"

"Sure you can. Call me tonight when you get home and let me know you made it safely."

"I will."

As agreed, Tanya called when she got in. That night we had a short conversation. The next evening, she called me as well. I couldn't believe we could talk for an hour, and she never brought up work. Finally, I was getting to know the softer side of Tanya. Things were going so well that she asked me to escort her to a black-tie business event.

She looked stunning in her black fitted dress with a slit on the side. We both had a great time at the event. When I took her home that evening, I walked her to the door and said good night. Before I could leave, she invited me out for a surprise date the following Friday. She said it was to show her appreciation. It wasn't necessary, but I was curious, so I accepted.

The week was long because my mind stayed on Tanya and what she had planned. The aroma met me as I neared her door. She wore a long-length turquoise cotton dress with the back out when she opened it. Her hair was put back into a ponytail. She looked so cute and down to earth.

Tanya greeted me with a hug, "You're awfully suited up tonight."

"I didn't know where we were going." With my eyes traveling up and down her curvy body, I offered, "You look good, but I wasn't aware this was a casual date. Maybe I should go home and change into something more comfortable."

"I got that covered. I thought you might enjoy dining in. The washroom is down the hall, the first door on the right. You will find a comfortable change of clothes."

"Something smells good. What's on the menu?"

"Grilled salmon, asparagus, and a loaded baked potato."

"Sounds great."

"Afterwards, I thought we might get in the spa."

"I didn't bring any shorts."

"Oh, ye of little faith. I've had that covered, too. Let me go and check on the salmon. After you change, can you join me back on the mezzanine?"

She had a beautiful, quaint backyard with a nice sauna. There was a table set for two, and she was grilling. I stood in the doorway for a moment and took it all in. It had been so long since I was in the company of a beautiful woman. I imagined she was mine, and I was coming home to her. She probed, "How do you like the clothes?"

Nodding my head, I responded, "You did well. I like the shorts, and the T-shirt is classic. Where did you find it?"

"The last time I was in Chicago, I picked that up. My dad has a store there. I'd forgotten about that shirt until I went through my closet the other day and remembered you said you wanted one."

"I thought you made a special trip to shop for me."

She blushed, "I had to get the shorts and shoes."

"I appreciate it. How much do I owe you?"

"You're my guest. It's just my way of saying thank you. Why don't you have a seat, and I'll fix your plate? Do you mind pouring the wine?"

"I'm going to pass. I'll pour you a glass, though."

We enjoyed dinner, then I got into the spa. When she went to change, I leaned my head back, closed my eyes, and relaxed. Replaying the evening's events as if I was married to Tanya, I would have come home and gone out on the terrace. She would be standing at the pit with her back turned from me. Eric Benet's "Just My Way" would play in the background. I would have hugged her from behind, kissed her on the cheek, and asked, "How was your day?"

She would say, "I got off work early, and I thought I would make you a special dinner."

I would sit on my special chair, and she would sit on my lap and tell me about her day. Over dinner, we would discuss our future, including four children. We decided that night would be the perfect time to start. Our passionate telepathy would lead us to the spa, where we would consummate our proposal. We'd continue making love all night and then morning.

My pure daydream that had turned into an erotic fantasy was interrupted. Tanya's beautiful long legs were getting into the spa, followed by a two-piece blue bikini.

Her body spoke so loudly to my flesh that her first words came out as blah, blah, blah. Close behind, followed by deafness because now her breast cleavage was hollering, "Come and get me"! My eyes started sending messages to my body, "Houston, we're in trouble." My soul answered and said to my spirit, "Aboard the mission."

Tanya came close to me, and her eyes invited me for more, "what do you think?"

For obvious reasons, I didn't want her to get too close. So, I gently grabbed her shoulders to stop her from discovering my secret and deflected, "I think you have a beautiful home."

Still searching, she inclined, "Not my home, me."

"I think you are a beautiful, intelligent, ambitious woman."

She grinned, "No, what do you think about my suit?"

I smiled, "I think blue looks nice on you."

"So, what are you going to do about it?"

I forgot about my commitment to God. My flesh signaled it was in control. I dropped my guard, rubbed her face, and leaned in, teasing her lips. I was fixed on the prize and determined I was going all the way when her cell phone rang. She softly uttered, "I have to get that. Hold that thought. I am expecting an important call." My eyes followed as she exited the spa and went into the house.

Since she didn't return after about five minutes, I collected myself and realized the phone call was indeed my way of escape. Remembering my commitment, I decided I'd better leave.

I toweled off and entered the house where Tanya was putting down her cell. She explained, "I'm sorry, that took longer than I thought. Where were we?" She pulled the string to the top of her bikini, dropping it to the floor.

I went over to her, put my towel around her, and offered, "We can't do this."

She grabbed the towel and queried, "Why? Don't you want me?"

Those riveting words reminded me of Tangi. I knew for sure I had to get out of there. I responded, "I think you are a beautiful woman, but I'm celibate."

"You don't have to lie, Anthony. If you don't want me, say so."

"I would, but it's the truth. I'm celibate."

"What was all this for? Why did you lead me on?"

"What are you talking about? Tanya, you invited me to dinner. You wanted to get in the spa. You came on to me. I had no idea you would want me to sleep with you."

"I don't think you're celibate at all."

"I told you it has nothing to do with you. You're sexy, and I'm attracted to you."

"You can't possibly be."

"Why not? I wouldn't be here if I weren't attracted to you."

"Cause you're one of those down-low brothers looking for a cover girl."

"Did you just call me gay?"

"No! I called you a down-low brother. If you came out of the closet and were honest with your-self and others, I could respect you more."

"Oh, I see. I must be down low because you're so fine and irresistible. Get over yourself, Tanya."

"Well, if you were a real man...."

I interjected, "If I was a real man, what? I'd hit it with no regard for the consequences? Why can't it be I'm respecting myself, you, and my God?"

"Because."

"Be quiet, Tanya. That was a rhetorical question. It doesn't warrant an answer. I will show you what a real man does when he's been insulted. He removes himself from the presence of shallowness."

I started to the bedroom to get my things when Tanya yelled, "Well, leave then!"

I lunged, "Without a doubt, but I'm sure you needed to say that to remain in control." Then I got my clothes and left. All the way home and all night, I was conflicted within myself. My flesh was so angry. The anger provoked my ego and made me want to go over and show Tanya my manhood through my loins. All night, I tossed and turned. My deviant, predisposed mind was consumed with all the ways I wanted to have her body.

In the morning, I was awakened by a phone call from Tanya. She informed me that I had left my iPad over there. I decided to pick it up after work.

Red was starting to be a conundrum because she wore a red fitted dress that had me hypnotized. As she walked over to the counter, my eyes traveled behind, noting every curve. My lustful thoughts wanted to have her body. In those thirty seconds it took Tanya to retrieve my iPad, in my mind, I had her in at least four positions. My spirit beckoned me to pull my mind into subjection and escape immediately.

After she got my iPad, she stood in front of me. Her arms dropped, and so did her countenance, "Anthony, I'm sorry. I don't know what came over me last night. I was wrong." She started crying, "I wanted you to want me. I felt rejected."

Tanya wore transparency and vulnerability well. I'd never seen it on her, and it was attractive. The lust that was roaring inside me and her tears weakened my resistance. My mind no longer wanted to be subject to the spirit. At that moment, it wanted to please my flesh. I proposed, "Don't you know how to get what you want?"

She uttered, "No," as her tears increased.

I pulled her to me by her waist and slipped my hands down past her backside to a previously off-limits place. I started kissing her face, neck, and then some. My flesh didn't care, and neither did hers. She answered the invitation by returning gestures. Before we knew it, we were all in. Our clothes left a trail as we traveled to her bedroom to complete the unspoken symbolic communication we'd started.

Afterward, she fell asleep lying on my chest. I ran my fingers through her silky hair and looked toward heaven. My inner thoughts told God I would make it right and marry her.

I continued to lay fantasizing about how life would be waking up with my wife. We'd lay and talk for a while. The kids would run into the room and jump in bed. We'd get up, and all have Saturday morning breakfast, French toast, eggs, and turkey bacon. We'd have our choice of cranberry or orange juice with pulp.

My daydream suggested my reality. Getting up and making Tanya breakfast or taking her somewhere would be nice. Once she rolled over, I got up and took a shower. When I came back into the room, she opened her eyes slightly. Looking in my direction, she murdered the moment by saying, "Hey, I didn't know you were still here. Text me when you get home."

My own history taught me what those words meant. I'd said them to so many women. Translation: you don't have to go home, but you're not staying here. Instantly, I felt how I must have made so many women feel when I propelled them into the walk of shame. Cheap.

I went home, fell on my knees, and prayed for forgiveness. I'd made a vow that I would not sleep with another woman unless she was to be my wife. I determined I would make things right with God by making things work with Tanya. I knew she had issues, but I used the excuse that everyone has baggage. She and I would work through hers together.

I fell asleep and dreamt of my angel. This time, it was sad. She and my son stood in the park, licking an ice cream cone. I called out to them. She turned to me and had tears in her eyes. I said, "What's wrong?" My angel just stood and continued to cry. I went to hug her, but she dissolved in my arms. I reached for my son and said, "Where did she go?" I watched him as he started running towards the forest. Tangi stood holding her hands out, beckoning him to come to her, but he ran past. I tried to run after him, but I couldn't move.

He ran into the arms of my angel. They both turned and faded into the woods. I stood there hollering, "Don't leave me! Please, don't leave me! Come back! I looked at Tangi, "Where did my son go?" She shrugged her shoulders.

I woke up panting and sweating as if I had been running. I laid back down and replayed the record of my life with Tangi and our unborn son. Then, I fell to my knees and cried out for God's help.

After that night, Tanya and I saw each other a few times a week. I vowed I wouldn't sleep with her, but we seemed to end the evening fulfilling the lust of the flesh. I never spent the night, though. As I traveled home, I would reflect on what the Apostle Paul said in Romans 7:18-25, "For I know that in me dwelleth no good thing: for to will is present with me, but how to perform that which is good I find not. For the good that I would I do not: but the evil which I would not, that I do. Now, if I do that, I would not; it is no more I that do it, but sin that dwelleth in me. I find then a law that when I would do good, evil is present with me. For I delight in the law of God after the inward man: But I see another law in my members, warring against the law of my mind, and bringing me into captivity to the law of sin which is in my members. O wretched man that I am! Who shall deliver me from the body of this death? I thank God through Jesus Christ our Lord. So then with the mind I myself serve the law of God; but with the flesh the law of sin."

After a while, I entertained condemnation, roaring loudly, "You are a hypocrite! How can you go to the Lord's house, yet you are committing fornication? How can you offer to take her to church after what you have done with her?"

Don't get me wrong. I still attended church, just not as regularly, and I never invited Tanya. I never even took her to my parent's house to meet them. Whenever it seemed like things were safe with Tanya and I wanted her to meet the family, she would do or say something to turn me away.

However, I did have the occasion to meet her parents. They were in town from Chicago, and she invited me to dinner. I got caught up with an artist and was going to be late. I telephoned and suggested meeting up with them later at her place. As soon as she opened the door, she let me have it, saying, "Anthony, you knew my parents were just in town for the evening. The least you could have done is to be on time."

I tried to quiet her, "Can we talk about this later? I'm here, and I can meet your folks now."

She said, "That's fine." Then we went into her living area.

Tanya did the introductions. Apparently, she'd been talking about me because her dad said, "So this is Anthony. We've heard a lot about you."

"I hope it was all good."

"Tanya tells us that you're quite a prestigious young man. You're in the entertainment business and graduated at the top of your class."

"That's true. To God be all the glory."

"Oh, you're a church-going young man?"

"Yes."

"I don't understand a God-fearing man not wanting any children."

"I beg your pardon?"

Tanya interjected, "Dad, I'm sure the last thing Anthony wants to discuss is kids and Jehovah."

I looked at Tanya in puzzlement. I had never heard her mention "Jehovah," and I never told her I didn't want children. Thinking I should follow her lead and change the subject, I sat down and continued to talk to her dad. We talked about sports, business, and old-school music.

When it was time for them to go to the airport, I even offered to drive them. It was an enjoyable ride until they got out of the car. Tanya could not leave well enough alone. She started in on me again. It sounded like blah, blah, blah, nag, nag, and nag. Inside. I asked, "Can someone find a housetop in the rain so I can go on it?" I finally said, "Enough, already!"

She returned to, "Anthony, seriously, you could not have been there for dinner?"

"What should I have done, Tanya? I had a meeting with an artist."

"Couldn't you have rescheduled your artist?"

"No, she's going on a media tour tomorrow."

"If you are going to be with me, you need to set some priorities."

"Excuse you! Do I ever ask you to put me before your work?"

"We're not talking about me."

"Let's talk about you. Jehovah? Are you Jehovah's Witness?"

"I was raised Jehovah's Witness but have not been practicing."

"Do you plan on it?"

"It's a strong possibility."

"When did I tell you I never wanted children?"

"It's not a big deal. I don't want kids, and I'm tired of my parents going in on me about it. So, I told them you didn't want them either."

"Don't you think you should have discussed that with me long ago? We have been seeing each other for nine months. You wait until I find out by meeting your parents that you don't want children, and you're Jehovah's Witness? When were you going to tell me?"

"It's a religion, not a disease. And it's my body."

"It's a religion with beliefs contradicting my spiritual principles, and I want children."

"Why do you want kids?"

"Why wouldn't I?"

"Does keeping your wife barefoot and pregnant make you feel like a man? Are you one of those old-time, oppressive types? You want to tie your woman down with kids so she can't have a career?"

"Tanya, if two people don't agree on those serious matters, they can't have a successful life together, especially religion."

"Who says your way is the right way?"

"I'm not arguing religion with you. You have the right to believe what you believe, and so do I, but...."

"But, what?" asked Tanya.

"Religion and family are huge. Would your dad want you and me dating if he knew I was Christian?"

"No."

"That's why you cut him off. You didn't want me to call you out about the kids, and you didn't want him to know I was Christian, did you?"

"I'm not going to talk about this. Let's go one better; what if we don't see each other anymore, Anthony?"

"Here we go again. Where did that come from, and why are you always coming out of a bag?"

"I don't need you questioning me."

"Oh, but you can question me?"

"Just take me home."

"Tanya, where did you think I was taking you? Isn't this the direction to your house? Oh, this is one of those times you have to control the situation. Okay, Miss Daisy, I'll get you home right away."

"Why do you have to be so darn condescending?"

"Why do you have to be so deceitful? I don't know who you are."

"That's not fair."

"Tanya, let's just drop it."

"Fine, let's."

For the rest of the ride, we both sat silently. I felt terrible about my part of the argument. As soon as we got to Tanya's house, I walked her to the door and offered, "I'm sorry. I didn't mean to be so harsh."

I braced myself for her return apology. She held, "Do you think your apology changes anything? You were wrong, Anthony."

"Wrong, for what?"

"You called me deceitful."

"Did you ever tell me you don't want to have kids? Did you tell your dad I was Christian? Did you tell me you used to be a Jehovah's Witness and perhaps are going back to studying?"

"How does that make me deceitful?"

"Never mind."

"No, tell me?"

"Tanya, you win. I don't want to fight anymore."

She unlocked the door, went inside, and didn't look back. Tanya just closed the door and left me standing.

I didn't bother calling when I got home. I wanted to give her time to cool off. We had an annual industry mixer the next night that we were supposed to attend together. Music executives, colleagues, and their spouses were going to be there.

I telephoned her all day, but she didn't answer. I went on to the mixer, figuring I would meet her there. My parents, all the fellows from work, and their dates were in attendance. I had previously told my parents she would be there. I wanted to see what my mom thought of her. Tanya walked through the door looking amazing, as she always did. I turned to my parents and touted, "That's Tanya."

Mom said, "She's a cute young lady. Invite her for dinner."

It wasn't until I stood up to meet her that I realized Tanya had a replacement hitter. She was in the arms of another brother. I was humiliated. Since I was already headed towards the door, I kept going until I made it home.

I was lying on my couch replaying the last two evening's events at midnight when the doorbell rang. I opened it, and Tanya immediately started pleading, "Can I come in, please?"

I stepped to the side, let her in, closed the door, and turned around to face her. In my mind, I'd planned that this would be a brief encounter, and then she would be leaving for good.

She tested, "Why did you leave so early?"

I crossed my arms in fury, "Surely you are not going to try to act like you don't know what happened. I felt humiliated! You knew my parents, colleagues, and friends would be there, and you showed up with another man."

"I didn't know your parents would be there."

"Oh, you just wanted to embarrass me in front of my friends and coworkers?"

"I wasn't trying to embarrass you. He was just a friend."

"I thought we were supposed to go to the event together."

"I changed my mind."

"That would have been fine, but when did I get that memo?" I walked over, sat on my sofa, and put my face in my hands. After thinking I had calmed myself down, I asked, "Was this my punishment for last night?"

She sat beside me, "I admit I was hurt and disappointed when you said I was deceitful. I asked Kyle to bring me because I didn't want to go alone. No. It wasn't to make you jealous or to humiliate you. I didn't realize what I'd done until I saw you leave." I sat quietly, not wanting to burst a blood vessel in my brain or choke her.

She inclined, "I'm sorry. If it's any consolation, I did finally meet your parents. Your mom said she'd love to have me over for dinner sometime."

The rage and anger inside me responded, "I'm sure my mom was only being polite. Besides, do you think I'd have you to dinner at my folk's house after that display of disrespect?"

She stood up, eased her coat open, and revealed her completely nude body, "I had come over here to make it up to you, but I'm leaving with all of this. You know where to find me when you come to your senses." She fastened her coat and then stormed out.

I couldn't believe this unbelievably intelligent, attractive woman came to my house and pulled the naked woman under the coat routine. From the perspective of any real gentleman, that was a turn-off. However, since she put herself in a position as a jump-off chick, I felt I would oblige her.

I got dressed, went to her place, and acted like a dog. I hit it and went home without saying, "Good night." Turnabout is fair play. Remember when she murdered the moment by saying, "Hey, I didn't know you were still here. Text me when you get home. That part!"

After that encounter, I saw Tanya differently. Despite what I told God, I knew she wasn't the one. There was no way I would ever marry her. Hindsight shouted at me. "You should have listened to your dad and never started seeing her in the first place."

I guess I was a man struggling in my flesh, suffering from loneliness, or just in pain. After that night, I kept seeing Tanya off and on. Anytime my flesh got weak, like a dog in heat, I would get with her. If I wanted company, I would keep it with her. It wasn't just me. Tanya was confused about what she wanted too. Times she wanted to be together, and there were times she didn't. She would break up with me when she didn't get her way.

My sister Sheila wasn't fond of her and surmised she was an opportunist. She claimed that Tanya only wanted to be with me when she wanted something.

That year and a half or more was an extremely emotional and spiritual rollercoaster. However, I did manage to get back on track with my vow of celibacy. I had not slept with Tanya for six months, nor did I plan to.

I'm sure Tanya thought I would get excited because she finally informed her parents that I was Christian. They accepted me so much that she asked me to join her in Chicago for the holidays. I was not interested in going. What was the point? In my heart and spirit, I knew our days together were numbered.

We had the biggest fight ever, and I was tired of it and her. When I got off the phone, I prayed for God's strength and deliverance.

Advice taken: I would have been innocent.
Advice ignore: I indeed betrayed myself.

Chapter 6

Can We Talk?

My guilty pleasure was the BMW. The smooth ride and exquisite look moved me. Sometimes, I liked to get in it, amp up my music, and ride down the coast. Every few years, I would treat myself to an upgrade. This time, I purchased a BMW that I had customized. Like a first date, I was stood up, and I couldn't take her home. There was an issue with the sound system. The next day, my ride was finally ready. She was pristinely dressed in navy, a sunroof top, and an engine that purred. The vibrant sound system was off the hinges and worth the wait.

Little did I know my life and my dreams were about to collide. The point of intersection happened when I returned to the studio that evening. Thirstiness led me into the lobby to get an iced tea.

On the couch was a young lady sitting with her legs crossed. The red in her sweater was calling out to me, but Tanya wasn't wearing it this time. Compelled to get a good look at her, I stood. Finally, she pulled the magazine that had previously been obstructing my view. Our eyes met, and I said, "Hello."

The lady in red was a familiar stranger. Delightful Déjà vu is how I would title that moment. I'd seen her before in all my dreams cast as an angel. Only now, I realized she could not have been. I recalled what Mom had said about dreams foretelling the future. Now, the future and present were intersecting. My spirit informed me that this woman was going to be my wife. Her look was distinctive, and she was beyond gorgeous. High yellow had to take a back seat to caramel brown skin because it was the new black beauty. No doubt, this was the most captivating woman I'd ever seen. I immediately loved and had to have her.

After getting my drink, I stopped on my way out for one more confirming glimpse at my future. It was indeed the woman I'd been dreaming about. Overwhelmed by my encounter, I hurried into King's office to share my experience.

He stood from his desk, "Hey, Anthony. Are you still going by your parent's house tonight? I need you to drop my baby girl off at home."

I could barely answer because I was distracted, but said, "Yeah, sure thing."

"Man, what is wrong with you? You look like you saw a ghost."

I took a sip of my tea, composed myself, and leaned on the desk, "I just met the woman of my dreams. This woman is going to be my wife."

"What?"

"I'm now a believer in love at first sight. She is as beautiful as I dreamt. I'm in love and don't even know her name."

"How are you going to not know her name? Did you talk to her?"

"For the first time in my life, I was speechless. All I could say was hi. What I should have done is bust some Tevin Campbell. "Can we talk for a minute? Girl, I want to know your name."

King smiled, "Undeniably, every woman likes a man who can sing. You need to go back and at least ask her name."

"You're right. I've got to get my future wife's number or something. Tell your daughter I'm ready to go."

King snickered, "Are you sure? I know you're on a mission."

"I'm good."

He and I started walking down the hall together. Just before we got to the lounge door, I stopped. King inquired, "What's going on?"

"The pretty lady is in there. She has on a red sweater. Look at her. Isn't she gorgeous?"

"Who?"

"The woman I was telling you about."

"Oh, I thought you saw this woman somewhere else. I didn't know you were talking about someone in the building."

King grinned, "Come on. I'll introduce you to your wife."

"You know her?"

King nodded and smiled, "Yes, that's my daughter."

"She's your daughter? Her name is Melinda, right? And I get to take her home? Tell me she doesn't have a man."

"Ask her. Hypothetically, if she was single, I would caution you, don't open a door with her before you are finished closing the other one."

I crossed my arms and smiled, "Are you saying I have your blessings?"

"If God said she's your wife, who am I to stand in the way? You have my blessings to pursue her once that whole Tanya issue is resolved."

"No doubt, I wouldn't bring her into that."

"More importantly, you need to get Melinda's blessing. She may not like you, Pretty boy."

"I'm not concerned about that. I got this."

"Oh, okay, "I got this." If you hurt my daughter, you will have me to deal with."

"I got you."

She stood up as we entered the lounge. King did the introduction, "This is Anthony. He's Ray's son."

Nodding her head, "It's nice to meet you, Anthony. I'm Melinda. Your father told me a lot about you."

I smiled. "I've heard a lot about you, too. I didn't know it was you when I came in earlier."

King snickered, "I've got to stay here a while longer. Anthony is going that way. He said he would give you a ride to the house."

"Okay, Daddy, that would be fine." King kissed her on the cheek.

I thanked God silently while Melinda and I walked toward the car. She was the first person who would be riding in my new BMW. I felt like she should. One day, the passenger side of my ride would be her permanent position. Incidentally, she was a real lady. She expected me to open and close her car door. As I was putting on my seatbelt, Tanya came to my window. She leaned down, not even acknowledging my new car. "Hey, I came by hoping we could talk. I see you have company."

I was happy I had company, not just because it was Melinda. I didn't feel like spending another evening arguing with Tanya.

I said, "This is Melinda. She's a friend of the family. Melinda, this is Tanya."

Melinda looked at Tanya and smiled, "Hi."

Tanya didn't say anything. She didn't even acknowledge she was there. I felt she was rude, so I said, "This isn't a good time. I'm going to take Melinda home. Then, I've got to get some sleep. I'm tired. Let's talk tomorrow."

In an angry tone, she fired, "Fine!"

Internal agitation and embarrassment were rising in me, "This isn't the time for this, Tanya."

"When is it going to be the right time, Anthony?"

Melinda looked at me and attempted to open the car door, saying, "I'll go wait for my dad."

Tanya countered with much attitude, "Good idea."

I leaned back in my seat and gazed at Melinda, "I told your father I'd take you home. Give me a minute."

I got out of the car. Tanya and I walked over about ten feet. She immediately said, "I thought things over, and since you can't seem to pencil me into your schedule to go to Chicago, we need to have a conversation when I come back."

"What did I tell you about ultimatums? And didn't we talk about this last night? I'm not going to Chicago. The only reason you want me to go is for status. I'm not your toy, your boy, or your boy toy."

"What are you saying?"

"I'm done talking about this. Let's give it a rest."

She stood, crossing her arms, looking into the night. I knew this wasn't the time to end things. I stepped close to her. Can we call it a truce? I'll take you to the airport on Sunday morning. We can talk things over when you return from Chicago, and I return from Detroit?" Then I leaned down and attempted to kiss her on the lips.

She turned her head and mumbled, "Save it. I don't need it."

"That's right, I forgot the terms of our relationship. It's all about what you need."

"Obviously not. I'm going to Chicago alone." Then she walked off.

I got back to the car feeling completely embarrassed and upset. I looked over at Melinda, "I'm so sorry."

"It's not a problem. I hope giving me a ride didn't cause an issue."

"Trust me, it's not about you."

"Is she your girlfriend?"

"Something like that. Tanya is beautiful, and I love her ambition. I'm an old-fashioned guy, and she's unwilling to compromise."

"What do you mean?"

"She is a career woman that doesn't want any children. I want lots of kids. She thinks I want to have children to keep a woman down."

"You don't want your wife to work?"

"I'm not saying that at all. If my wife works, it will be because she wants to. I don't want a daycare raising my children."

She inquired, "Where are you going to be?"

"I will be right there for my wife and my kids. I feel it's my responsibility to provide everything they need spiritually, naturally, and financially. Together, we will work it out."

"That sounds reasonable."

"My commitment to marriage is for a lifetime. I don't want to ever get divorced."

"You don't find a lot of guys with those values anymore. That's special."

"You might think it's special, but many women would disagree. Tanya would be one of them."

"Oh, I see."

I braced myself and took a deep breath. "What about you? Are you dating anyone?"

"I'm just coming out of a relationship. His name is Trevon."

My stomach grew in knots, "Kind of?"

"Yeah, he wants to get back together."

"But?"

"He's a good-looking man with several women interested, and I don't trust him."

"You don't trust him because of other women or because he's given you reasons?"

"He's given me lots of reasons."

"Did he cheat on you?"

"I'm not sure, but I believe so. I've never been with Trevon. He was always pressuring me for sex. I think that's why he was with other women."

"You guys haven't slept together?"

"Never."

I was surprised but pleased at what I had just heard, "Why?"

"Don't laugh, Anthony."

"I won't."

"I've never been with anyone. I'm waiting for Mr. Right."

"You sound like an old-fashioned girl. You won't find values like those anymore." We both started laughing.

Getting acquainted became organic while traveling down the Ten freeway. Crenshaw Boulevard welcomed her as we exited to streetlights and small businesses closed for the evening. It all made for a conversation about my city life and her rural Georgia experience.

Up the Baldwin Hills, we traveled winding roads until I pulled in front of her parent's house and turned off the engine. I sat back, anxiously wanting to rekindle the conversation we had previously started. I offered, "Melinda, I don't think it's excusable for him to be with other women because you're not sleeping with him, but I could imagine that would be hard."

"What do you mean?"

"Hard for him not to want to be with you intimately. It takes a lot of strength – especially when a woman is so attractive, sexy, and appealing."

She blushed, "I don't know how hard it is. I just wanted Trevon to be honest. I believe as long as two people are truthful with one another, there is nothing you can't work out."

Those words were music to my ears. I nodded my head and smiled, "I agree. Why did you think I'd laugh?"

"I'm a virgin, Anthony. I've been laughed at. Guys have dumped me because I wouldn't do it. I know everyone's doing it," she said as she made quotation signs with her hands. "Since I was younger, I've always said I was only going to make love to one man, and that man will be my husband."

She leaned her beautiful head back and closed her eyes. "For my honeymoon, I want the linen on the bed to be all white, including the comforter. I want white rose petals to be sprinkled all over the bed. There will be beautiful, white, scented candles on the nightstands. We'll toast with champagne. There'll be soft music playing."

I closed my eyes and shared in her dream. I knew one day I needed to make her vision our reality. "What will be playing?"

Allowing me to share her fantasy, she smiled and obliged, "Something by Eric, Luther, or Teddy."

"Melinda, you don't have anything to be ashamed of. There's nothing wrong with having high standards or dreams of linen and white roses."

She said, "A lot of guys wouldn't agree with you, and Trevon would be one of them."

I sighed and smiled, "The right guy will respect you and wait. I think it's beautiful. I guess we're both old-fashioned in our own way."

"Anthony, this is our secret, right?"

"Your secret's safe with me."

She laughed and went on to another subject, "You have a nice car."

"Thanks."

"We're supposed to come to your parent's house for Christmas dinner. I'm looking forward to meeting your family. Will you be home?"

"I don't live with my parents. I have a place in the valley, but I'll be there."

"Is Tanya going to be there too?"

"No, she's going to Chicago for two weeks. She's leaving on Sunday morning."

"Why aren't you going with her?"

"I wanted to spend Christmas with my family because I will be traveling for about a month afterward. Besides, she and I are going through a lot right now. I think it would add to the confusion."

"Well, I hope everything works out for you."

"I've been praying about it. I know God will give me the answer."

"You're a praying man, Anthony?"

"Some would call me a Holy Roller. Does Trevon allow you to have male friends?"

"What does Trevon have to do with this?"

I blushed, "Just checking. I would love to show you around while you're out here."

"Does Tanya allow you to have female friends?"

"Trust me. She wouldn't even notice."

"I just got here earlier today. I don't know what my parents have planned."

"I am taking Tanya to the airport Sunday morning, and then I will go to church. Traditionally, we have dinner at my parent's house on Sundays. After that, my sister, brother, and I will take you to Beverly Hills and Hollywood if you'd like."

"That would be great! I'm looking forward to meeting Howard and Sheila. Well, I'd better go inside. I know you're tired. Thanks, Anthony. It was nice meeting you."

Before we exited the car, I secured her cell and the phone number to the house. After walking her to the door, I got one more look at the total package. Her smooth, beautiful brown skin and shoulder-length, un-weaved hair was all a plus. When she smiled, it caused her eyes to twinkle. Her body, all I can say is, wow!

Like a lovesick little boy, I walked to my car and sat there momentarily, reflecting on our evening. I noted how easy she was to talk to. Melinda was strong and confident enough to save herself for the right man. More importantly, she was God-fearing.

I started my car and made my way home in a fog. Once I got there, I took a shower and tried to watch a little TV. All I could do was think about this woman. I wanted to hear her voice again before I went to sleep, so I dialed her number and lay back on my pillow. We stayed on the phone until 3 AM, sharing our dreams, desires, values, family, and God. We talked about my music and her passion for owning an accounting firm and someday authoring a book. Undoubtedly, we wanted several of the same things in life.

Our current relationships were discussed, but only a little. I was careful not to talk negatively about Tanya. Nor did I tell her she and I were on the verge of breaking up. It would have been disrespectful.

She told me all about Trevon. The little I did hear made me not like this guy. Judging from what she told me, she was right to eliminate him. He was clearly a cheater.

Before we hung up, I told her about Tangi committing suicide, but I didn't tell her it was at my place or about the baby. I appreciated her understanding.

It was essential to me for Tanya to have a good time in Chicago with her family. The last thing she needed was to concentrate on our issues. For the past week, every conversation we had somehow ended in an argument.

Sunday morning, I got up early and took Tanya to breakfast. I initiated the conversation to break the apparent silence asking, "Will you call me when you get there and let me know that you arrived safely?"

She didn't look at me but glared out of the window, "I can do that."

"Promise me you are going to have a good time?"

She turned her eyes and finally looked at me, "How am I supposed to, Anthony?"

"Tanya, what can I do short of going with you?"

"This isn't just about that. It's about everything."

"I thought we were going to call a truce until we both got back and could talk about it?"

She smacked her lips, "Your idea, not mine."

"We have an hour before you need to be at the airport. What's on your mind?"

"Are you in love with me, Anthony?"

"Wow. Where did that come from? Love has never come up in the two years we've seen each other."

"That's my point."

She looked so vulnerable. It moved me to want to hold her. I summon the waitress for the check, "Let's get out of here."

"Is this your way of avoiding the subject?"

I put the cash in the black billfold to pay the check and tip. Then I got up from my seat and extended my hand to Tanya, "No. I just want to get out of here and go somewhere we can be alone for a moment before you leave."

She stood up, and I hugged her around her waist, kissed her lips, and looked into her eyes, "Is that okay?" She blushed and nodded her head yes.

I took her by the hand, "Let's go then." Inside, I was thinking, "She blindsided me with that question. How am I going to get out of this jam without an incident? I knew I wasn't in love with her and didn't want to hurt her."

As I put the key in the door and unlocked it for her to get in, she stood with pouting eyes, "You're not going to answer me, are you?"

I pulled her close, held her tight, and kissed her sensually. She returned my affection. Afterward, I looked into her eyes, "Of course I love you. Do you think I would go through all the drama if I didn't?"

Tanya got in the car without responding. I closed the door behind her, got in on the driver's side, and sighed with relief, thinking, "I dodged the love bullet."

Not so, because she continued as I pulled out of the parking space, "Anthony, I know you love me as a person. That's not what I asked. I asked if you were in love with me. But you are right. Let's table this discussion until we have more time to deal with it. The more I think about it, the more I realize we need this time apart. It seems we are at a crossroads in our relationship."

"You're right."

We continued with casual conversation, but her heart appeared heavy. Confirmation came when we got to the airport.

She insisted I drop her at the curbside, although I had offered to go inside with her.

After leaving the airport, I went to my church. The message really hit home. It came from Philippians 3:13, "Brethren, I count not myself to have apprehended: but this one thing I do, forgetting those things which are behind, and reaching forth unto those things which are before, I press toward the mark for the prize of the high calling of God in Christ Jesus."

The pastor talked about how some of us were so bound to our past that we couldn't receive our promise. Sitting there, somewhat perplexed, reflecting, "I've been in an off-and-on relationship with Tanya for two years. My heart and spirit knew the relationship was at a dead end. It was unhealthy for me in every way. Yet, I had a hard time letting go.

In contrast, I loved Melinda the moment I laid eyes on her. So far, she is everything I prayed and asked God for. I could not receive my promise because I was still tied to my past.

After church, I went to the car wash and got a haircut before going to my parent's house. King and his wife were in the living room fellowshipping with my parents. There was no sign of Melinda. I greeted everyone and noticed Sheila wasn't there either. "Where is Sheila?" I inquired.

Mom said, "She went to the store. She should be back in a minute."

I entered the den, where Howard was kicked back onto the couch, watching the game. That's when I first noticed something was going on with him. "What's up, Man?" I asked.

"I'm just watching Cleveland putting a whipping on the Braves."

I sat on the couch, "What's the score?"

"Twenty-one to nothing."

"What quarter are they in?"

"The second."

"That's definitely a whooping."

I watched the game for a few more minutes, then inquired, "How's school?"

"I see Sheila's been opening her mouth."

I moved forward in my seat, "No, she hasn't, but now I'm curious. What's going on that has you going in on Sheila?"

"Nothing, it's all good."

"I don't believe that Howard. I'm going to let you have it for now, though. I wanted to take King's daughter, Melinda, to Beverly Hills later. Do you want to come?"

"Not if you and Sheila are going to gang up on me."

"You said nothing was going on, and it was all good. So, what is there to gang up on you about?"

"Nothing, nothing at all."

"Clearly, it is, but we won't deal with it today. Are you in?"

"Alright, I'll go."

I was perplexed, wondering what was going on with my little brother. I didn't want to press him, so I talked about the commercials, the game, and social media. After about twenty minutes, I entered the kitchen to see what was holding dinner. Sheila was mixing the punch.

I was alright when I saw Melinda putting the dinner rolls in the oven. She and I exchanged playful salutations until Sheila asked, "What do we have here, you two?" We both started laughing.

We had dinner in the dining room as we usually did. Melinda sat between Sheila and me. The conversation between the families at the table was fluid and natural. It was as if our families were already related.

Usually, Howard was the classic youngest child. Baby Brother had the syndrome to go along with it. He was typically the entertainer at family functions while I sat quietly. Howard was a good dancer, but not that good of a singer, and definitely a comedian. Sheila was his coconspirator and would encourage or inspire his antics.

I played basketball and baseball for fun, but Howard was an all-around athlete. He dominated every sport but mastered basketball. My baby brother struggled to get A's in math. Like Sheila and I, he was good in other subjects. My parents would not have it any other way.

This particular Sunday, he wasn't saying much at all. I believed he was trying to stay under Dad's radar. He didn't want to risk being called out for whatever was happening at school. Hindsight, trouble was raging.

After dessert, Howard, Lisa, Melinda, and I went to Beverly Hills and Hollywood. I ensured she sat in the seat that ultimately would belong to her—by my side in the passenger seat.

Before going home, we went to the studio. I introduced Melinda to Ricky and Daniel. Daniel invited her to attend his holiday party, which was going to be that Friday night. I was glad she accepted the invitation. Until she and Sheila decided they'd come together. Sheila told Melinda that there would be a lot of fine, single men there. Insecurity got a hold of me momentarily until reality reminded me Melinda wasn't mine yet. Then again, what God has for me is for me.

Advice taken: Innocent.
Advice ignored: I could be betraying myself.

Chapter 7

I Can't Make You Love Me

We took Melinda home and stayed until the Kings arrived. Afterward, I dropped my siblings at the house, grabbed some leftovers, and went home. Just before I got there, Tanya called my cell. I answered and asked, "Hey, how are you doing?"

"I'm good."

"And your flight?"

She said, "It was okay."

"I feel you."

"What did you do today?"

"Church, and then I went to Sunday dinner at my parent's house. King and his family came over. Sheila, Howard, and I took their daughter to Beverly Hills and Hollywood."

"The young lady you took home the other night?"

"Yeah, she's here for the holidays. She lives in Atlanta."

"Oh, I see. Did Melinda enjoy herself?"

"I think so."

"That's good."

"How about you?" I asked.

"I came straight to my parent's house from the airport. My sisters and my brother-in-law joined us for dinner. I was glad we didn't go out because I wasn't feeling it. I'm so tired. I'll text you my itinerary for my return trip. My folks told me to say hello, and they were looking forward to seeing you again."

"Tell them hello."

"I will."

"Well, get some rest, and I'll talk to you soon."

"Anthony, while I'm here, it might be a good idea if we do not talk. I have a lot of thinking to do. I'm sure you do too."

I felt like she was playing her usual games, and I was not going to buy in, so I indulged, "Are you sure that's what you want?"

"I'm positive."

"Alright, but I'm here if you need to call."

"Yeah, I know, but I won't."

"Tanya, why... never mind."

"What?"

"Nothing...."

The conversation left me with thoughts resting in my head for a while. There are times I enjoy being with her. Then, there were times when our relationship was polarizing. Just for a second, my mind drifted to Howard. Then, I dismissed the idea that anything serious could be wrong. My thoughts embraced my wonderful day with the King family and mine.

Over into the midnight, nightmares of Howard being chased by images of death captured and held my attention. The two images were large in stature and about six feet tall. Finally, he was caught by one of them. The figure penned Howard to a wall by his neck. His feet were dangling as my brother was kicking and screaming. I woke up pleading, "The blood of Jesus." My difficult night drove me to lay prostrate before God that next morning.

Afterward, I went to work for a few hours and got my travel schedule. Before leaving the studio, I dropped by King's office. He and my dad were in there. Dad greeted me, trying to be current, "Hey, Son, what's it looking like?"

"I'm on my way out. I have some errands to run."

"Alright."

"What's going on with Howard? I got the impression yesterday that something was up with him."

Putting his fingers together, "He's this close to walking into a full-ride athletic scholarship. Now he's saying he doesn't want to play basketball this year. Besides, he's having issues in his 7th-period calculus class."

"Well, Dad, you know math is not his thing. He's doing well getting that far."

"I don't know. There could be more to the story. Howard has been hanging around with these knuckleheads, too." Said Dad.

"What knuckleheads?" I asked.

"This young man that moved in down the street named Montel and a couple of his friends."

"Dad, what's Montel's story?"

"I haven't gotten the chance to meet him. He's never really been to the house. The two times he did come down, he and Howard stayed outside."

I suggested, "That sounds suspect. Howard usually doesn't roll like that. When did Howard start dealing with him?"

"He met Montel at school. The young man has a car, and Howard started riding home from school with him."

"I thought he was carpooling with Corey."

"Corey's dad was dropping them off and picking them up. Howard is smelling himself. He's claiming he's too old for someone's dad to be dropping them off."

"I can't hate on him. I remember being that age. The last thing I wanted was for you or Mom to have to take me anywhere. Then again, that's why I got a job. Howard is too busy with the sports and stuff to work as I did, though."

Dad agreed, "That's why I'm not trying to have him work. He knows how to drive, and he has his permit. We will get him a car when he does what's necessary."

I said, "It sounds like he's distracted."

Dad added, "It doesn't make sense to get this close and give up on the prize. This is what Howard said he wanted."

"That's true. I'll get with him sometime this week and see where his head is."

"I hope it helps." Then Dad transitioned, "How's Tanya?"

"I spoke to her last night. She made it home safe. We are going to have that talk when she comes back."

"Well, you have to do what you have to do. It's been a long time coming. There is no need to prolong it."

"You're right."

King inquired, "How long have you been with her."

"Off and on for two years."

Dad cosigned, "Two rocky years of wasted time. He knew after the first date that she wasn't the one."

"I know, but I got lonely, and time went on. Now, here we are after two years. We have no foundation and definitely no future."

"She is smart as a whip and gorgeous. But there needs to be more than that when seeking a wife. Let it go as soon as you know that's not the one." Said Dad.

"I'm kicking myself because I didn't heed the advice. Now I have the woman of my dreams in front of me, and I'm unprepared for her."

"King, he has been talking about this woman of his dreams for at least three or four years. "

"Well, I met her the other day. She was just as I described. She even had on the red sweater."

"No kidding. Where did you meet?"

"Right here at the studio. It's King's daughter, Melinda."

"Melinda?" He looked at King, "Is that right?"

"He came into my office like he had just seen a ghost. Your boy was so speechless that he didn't even ask her name. I told him he could pursue her after he handles his business with Tanya.

Melinda has been through a lot lately. She doesn't need the drama."

"You're talking about Trevon?"

"She told you about him?"

"Yeah, she did. Guys like him make it hard for brothers like me."

Dad interjected, "Brothers like you? I'm going to have to call you out. You haven't always been right."

"That's past stuff. God threw that in the sea of forgetfulness years ago. I'm a changed man now."

"I was not talking about years ago. You have come a long way since then. I'm talking about now."

"Oh, that. I stand corrected. I don't have any right to judge Trevon because I led Tanya on. I am getting that straight now and giving Melinda space in the process. Know this, King, when the time is right, I'm going after her. Mr. Trevon is going to have to move out of the way. He can't have her."

King digressed, "Melinda said she enjoyed herself yesterday."

"I have something I need to do today that she might be interested in. I'll call her and see if she's available."

After leaving work, I telephoned Melinda. She agreed to go with me to the mall. I stopped by my parent's house on the way to the King's. While I was there, I intercepted a phone call from the school. They said Howard was absent from his last class the day before. I didn't think much of it. I figured he had a doctor's appointment or something."

When I got to Melinda, she expressed discomfort with spending time with me because I had a girlfriend. Once I put her fears to rest, she and I went to the mall and picked up the music I was looking for. We also traveled through the mall doing a little more shopping.

Melinda admired a beautiful black dress in the window. I suggested she try it on. While Melinda was in the dressing room, I sat outside daydreaming. She was my wife, and I was waiting for her to come and model the outfits. I knew I had it bad because I had never waited on any woman while she shopped.

After the mall, we picked up Sheila and went to the health club. We all lifted weights together, and then Melinda and I got on the treadmill while Sheila ran around the track. I told Melinda about my childhood in L.A. She shared about her childhood in Georgia.

Sheila and I took Melinda home and stayed for a while talking to her parents. When the visit ended, Melinda walked us to the door. She and Sheila embraced. Then Sheila mysteriously went out to the car. I followed after Melinda, said good night, and I kissed her on the forehead.

I got in the car to Sheila, snickering, "I thought I should come to the car so the two of you could be alone."

"That wasn't necessary."

"Indeed, it was. I saw the kiss on the forehead."

"I kiss you on the forehead."

"And who else?"

"Mom and Tanya..."

"Mom and Tanya, who is sort of your girlfriend... That's my point."

"What point, Sheila?"

"You like her, don't you, Ant?"

"She's nice."

"I know you, Ant. All this time you're spending with her. You don't even spend this much time with Tanya, who is sometimes your girlfriend."

"She's sometimes my girlfriend?"

"Sometimes you two are together, and sometimes you're not. I can't keep up."

"What's up with you, Sheila?"

"What are you talking about?"

"All this Tanya stuff."

"Ant, I can tell you are not into her."

"I like her."

"Since you have called yourself "liking her," have you ever bought her to dinner at Mom and Dad's?"

"No."

"And there you have it. Yet, every time I turn around, you are somewhere with Melinda. I know you're feeling her, and she's feeling you too. You two need to just hook up."

"She has a man, and I'm dealing with Tanya right now."

"Melinda has pretty much kicked that trifling dude to the curb. She is not even wearing the ring. And you need to stop dealing with Tanya because you know that's not you."

"What ring?"

"He asked her to marry him before she came out here. He gave her a ring and asked her to think about it."

"Well, maybe I will just focus on me and my career."

"You're just saying that because you are scared to step to Melinda. Forget Tre' whatever his name is."

"I'm not scared of anything, Sheila."

"What are you waiting for then?"

"What are you waiting for? I know you are feeling that preacher at church."

"The Bible says a man that finds a wife finds a good thing and obtains favor from the Lord. That brother is going to have to find me to get his favor. I hope you don't let your favor get on the plane without telling her how you feel."

By this time, we were pulling in front of my parent's house,

"Sheila, I'm not trying to skip the subject, but what's happening with Howard at school? The other day, I was just randomly asking him about it. He went in, talking about you running your mouth."

"That little simp."

"Don't you start, Sheila."

"I'm going to give him a break because it appears he's having a delusional breakdown. I usually have his back. He doesn't want me to tell Mom and Dad the whole story."

"What story?"

"He's been hanging with this trifling dude, Montel."

"Dad told me about him. He lives down the street, right?"

"That's all Dad knows. He has a bad reputation. Rachel, a friend from work, told me he used to sell drugs."

"Why didn't you tell Dad?"

"I'm giving Howard a chance to fix it."

"That's real. Well, you need to tell if he keeps it up. Montel sounds like bad news."

"Montel came over to the house several times when Mom and Dad weren't there. He has a foul mouth, and he even smokes."

"In the house?"

"No. I was coming up the walkway, and Montel was smoking in front. Then he had the nerve to say, "Hey, Miss Lady." I wanted to punch him in the throat."

"Dad would have a fit if he knew about that."

"Exactly. I want to give Howard a chance to straighten out his situation first, Ant. I told Howard he had better not have him in our house, or I was telling. I would want you guys to do that for me."

"It sounds like the situation is already getting out of control. Howard's grades are slipping, and he's talking about not playing basketball. I told Dad I would talk to him and see where his head was. I'll get with him."

"Better you than Dad."

"That's for real. I'm not coming in. I'll wait until you get inside, though."

"Okay, Ant, but think about what I said."

"About what? You said a lot."

"About Melinda."

"Good night, Sheila. I love you."

"I love you too." She kissed me on the cheek and got out of the car."

That night, I went to bed and thought about all the conversations I had that day. I was growing more concerned about Howard, and I admit, I was surprised about Melinda. Trevon gave her a ring, but she didn't tell me. Perhaps obtaining my favor was going to take more work than I thought.

The next evening, I went over to her house. Sheila had been over there most of that day helping Mrs. King. Melinda and I dropped Sheila off at home because she had to go to work.

Melinda had never had a pastrami sandwich. I thought it would be dope if I took her to get one. It was still early after we left Samos, so we went to the Theater and saw a movie. We shared popcorn, Red Vines, and a Coke. We had such a good time.

After taking Melinda home, I went to my spot and took a shower. I wasn't very sleepy, so I went into my music room and turned my sound system up. I was listening to Tank's version of, "I Can't Make You Love Me." It prompted me to sit at my keyboard and write new music. Melinda was in my head and was my inspiration.

That night in bed, my thoughts about Tanya and me and our relationship were inundated. Hindsight followed, telling me, "I should have never started dating her. All the signs pointed to NO because we had no spiritual foundation. My loneliness, ego, and lust took us on an emotional journey that neither of us needed, especially when I knew there would never be a future with the two of us."

Retrospect echoed, "You should have been the spiritual example and the friend Tanya needed." Realization followed, "Now she has new baggage to deal with, "mine." There was a mess before me that I created. Now, in walks Melinda, who already overwhelmingly had my heart."

I began to hurt for Tanya. Condemnation tried to tell me I was unworthy of Melinda. Citing, "I was the same creep that also made mistakes with Tangi." The liar wanted me to believe I had not changed and never would. Quickly rebuking that thought made room for conviction. Tanya suggested that we had a lot of thinking to do. She was partly right. I had a lot of praying to do as well. It was time for me to stop trying to fix everything. I turned over on my face and cried out for God's help.

Revelation awakened me in the night and informed me that I needed to forgive myself and ask for Tanya's forgiveness. There was also a need for the inevitable conversation with her. Then, a real friendship could grow.

As far as Melinda was concerned, I needed to start by listening to her and being a friend. While I was still in a relationship with Tanya, I had to respect boundaries and learn from my past relationships. My loneliness, ego, and sexual desires had to take a back seat to the needs of Melinda. As the Apostle Paul said, "Love thinketh not himself."

Advice taken: Innocent.
Advice ignored: I'd get off track again.

Chapter 8

You Got It Bad

Friday had come, and Melinda and I had not communicated for a few days. Being around her sent me into a tailspin, and I needed to gain control of my emotions. The next chapter of my life played out like the lyrics of Usher singing, "You Got It Bad."

Mom had agreed to make me an ultimate omelet. So, I was at the house standing in the vestibule, looking through the mail when Sheila came down the stairs and announced, "Hey, Ant. I can't wait until tonight. There are always fine men at Daniel's parties."

I teased, "Is the preacher going to be there?"

She fired back, "No, but Melinda is. Not only will she be there, but there will be a room full of eligible bachelors. You and I know she is gorgeous. If you don't step up your game, one of them could potentially be her Boaz, my dear brother." Then she strolled into the den.

Mom was at the stove in the kitchen. I hugged her from behind and kissed her on the cheek, "Is that my favorite sausage cooking?"

"Yeah, Al and Janet Roberts were out here. They came over for dinner last night. He bought your daddy five pounds of sausage this time. You can only get them in North Carolina."

"Good old Al. My man."

"How long are they going to be out here?"

"They went back this morning. Have a seat. I'll make your omelet."

I sat on the stool at the kitchen island and asked, "Dad's gone to work already?"

"Yes, he is. He told me about your dilemma."

"Which one?"

"Both."

"I've been praying about it."

"It's amazing that you have been dreaming about Melinda for years. I would not have believed you if you had not been telling me all along. She is a sweet young lady."

"Mom, she's beyond sweet. The craziest thing is I love this woman with all my heart. I met her over a week ago and will marry her today. She does something for me that no woman ever has, and I've never even kissed her."

"That's powerful."

"I have to be patient, though."

"And you've got to do right by Tanya."

"Dilemma number one. I feel bad about our relationship. I didn't do right by Tanya from the beginning."

"All you can do is do right by her now."

"Yeah, I will as soon as she comes back. Do you mind if I wash your car?"

"It's that bad, Son? You need to have the ultimate omelet and wash the car?"

I smiled, "I need all the therapy I can get right now. I need the omelet to cure my woes for Tanya. I need to wash the car to work off my frustration of not being able to have and hold Melinda."

After breakfast, I went out to wash my mom's car. When I saw Sheila coming out of the house with her purse on her shoulder, I shifted my eyes down the driveway. Melinda was in the driver's seat of her dad's car. I put the sponge in the bucket and went to say hello. The gorgeous lady still looked pretty with no makeup and hair pulled back in a ponytail. I rested my forearms on the window seal and said, "I haven't heard from you in a couple of days."

"Not since Wednesday," She responded.

Like a thirsty man, I suggested, "You know the phone rings both ways. You can call me too."

"Okay, but I hope you don't get tired of me."

I said, "Sheila, can you give Melinda my numbers?"

"Which number?" She asked.

"All of them." Sheila blushed and nodded, "Of course, big brother. I can do that."

That evening, I went to the party solo. Some fellows and I were talking shop when Melinda and Sheila entered. Man, that woman looked fine. But I didn't approach her. Using restraint, I observed from afar as Sheila introduced her to the other guests, mostly the men. About an hour later, I saw Melinda at the bar alone. I seized the opportunity and walked over. She had on the black dress from the mall. The three-inched black strapped sandals she wore caught my attention and directed it to her lovely legs. I complimented, "Melinda, I was right."

She smiled, "Right about what?"

"You look good in that dress."

She countered, "Thanks, Anthony, you don't look bad yourself."

I observed her glass, hoping it wasn't alcohol, and asked, "What are you drinking?"

"7-up." Relief caused me to grin.

Melinda probed, "What's going on?"

I blushed and nodded, signifying approval, "You really look good."

Blushing, she asserted, "You're embarrassing me, Anthony."

Ricky walked up and joined the conversation, flirting with Melinda. She playfully entertained him. At some point, Ricky rubbed her arm, "Do you have plans for tomorrow?"

I thought, "Bruh, don't do it." Then, I held my breath in anticipation of her response.

I exhaled when she replied, "Yes, I do."

Ricky resolved, "Maybe I'll call you sometime next week before you leave, and we can do lunch."

"Okay."

After he walked away, I crossed my arms and said, "Should I have dismissed myself?"

"No. Why do you ask?"

"Melinda, Ricky is single. He wants to take you out."

"I'm aware, but I'm not interested in him like that."

"I'm not the one you should be telling. I don't want you to get hurt. This is LA, and you have to be careful. If you are going to come right with him, do so. If not, make the lines clear. Don't be a tease."

"What does that mean?"

"Yes is yes, and no is no. Mean what you say and say what you mean." I walked away, realizing I had it so bad that I acted like a jealous boyfriend. About fifteen minutes after that incident, embarrassment and I left.

I woke up early on Saturday morning and went to my parent's house. They were gone for the weekend, so I thought it would be an excellent time to connect with Howard. I went into the kitchen where Sheila was cooking. "What's going on, big brother? What brings you to this side of town?" she asked while opening the oven.

Dad told me they would be out of town this weekend, so I'm taking Howard to breakfast. That way, I can see where his head is. Then, I'm supposed to connect with Melinda.

"Sheila smiled, "What do the two of you have planned for today?"

"She said she would give me some ideas to decorate my downstairs bathroom."

"Why couldn't Tanya do that?"

"You know that's not her thing. I mentioned it to Melinda, and she jumped at the chance."

"The plot thickens."

"What plot, Sheila?"

She leaned on the counter and smiled, "The love story unfolding before my eyes."

"There you go with your conspiracy theory. Why can't it be that the two of us are just friends?"

She asserted, "A, because you didn't invite me. B, because I know my big brother, and C, I saw you low-key checking her last night. By the way, what happened at the bar?"

"Nothing happened out of the way."

"Melinda said you got upset about something."

"She, Ricky, and I were all talking. I left right after that."

"Yes, without even saying goodbye. Something is up."

"Everything is not a conspiracy, Sheila."

She went to the stove and started stirring the grits, "Uh huh...Well, she thinks you're mad at her."

"I'll straighten things out with her this afternoon. What do you have planned for today?"

"Oh, since I called you out, you want to play like you were going to invite me all along."

I smiled, "You're a mess." Then I transitioned, "How's the preacher?"

She looked up and, with a snicker, revealed, "He and I are going to brunch today."

"Then why are you eating breakfast." I asked.

"Because I don't want to be ordering a lot of food."

"In other words, you don't want him to know you're greedy. You need to keep it real."

She playfully punched me in the arm, "Shut up, Ant. You're the one that needs to keep it real."

I transitioned and asked, "Is Howard up?"

"Probably not. That boy was on the phone with some girl all night."

"Let me go wake him."

"There's enough breakfast if you want to eat here. I can eat in the den if you want to talk to our baby brother alone."

"I'll let you know, Sis."

"I knocked on Howard's bedroom door and went in. He was asleep with his back turned. I sat in his desk chair and pulled myself beside his bed, "Howard, wake up."

He stretched and turned over, "What time is it?"

"About 8:45."

"Bro, it's Saturday, and Dad is not here. I'm sleeping in."

"I thought you might want to hang out with me today."

"What you got planned?"

"I was going to see if you wanted to go to breakfast, then Melinda and I were going to go to my place."

"What. You need a chaperone, Bro?"

"No, I don't need a chaperone. We're just friends."

"Right…right..." He says facetiously, "Now, is that the story we're telling Tanya, her daddy, or…?"

"It's the truth."

"As Tamar would say, "Them lies you tell. Melinda is fine! Are you trying to get me to believe you're not feeling her? No cap. If you're not, I will have to start wondering about you, Bro. Let me know cause if you're not going to, I'm gonna holler at her. She might like a younger man."

"Man, be quiet and get up."

"Is Sheila going?"

"Nah, she has a date with that Preacher."

He sighed and said, "I'm going to have to pass. Being the third wheel will mess up my street cred."

"You have no street credit."

"I have more cred than you and more game."

"Is that why you are sleeping with a hard, un-animate object?"

"I just have to go to the restroom."

"Dude, I'm talking about your phone. It's next to your pillow. Are you going or what?"

"I'm down for breakfast but I'll pass on the chaperone gig."

Shaking my head, I said, "Sheila cooked so we can eat here. We need to talk later, though."

"About what?"

"I want to see what's going on in your world."

"You need some player tips. I'll teach you."

"I stopped playing marbles years ago. That's all you can teach me. I'll see you downstairs."

We all ate breakfast together, and then I headed to Melinda's. Embarrassment accompanied me because I thought I was the only one who had noticed that I acted out of character at the party. Once I was in Melinda's presence, she made me feel comfortable. Her warm smile and tender voice told embarrassment to subside. However, I knew I would have to address my behavior so she would not feel uncomfortable. On the ride to my house, I said, "I'm sorry about last night. I had a lot on my mind."

"What do you mean?"

"When you, Ricky, and I were at the bar."

"Yeah, I thought I had said or done something to offend you."

"No, it was me."

She glanced my way, "So it had nothing to do with me?"

I didn't want to lie, nor was I ready to expose her to my reality. Therefore, I reiterated what was most of the truth, "No, it was me."

"Remember what I told you about honesty?" She asked.

"Yeah, I do."

"If I ever do something that offends, please tell me, okay?"

I glanced at her and agreed, "Yes, I will." I appreciated her sincerity and appreciation for truth and honesty.

After giving Melinda the tour of my place and letting her give me feedback on my bathroom, we settled in my music room. I shared some of my original songs, which she complimented. Little did this beautiful woman know she was the inspiration for the last piece I had written just days before.

On the drive home, I mentioned being hungry. Melinda insisted I come over, and she would cook for me. Curiosity had me wondering if she could. I offered to buy the food, but she would not let me.

When we got to her place, Melinda telephoned and invited Sheila and Howard to join us. Sheila came through the door smiling, "I'm in love."

I cut in, "Where is Howard?"

"He was going to come, but when that silly girl called, he decided to stay home."

"Howard has a girlfriend?" Melinda asked while closing the door.

Sheila responded sarcastically, "He has a bunch of little girls calling him. He thinks he's a player."

"He is a little cutie. I can see why they like him." Said Melinda.

Sheila offered, "Don't you all want to know how my date went?"

I said, "Not really."

"Anthony, don't be a hater. Melinda, you want to know, don't you?"

"Of course, I do."

Sheila's cell phone rang, so she said, "I've got to tell you later. That's him calling now. Where can I take my call?"

"You can take it upstairs in my room."

I loved the way Melinda related to my family and me. It wasn't my intent if she and I appeared to be a couple, and the lines were becoming smeared. I was just being me, and this woman allowed me to.

She was comfortable in her skin and never pretentious. It was a breath of fresh air. I didn't fantasize about Melinda being my wife as I did with Tanya. I couldn't afford to. The cost of having her in my fantasy and then finding out I would never have her was a price I didn't want to pay. She occupied space in my heart that was only reserved for the woman who would be my wife.

In the kitchen, I took pleasure in acting as Melinda's sous chef. She really could cook. She fried some red snapper and made smothered potatoes garnished with green onions. Melinda made us some Georgia sweet tea, my favorite drink after that day. After eating, she and I cleaned the kitchen and entered the den.

It was an excellent way to spend a Saturday with my fictitious girl. She and I sat on the couch, discussing my upcoming trip to Detroit. Our interaction was normal and fluid. I wanted, felt, and reacted like she was my lady, and I was her man.

The distortion started to become overwhelming and frustrating. I had concluded that I couldn't be around Melinda unless she were mine. Once I left her that day, I had planned not to see her anymore while she was in LA.

Melinda asked me to text Howard to see if he wanted me to bring him a plate. He didn't respond. My gut told me I needed to check on him.

After a while, Sheila got off the phone, came downstairs to the den, and asked Melinda and me to go to Santa Monica Beach with her and Damien. I didn't think that was a good idea. I gave several excuses that all fell dead. I surrendered after I saw Sheila's persistence.

We agreed to meet back up in a couple of hours. I wanted to go home, change, and take care of a few things. Those things included checking on Howard.

Melinda made a plate for me to drop off to him. A raggedy old model Honda occupied the space in the driveway I'd planned on pulling into. I went into the house and did not see anyone in the den. It appeared that Howard had company. So, I went into the kitchen to put Howard's food down.

I thought I smelt weed. The scent led me to the glass door leading to the rear of the house. I walked onto the terrace and found some young dude with a female on his lap. They were hugged up, and a lit joint was on the table in a makeshift ashtray.

I said, "Excuse me." They sat up quickly. I continued, "Where's Howard?"

The dude said, "You must be Howard's brother, Anthony."

By now, I was fuming and responded, "Yeah, I know who I am. Where's my brother?" I sighed, "Never mind, I'll find him."

I stormed upstairs to his room. As I neared his closed bedroom door, I could hear music. I knocked and went in. Apparently, he was about to get busy. This young female sat straddling his lap with her top off. Howard and I locked eyes. Then he jumped up when he heard me firmly, rhetorically ask, "What do you think you're doing?"

"Get these people out of Mom's house." Shaking my head, I walked out and went downstairs.

Dude and his girl were leaving. He said, "Tell Howard I'm out."

My brother and his girl came downstairs. I heard the door close, so I knew she'd left. Howard entered the kitchen, grinning, "Man, why did you wreck my party?

I was about to put it down." He looked at the plate Melinda sent him on the counter, "Is this for me?"

With fury, I lunged, "Are you serious right now? You have some dude acting like he's a resident of the house. He was sitting by the pool, smoking a joint, with a trick in his lap. You're upstairs with another one, with God only knows what was about to jump off in our parent's house, and you don't feel the need to explain?"

"It was only weed, and you can't say you weren't hitting it when you were seventeen."

"It's not about what I was doing. Don't try to play it down or deflect. This is our parent's home, and you are disrespecting it by letting dude act like this is his house and having drugs here. Then you want to stroll down here and act like I'm your boy. I am ten years older than you. I'm never your boy when you're acting a fool and being disrespectful. In fact, we can't be boys until you become a man. A man gets his own spot. He doesn't infringe on his parents."

"Man, you act like you're so perfect."

"Again, we're not going to deflect. This is about you being disrespectful. Get your stuff together. I'm going to make a run. Then I will be back to get you. You're coming home with me."

"Man, I'm not going nowhere. You're not my daddy."

"I'm your daddy this weekend."

"I don't need a babysitter."

"It's not about you needing a babysitter. You are disrespecting our parent's home. I'm not going to banter with you, Howard. We can handle this in two ways. You can deal with me, or you can deal with Dad. I've got to make a run. When I come back, be ready."

Later, Damien drove Tanya, Melinda, and me to the pier. We got on several rides. I will never forget the roller coaster revelation that changed my life. It was having mechanical problems, and Melinda and I got stuck at the top for a while. We decided to play the games once we got off the rollercoaster.

Damien and I bonded at the basketball hoops. We occupied them so long that Melinda and Sheila went and played other games, came back, and we were still there. Once it got dark, Sheila broke up the game by saying, "Okay, guys, don't forget about Melinda and me."

Damien agreed, "You're right. Let's get our prizes." He won three medium-sized bears and gave them to Sheila. I traded four medium bears for one large brown stuffed bear with a red bow and gave it to Melinda.

Melinda and I got some popcorn and coke. Sheila and Damien purchased cotton candy and started walking further down the pier. I wasn't feeling my baby sister going down the pier without me. Sheila started acting a little salty. I didn't care. I figured she'd get over it. Damien convinced me he had good intentions, so I let her go.

Melinda and I sat on a bench at the beginning of the pier. I wasn't saying much to her because I was in thought about Howard and my inevitable discussion with Tanya. She interrupted my moment with a conversation about Sheila and Damien. Then she stood up, gazed down the pier, and shared, "I want to see the ocean. Do you want to come?"

Leaning forward, I rested my forearms on my legs; clinching my hands, I said, "No." Truthfully, heck yeah! I wanted to walk down the pier with her, holding her hand. I would look into her eyes, tell her I loved her, and then kiss her. I didn't want to risk making a fool out of myself. I couldn't watch her walk away. So, I just put my head down.

I eventually sat back and started thinking about Tanya. I thought about how drop-dead gorgeous she was the day I first met her. I framed a picture in my mind of the way she looked in that red dress. The tempo changed when my memories turned south, calling my attention to how she snapped at me, labeling me as arrogant.

I gazed back and remembered how she blushed when I first gave her flowers. After dinner, that precious moment was interrupted by her having a fit because I paid the bill. The gentleman in me wanting to open the car door for her was marked as a travesty.

My heart softened the first time I saw her show real emotions. Me trying to comfort her led to her walking out on me. I remember the night we made love. Her coldness wanted me to go home. My heart hit rock bottom when I recalled the time Miss Lady showed up to the industry dinner on the arms of another man. Spellbound, I thought of the many times we had broken up and the many times we argued.

I glanced over at the roller coaster. It caught my consideration as I paralleled how it would stop and start, go up and down, to our broken relationship. My stomach was in a knot, and I started feeling like I was going to be sick. I got up and traveled down the pier. My emotions were beginning to get out of control, so I started praying, "God, I'm hurting, and I don't know what to do. I need some relief. Please help me! Show me your love."

At that moment, I looked up and saw Melinda. She was standing at the rail looking into the water. It had turned cold, so she was shivering. Instinctively, I went over. From behind, I wrapped my arms around her, gently pressed my body, and then my face against hers. She intuitively nestled into my arms where she belonged. I held her closer. The intimacy felt so natural—so good, but she was not mine to have or to hold.

From where we were standing, we could see the roller coaster. My inner thoughts spoke audibly from my mouth, "A relationship can be like that roller coaster. As soon as you realize it's not going to work, at some point, you have to get off and not go on that ride again. They say the definition of insanity is "keep doing the same thing and expecting a different result."

The many times Tanya and I tried to break it off, we found our way somehow back. I needed to get off our love rollercoaster and never get back on again.

The ride on the way home from the beach was crazy. Melinda fell asleep and naturally leaned over, and I received her onto my chest. As if it was expected, without thought, I kissed her on her forehead and stroked her hair.

Damien dropped Melinda and me off at her house, where I'd left my car. I walked her to the door. The comfort became too familiar as she and I mutually moved close to one another. Face to face, we locked eyes as she and I shared a speechless, nonphysical, intimate moment. I wondered if she was feeling the same way as me. Was it possible our chemistry was clearly illuminating to everyone else but her? Lip-to-lip and tongue-to-tongue would have been the next obvious place to go. But I took her key, put it in the door, and said, "Good night."

My baby sister was shaping up to be a classy lady. After I left Melinda's place, I went to my parent's house. Damien was sitting in the den chilling with my brother. Addressing Howard, I asked, "You ready to go?" Without saying a word, he got up and headed for the door.

Before leaving, I yelled up the stairs, "Sheila, I'm out," and said my goodbyes to Damien.

She hollered, "Ant, wait! Then, she came running down the stairs with her bags. When she reached the bottom, I asked, "What's up? Howard is going with me."

"Wait for me?"

"I thought you were staying with Melinda?"

"I am. Hold up a second." She called out to Damien. When he entered the vestibule, she said, "My brother is going to take me back to Melinda's."

"I could do that," Damien said while reaching for her bags.

She smiled, "It won't be necessary, but I appreciate the offer. I will let you carry my bag and walk me to the car, though."

What was going on? At first, I thought Damien had offended her, but I was conflicted because she was smiling. I followed Sheila's lead. He walked with us to the car, kissed her on the cheek, and left.

As we pulled off, I probed, "What was that all about?"

"I didn't want him to think I was needy or easy.

"Did he say something out of the way?"

"No, I really like him. I thought we should end the date there. I don't want us to become common."

I smiled, "I feel you."

The ride to my house was silent. I could tell Howard was wearing his feelings on his sleeves. So, I chose to avoid disrobing him with further conflict or conversation. When we got to my place, he camped out in the living room.

Sunday, he and I picked up Sheila and Melinda for church. Afterward, the four of us went out to dinner. When we got back to the house, my folks were there. Dad asked how the weekend went. I evaded lying by only highlighting the positive things.

Later that night, Howard texted me, "Thanks, Bro." Little did he know, I wasn't finished with him. It was just time for an intermission.

Monday, while Ricky and I were working on a project, he offered, "Man, King's daughter Melinda is fine. I've got to get with her before she leaves."

I ran my hand down my face, "Yeah, Man, about that."

He asked, "Is that you? I thought I sensed some chemistry between the two of you the other night."

"Yes, but I haven't stepped to her yet. She is the one."

"The one? Man, that's deep. What are you waiting for?"

"It's coming. I need to take my time. Anything good is worth waiting for."

"What about Tanya?"

"She's the reason I haven't stepped to Melinda. We have unfinished business."

"Yeah, I feel you, man. Alright. I'll fall back."

"I'd appreciate that."

"You got it. Just don't take too long. Melinda is the business. There's no need for both of us to miss out."

Melinda, her parents, and her brother Kenny, who had flown in that morning, spent Christmas Eve with us at my parents' house. Sheila's new boyfriend Damien was there too. We danced, sang, and played all kinds of games.

On Christmas Day, it was just my siblings and parents. My folks got me a new tablet. Sheila and Howard hooked me up with a Nike sweatsuit and the latest Jordans.

Everyone got either cash or a gift card from me. Mom prepared an incredible spread that included my favorites: mixed greens, cornbread stuffing, and glazed ham. I filled my plate twice and took a plate home. After dinner, Dad, Howard, and I settled in the den to watch football.

Later that evening, Sheila announced, "Anthony, I'm about to take Melinda and her parents their gifts. Do you want to come?"

I said, "No, but you can take her my gift." I got up, went into the living room to the Christmas tree, picked up the small package, and handed it to Sheila.

She asked, "What did you get her?"

"A gift card. Do you think that's appropriate?"

"Ant, you just met her. Of course, she would be happy to get a little gift card. Where is it, too?"

"Goldsmiths."

"Goldsmiths? She's hardly going to be able to get anything. That place is high-end. How much is it?"

"Five hundred. Do you think that's enough?"

"Now I know for sure you got it bad. You are into Melinda, and you've lost your mind. Five hundred dollars, Ant?" She sat down and suggested, "Seriously though, five hundred is over the top for someone you just met. What if the two of you don't hook up?"

"Who said I wanted to hook up? She's just a nice young lady, and I wanted to get something nice for her."

"You are in as much denial as she is. You know you are feeling her, and she's feeling you. You don't spend this kind of money on anyone."

"Yes, I do."

"You only gave me two hundred to Old Navy, and I'm your favorite sister."

"Sheila, you are my only sister."

"That's why you should spoil me more."

I smiled, "Yeah, right. What would you suggest?"

"If you hook up, give it to her on your sixth-month anniversary. You might scare her if you give her that now."

We embraced, and I said, "Thanks, Sis."

"Thank me by taking me to lunch when you come back."

"I can do that."

Sheila was right, and she bought me into reality. I didn't see Melinda before she or I left, but I did telephone her to say goodbye. She revealed a shocker when I asked, "What will you do when you get home?"

She contemplated, "Trevon is picking me up from the airport. I think it's time we had a conversation."

"Are you going to get back with him?"

"It's a possibility. I'll know when I get home. Being here in LA has allowed me to clear my head. He did ask me to marry him. Although I can't answer that question, I may need to give us a chance."

"So, you haven't completely decided?"

"I believe I will know when I see him, and we have a chance to talk. My dad asked me to pray about it. I have been praying day and night. I am sure I will get my answer. What do you think, Anthony? If you were me, would you get back with him?"

I forged, "Well, Melinda, I'm not you." Then I bit my tongue, put my desires on hold, and continued, "One person's pain threshold may differ from another's. What your dad told you is sound advice. I would only add to be open to what God tells you." Inside, I did not believe God would ask her to say yes to a guy like him.

Melinda said, "Thanks, Anthony, you are a good guy. I know you can't wait until Tanya comes back. You must miss her a great deal."

"I just hope she had a good time with her family."

"Well, I know you are going to be busy working. You still try to have a good time on your trip."

"I will."

Melinda suggested, "Let's keep in touch. Call me now and then."

"And you do the same."

"Definitely. It was nice hanging out with you and Sheila. I mean it. I don't know what I would have done without the two of you."

"Well, you can return the favor if I ever come to Atlanta."

"You can count on it. Maybe you can meet Trevon."

"Maybe so."

That phone call left me completely discouraged. Perhaps the dreams were a lie, or God was punishing me for not obeying Him. My mind told my heart to be afraid. Fear helped me not to call her. Fear also convinced me to give up my fight for favor and give her space to work things out with Trevon. The ounce of courage I had left told me to leave the door open for her to walk through if she wanted to.

Even though it appeared Melinda and I were not going to get together, I knew I still needed to close that chapter of my life with Tanya. I contemplated going back to how I was before our relationship. I would remain celibate and not date unless it was the woman God had for me. Work and church would again become my mainstay.

Advice taken: Innocent:
Advice ignored: I could get betrayed.

Chapter 9

Let's Just Kiss and Say Goodbye

Fear did not want to meet with argument, so I was not looking forward to having the necessary conversation with Tanya. For strength, I prepared myself by committing to a time of prayer and fasting. She returned from her trip a few days before I did.

Clearly, Tanya was as anxious as me to talk. The evening I returned, she came to my place before I could unpack. We greeted one another with a kiss on the lips and a hug. She proceeded to take off her coat. I finished helping her. After putting her jacket on the coat rack, I turned and looked at her standing.

Stunning is the word that describes her with the sexy red pantsuit that gloved her body. Her breast peeked out from the suggestive little top she had on underneath. I admired her straightened hair that lay on her shoulders.

Her silver and diamond earrings sparkled. I complimented, "You look great. I feel underdressed in my jeans. It looks like I should be taking you out."

She blushed, "You're fine. I just came back from an event."

"How was it?"

"It was cool."

I offered, "Can I get you something to eat? I have a chicken baking in the oven."

"You cooked?" She asked.

"Yeah, I did."

"I'm not hungry. I want to sit down."

As she moved toward the couch, my eyes followed behind. I thought, "What's really going on? What is Tanya up to? She knew I loved to see her in red."

I sat beside her on the couch, "How was Chicago?"

"I can't complain. I spent time with my family, which gave me time to think."

"Oh, yeah?"

Before I left, I asked if you were in love with me, but you couldn't answer. That spoke volumes."

I thought, "Here we go. Let's get ready to rumble", but I said, "It caught me off guard."

"It should not have. If you were in love with me, it should have been natural. Anthony, we've been involved for over two years. We don't have anything to show for it. No commitment or anything. We've never even exchanged I love you."

"It's not like the last two years have been all uphill. It has yet to be consistent. It's been rocky at best. One gigantic roller-coaster, but we both have responsibility in that."

"I didn't say I've done everything right. I'm just tired of this relationship being stagnant. We are no further now than our first date. At one time, we at least used to sleep together occasionally. Now, we don't even do that. It hurt my feelings that you wouldn't even come to Chicago."

"I'm sorry."

She stood and said, "Don't be. Your parents live here in the city, and you've never even taken me to their house. It made me start thinking and taking a long look at us. We're so caught up in our careers that I think we tolerate each other."

"Are you saying you're not in love with me either?"

"I care for you. But you want too much from me. You're old fashion, and I'm not Clair Huxtable."

"What's wrong with Clair? She was a good catch and a beautiful, intelligent, sexy woman. Not to mention, she had a career, children, and a husband who loved her."

Tanya declared, "That's my point. I don't want kids. My career is very important to me."

"I can respect that, but I want my Clair Huxtable."

"Would you be willing to have Clair without the children?"

"Having a family is important to me, Tanya."

"Then you can't have me, Anthony."

I asked, "Are you giving me an ultimatum? I have to choose between you and giving up my desire to father children, or we can't move forward?"

"Why should we continue to go on and we've reached a point of impasse? Clearly, the children are a deal breaker for both of us."

I offered, "Do you want to break things off again?"

"Yes, I do, for good this time. We need to go our separate ways and stop the off-and-on-again madness."

"Are you sure that's what you want?"

"Take a good look at me. Are you sure that's what you want? I'm a good woman, and I doubt you will find your Clair."

I surmised, "Oh, this is the game we're playing tonight, all in or all out? Is the sexy red pants suit a bargaining chip?"

She admitted, "Absolutely. You have to always bring your A-game."

"How about leaving the games at home and just bringing yourself? I guarantee you'll get better results."

She said, "I'm not willing to give any more of me."

"That's your choice. As I said, I can respect that."

"It's time for us to move on with our lives."

I offered, "This is the first time we had an intense conversation, and it ended peaceably."

Tanya said, "On that note, I will say good night so it can stay that way."

I got her coat and met her at the front door. After helping her, we embraced, and I offered, "Take care of yourself."

She concluded, "I will."

I followed the script written by The Manhattans. Tanya and I kissed for the last time as a couple and said goodbye. The situation was bittersweet. Tanya was going to be missed. She filled some of my lonely days. At the same time, I could move on with my life. Unfortunately, there was no Melinda to move on with.

After three weeks, Melinda still had not called. She spoke to Sheila from time to time. My days were often filled with thoughts about her. Mostly, I imagined her with Trevon. I tried to get her off my mind, but still loved her greatly. I didn't have the right to, but I felt like a jilted lover.

However, there was a shift that changed my perspective. Dad, King, and I went to a ball game in which we had box seats. We were waiting for the game to start when King solicited, "Have you talked to Melinda lately?"

I offered, "No, the last time I talked to her, she said Trevon asked her to marry him. I thought I would give her some space."

"Is that so? Hum. Are you sure? She hasn't mentioned him to her mother or me."

"Yeah, Melinda told me she wanted me to meet him when I came out. That hurt right in my gut. I love her to death and don't like that dude."

"Dad chimed in, "What are you going to do? Are you just going to sit back and let him have her? I thought you said she was the woman of your dreams. What God has for you, it is for you."

"What should I do, Dad?"

"Go out there. Tell Melinda how you feel."

I said, "She's all into him."

Dad countered, "She doesn't know you're all into her. Is she worth fighting for?"

I snickered and asked, "Literally?"

"No, Man, figuratively."

"Yes. I can't get Melinda off my mind."

King crossed his arms and sat back, "She's my daughter, but I still say you got to go for it. You missed the opportunity once. Besides, what would I do with Trevon as my son-in-law?"

That night, after Dad and I dropped King off at home, I went to my parent's house. I was a little hungry and went into the kitchen for a snack. Sheila and Damien were sitting at the table eating.

Sheila greeted, "Hey, Ant."

"Hey."

Damien stood up, "Hey, Man, do you want to share? We have plenty?"

"What do you have?"

"Take out from Titphalith Yem's, shrimp broccoli, and fried rice. Help yourself."

I got a plate from the cabinet and joined them at the table. As we ate, I asked, "Sheila, how is Melinda?"

"You haven't talked to her?"

"No, not for about three weeks."

Shaking her head, "Brother, brother, brother."

"What?"

"Three weeks?"

"Yeah, the last I talked to her, she was trying to work things out with Trevon."

"When was that?"

"Before she left."

"Oh no, I talked to her yesterday. I don't think she got back with Trevon."

"Hum, really?"

"I'm more than sure."

"I'm going to be going out there soon. Maybe I'll look Melinda up."

Sheila offered, "I'll tell her you're coming."

"No. I'll work it out, but thanks."

Damien chimed in, "When I saw you two together, I thought you were already a couple."

Sheila added, "I told him that. He didn't want to believe me."

I smiled, "Well, we'll see what's up. I'll make Atlanta the first stop on my scouting tour."

"That's what I am talking about, Big Brother. Go get your girl."

I was so excited about the news that I went home that night and put together my tour schedule. My trip was going to begin with five days in Georgia.

First thing in the morning, when I went to work, I immediately called my assistant Anita into my office. She came in and sat down, "What's going on, boss?"

"I need you to make travel arrangements for next week."

"Where to this time?"

"I'm going to start with five days in Georgia. I want to get there next Friday morning and stay until Tuesday evening. Call Vernon Thomas at Scorza Studio and tell him I will meet with him on Wednesday afternoon. I need him to have all the artists he wants me to see on Thursday. Leave my ticket from New York open-ended just in case I need to go somewhere else."

"I always leave your tickets open. Who are you meeting with in Georgia?"

"I'm not meeting with anyone, particularly at the studio. I'm going to take care of some personal business for a few days and do some scouting the rest of the time."

"I will take care of it right away."

Two hours later, Anita returned to my office and confirmed, "Okay, your Airline reservations have been taken care of. I also booked your hotel at the usual spot in New York. What hotel would you like to stay in when you go to Atlanta?"

"Have a seat. Let me get King on the phone." I dialed his extension, "King, can you recommend a hotel in Atlanta near Melinda's place? I also need her home phone number."

"You decided to go?"

"Yeah, I've got to see her. I'm going out there next Friday. Can you keep it under wraps? I want to surprise her."

"Absolutely. The Embassy is the best place to stay. It's about fifteen minutes away. Let me run down Tracey's phone number, and I'll get that to you."

"Okay. Thanks."

I hung up and said, "Anita, book me a suite at the Embassy. Also, I was hoping you could order a box of See's Candy. Make sure there are a lot of Almond Squares. She loves those. I need the candy and twelve long-stem red roses waiting for me when I get to my hotel."

"Red roses. Are you sure? You never send red roses."

"I'm positive. I'm also going to need a nice car."

"Are you going to pick the car up from the airport or have one waiting at the hotel?"

"Have it waiting at the hotel. Let the car service pick me up from the airport."

"Okay, I'll take care of everything. It's been a long time since I've seen you this excited."

I blushed, "I can't remember ever being this excited. Melinda is the woman of my dreams."

Friday couldn't get there quick enough. Anxiety made me behave like a little child waiting for a memorable excursion. I didn't sleep nights, reminiscing about my time with her in LA.

On the day of the trip, I was dressed two hours before the car service was to pick me up. On the plane, I rehearsed in my mind over and over what I would say. I called her cell in the car on the way to the hotel. There was no answer, so I called the home phone and spoke to Tracey. She didn't give me the details but confirmed that Melinda was no longer seeing Trevon. Together, she and I conspired for me to surprise Melinda that evening. I got off the phone and said a resounding, "Hallelujah!"

After checking into the hotel, I went directly to my suite. Sitting on the dresser was a vase with a dozen red carnations and the box of See's Candies. I was a disappointed that the wrong flowers were delivered. The florist informed me that there was a mix-up with the order. They assured me they would replace them within the hour.

I arrived at Melinda's place promptly at six, rang the doorbell, and there was no answer. I waited for a few minutes and rang the doorbell again. Melinda's friend Tracey answered. She put me in the mind of Regina King or K. Michelle, only she had dreadlocked hair. Out of my peripheral, I saw Melinda coming down the stairs. So, I directed my full attention toward her.

Oh my, she looked so beautiful. I'd never seen her hair that way. She knew how to dress. My girl wore a lovely black pantsuit, a white ruffled shirt underneath, and some high-end red shoes to accent. She greeted me, "Oh my God, Anthony. Come on in. I'm so surprised."

While handing her the flowers and candy, I said, "I hope it's a pleasant surprise."

"Don't be silly. You're always welcome. You don't need an invitation."

Getting right to the business, I pulled her close, looked into her eyes, and rubbed her face gently with my finger, "You look so good." My heart began to break when I looked into her eyes and saw she'd been crying. I asked, "Have you been crying?" She looked down, then up into my eyes.

I said, "I've missed you."

As long as she allowed me to hold her, I planned to. And I did until Tracey's voice echoed, "Let me take those flowers and put them in water."

Melinda handed Tracey the flowers, took my coat, hung it on the coat rack, and invited me to sit down. She sat next to me.

Tracey returned to the room and told us she would spend the evening with her boyfriend, Reggie. Before she left, she kissed Melinda on the forehead and said, "I love you. I need you to be okay. You have a good time tonight, and I will see you later." Those words confirmed that something was going on with my girl.

After Tracey left, it was silent for a moment. I was trying to figure out what I should say. When I had rehearsed it in my mind, I had not just seen tears in her eyes. I didn't want to come off as selfish and insensitive.

Melinda broke the silence by saying, "I'm glad you came. What are you doing out here? How long are you staying? Where are you staying?"

"I've been here since early this morning. I'm working. I'm here until Tuesday evening. I'm staying at the Embassy, and I'm here at your house because I wanted to take you out."

"Wow! You said a mouth full."

"You asked me a lot of questions. Now it's my turn. When are you moving to LA?"

"When school is out."

I took a deep breath and asked the dreaded question, "What about Trevon?"

She rose and walked toward the fireplace, "There is no more Trevon."

I could tell that this was the source of her pain. I asked, "What happened? Is that why you have been crying? You can tell me."

"Trevon and I are done. Remember when I told you I thought he was cheating?"

"Yeah."

"Well, it was confirmed the day I got back from California. I found out he got someone pregnant."

Inside, I was heated enough to find Trevon and punch him in the face for hurting her. On the other hand, I knew she was better off without him. I was also glad I was there to comfort her. I desired to replace all the hurt he afflicted with my love.

Stroking her lengthy hair, I offered, "Melinda, I could…" slipped out of my mouth and replaced itself with silence.

She probed, "What's wrong? What's on your mind?"

I gently took both of her hands, "It's not what's on my mind; it's what's in my heart. I've only got to know you briefly, and it's been a month since I last saw you. I've missed you. Can I confess?"

"What?"

"I planned to work in Atlanta because I needed to see you."

She blushed, "Why? What's going on?"

"I can't get you off my mind."

"What about Tanya? And you said you weren't interested in getting with me."

"Trying and wanting are two entirely different words. Although I wasn't trying to get with you, I wanted to." I slipped my hands around her waist and pulled her closer to me. "I wasn't trying to get with you, and Tanya was still in the picture."

"And now?"

"We broke it off when she came back from Chicago."

"Why did you break up?" She asked.

"Our values are so different."

"But she is beautiful, smart, and ambitious."

I agreed, "Yeah, that's true, but."

"It didn't have anything to do with me, did it?"

"Not directly."

"Anthony, I don't understand. Explain that to me."

"Tanya and I had been in an off-and-on dead-end relationship for two years. Right before you came, we were on the verge of breaking up. It became clear the night you and I went to the pier and got stuck on the rollercoaster. It was time to end things. I have always believed that there was that one woman in the world for me. I had started giving up. But when I walked into the studio lobby and saw you sitting there, I was attracted to you. It was love at first sight. The times since then that we've spent together have been good. I knew you were a special lady. You have a beautiful spirit. You're intelligent, talented, pretty, and a good friend. I want us to build on that friendship. I told your dad I wanted to pursue you."

"What did he say?"

"I had his blessing. Good luck, respect you, and if I violated you, he'd kill me."

"My daddy is a mess."

"If you were my daughter, I'd feel the same. I will always respect you and never violate you in any way. When I noticed you had been crying tonight, I just wanted to love you. I don't ever want to see you hurting." Running my fingers through her hair, I shared, "You look more beautiful than I remember."

She blushed, "Thank you, and you are more handsome than I recall."

"You've had my heart from the first day I saw you. I don't know how to explain it. I knew I loved you and had to have you. Melinda being in love is a decision. I've been permitted by your father to pursue you. I need you to allow me to love you."

"But I live way out here in Atlanta. How is that going to work?"

"I know we live miles apart right now. We'll talk every day. I'll see you every chance I get. No doubt you've been told this before, but I swear I will never cheat, disrespect, or ever leave you. I need you to say you'll give us a chance."

It's as if Etta James was singing in the background of my mind "At Last."

I leaned closer and looked into the deepening of her eyes, "Can I kiss you?"

She nodded her head yes. I pulled Melinda closer, pressed my lips against hers, and kissed her passionately. It felt so right when she reciprocated and melted in my arms. I enjoyed every moment. After what seemed to be about five minutes, she stepped back, "Whew, this is heavy. I don't know how to take it. You've been a friend. I just never imagined you felt the way you do."

I offered, "I can be a friend and more. I have to have you in my life in a more intimate way. If you need time, I'll wait. I need you to want this, too."

"Wow, this is heavy. I need to think."

"While in town, I would love to spend time with you. After I'm gone, will you think about us and let me know?"

"Anthony, I think you are so handsome, nice...."

"But...?"

"There is no but. I think the world of you. Let's take it slow and see where it goes, okay?"

"We can do that."

After talking, I took her to dinner and Tyler Perry's latest play. It felt so good being with Melinda again. This time, it was even better because she was now my lady.

That evening, she and I went back to her place. I put wood on the fire and shared some of her See's candy. We cuddled on the couch as we continued to talk. It was 3 AM when I left, but not before planning to take Melinda to lunch and a musical at a church the next day.

While preparing to leave, she got my coat, helped me put it on, and walked me to the door. I kissed her on the lips and told her I'd call her when I got to my room.

Before I could leave, she softly called out. "Anthony?" I turned, and she walked up close to me. "The evening we went to the beach, I remember Damien dropping us off at my house. When you walked me to the door, I felt something was happening between us. Was it me or?"

I rubbed her face and confirmed, "It was happening."

Her eyes invited me to consummate the unspoken, nonverbal, intimate moment we'd started in Los Angeles. Holding her tight, lip to lip and then tongue to tongue, passionately our moment, our time, at last, I loved her more than anything or anyone but God.

The following day, I was awakened by a phone call from Anita, "Hey Anthony, I was just calling to see if you need me to do anything today."

"No. I'm good."

"Okay, let me know if anything comes up."

"Oh, there is one thing. The order for the flowers was wrong. They sent carnations when I specifically asked for roses. She shared her candy with me last night, and I noticed only two Almond Squares in the box. I checked my notes and asked that you ensure a lot was in there. Two doesn't constitute a lot."

"I'm sorry. I will check into it. I don't know what could have happened. I hope Melinda wasn't upset."

"She wouldn't be. She's too gracious. But I did. When I ask for something to happen, I need it to happen. I shouldn't have to justify what I need it for."

"You're right. I'm sorry."

"Anita, people mess up now and then. Melinda is very special to me. This is the first time I have come out here to see her. The flowers and the candy were wrong. What would I have looked like showing up at her door with some carnations? That's too much for one day."

"I understand, but I had Tyra…."

"You had Tyra do what? Anita is the one in charge, right?"

"It won't happen again."

"We've been doing this for a minute. You know how I like things."

"You're a man of excellence."

"That's right, and when it comes to Melinda, I need Anita to ensure things are done excellently."

"I got you."

"Have a good day. I'm not going to need anything. As a matter of fact, take the rest of the weekend off. I'll hit you up on Monday."

"Have a good weekend. Tell Melinda hello."

"Will do."

I picked Melinda up at about eleven. After brunch, she and I went to the Aquarium. Then, the Martin Luther King Museum. Later that evening, Melinda and I attended a Gospel Concert at a church in Atlanta. After the concert, one of the singers I came to see introduced Melinda and me to the pastor, who invited us to come back to service on Sunday.

Sunday morning, I picked Melinda up for service. Coincidently, she had on a navy dress that complemented the navy suit I was wearing. During praise and worship, all I could do is to thank God. After all the awful things I'd done to, and with Tangi, Tanya, and all the rest, He still blessed me. Not only did he forgive me, but He also kept His promise. I knew he'd given Melinda to me, and I vowed I'd always love her. Tears flowed from my eyes. Lifting my hands, I worshipped my God. I didn't care who was looking. Nobody knew the grace and mercy He had extended to me.

After the pastor finished preaching, he called Melinda to pray for her. As the pastor prayed, I prayed for her silently. She did the cutest thing when I took her to Ruth Chrisp's Steakhouse for dinner that evening. When the check came, she said, "Let me pay. You are here visiting me."

I blushed as I looked at the two hundred- and ninety-one-dollar check, "I don't think you want to pick up this one."

"I can afford to take you to dinner."

While still smiling I said, "I'm sure you can. When we go out to dinner, I'll pay. When you cook me dinner, you pay. How about that?"

"Are you saying you want me to cook something for you?"

"Miss Lady, you can burn. I will never turn down your cooking."

"How about Monday night?"

"Sounds like a date."

Later that evening, I went back to her place. Tracey, Reggie, Melinda, and I had banana splits and played Uno and Scrabble until I left at 10 PM. I left early because I had to get up at dawn the following day. A lot of good that did. When I got to the hotel, I called Melinda, and we talked until midnight.

Monday morning brought disappointing news. Anita informed me that I had a conference call with Vernon from Scorza Studios at noon. On the call, he'd gotten the impression I would be there Tuesday instead of Wednesday. He'd booked the artist for Tuesday and Wednesday and had booked meetings for us all day. While on the call, I checked the computer and found I'd have to leave Monday evening to make my first appointment in New York for Tuesday. By the time I got off the call, it was 2:15 PM. So, I got my things packed and checked out of the hotel.

I knew I could not have dinner with Melinda, so I decided to go by her house early and let her know.

I pulled into the driveway behind Melinda, who was arriving from work. I met her with a hug and a kiss on the lips. She said, "You're early," As she attempted to get some shopping bags out of the trunk."

"I know. Let me help you get those groceries." I got the bags, and she got a vase of flowers and the card from the passenger side of her vehicle. Admittedly, I was curious about the flowers but didn't want to sound like a jealous boyfriend and ask.

Once we got inside, I put the groceries on the counter in the kitchen. Melinda put the fresh flowers in the trash next to the counter. I noticed Trevon had signed the card, but I did not comment. I just sat on the stool. She came over and stood in front of me. I pulled her to me by the waist and kissed her on the lips.

Melinda pulled back and started straightening my tie, "I wasn't expecting you so early, but I'm glad to see you."

I sighed, "I had a conference call this afternoon. I have to leave in a couple of hours."

"What do you mean?"

I hesitated, "I have to go to New York earlier. My flight leaves in three hours."

"What about dinner?"

"We only have an hour, and I would hate for you to spend that time in the kitchen. I'll pick something up at the airport."

She was so cute when she whined. "I was just looking forward to seeing you one more night."

"I know. I was looking forward to your good cooking and spending time with you. I rubbed Melinda's face with the back of my finger. I'm sorry. I'll make it up to you."

"If we date, is this what it will be like?"

I could tell she was even more disenchanted than me, so I offered, "It's disappointing because we were expecting more time and got blindsided. We only have a few months until you graduate. You will be in LA all the time then."

"Will you?"

"No, but we'll be sure the time we spend together is quality. I travel a lot right now. It won't always be this way. I never had a reason not to."

She didn't say anything. I didn't want to risk losing her, so I forged, "Will you give us a try?"

Melinda looked up at me and said nothing. But I could sense she was afraid, and perhaps she wasn't ready for us.

I offered, "I'm not going to pressure you. I'll give you some space and let you think about it."

Melinda said, "Okay." Then turned around and leaned on the stool in front of me. Her head fell back. I held her tight as we said nothing for a while.

Advice taken: Innocent
Advice ignored: Betrayal

Chapter 10

When Somebody Loves You Back

My business in New York kept me longer than I had expected. I had already been there for eight days and buried myself in my work. It helped me keep my mind off Melinda because I wanted to give her space. While there, I received several texts and voice messages from Tanya, wanting to talk. They went unanswered.

I came to my room after a day inundated with meetings on Wednesday evening. I took a shower and ordered dinner by way of room service. After eating, I turned the television to the oldies station. Teddy Pendergrass came on singing, "When Somebody Loves You Back." My thoughts shifted to Melinda. I wanted to get her off my mind, so I turned the TV off. That didn't work, so I pulled out a book. The words, nor could the pictures, hold my attention. I hadn't spoken to her in over a week and longed to hear her voice. I picked up my cell and scrolled down to her number. Then I put the phone down. I repeated those steps about three times in one hour. Finally, I pressed the number. She answered with excitement, which immediately put me at ease. I invited her to Mammoth Mountains with me, Ricky, Daniel, and their dates. She was apprehensive, fearing her dad would not be down with it. I assured her I would deal with King.

The minute I finished talking to Melinda, I knew I had barked up a giant tree. King. Nonetheless, I telephoned him at the studio. He answered, "Hey, Son, how's it going? Or am I going to be calling Trevon, son?"

"What God has for me is for me. You know that's my lady."

"It might be your lady, but she will always be my baby."

I swallowed and thought, "This conversation isn't going to turn out well." But I forged ahead. "My visit with Melinda went well, Pops." We both laugh and then I seize the moment, "Hey, I was wondering how you would feel about me taking her to the mountains. A group of us are going. I would pay and make the arrangements, of course."

"I think she would love that. I spoke to her last week after you left. She told me you two were an item. I was being face-tious before. Thank God that Trevon is a thing of the past."

"Indeed, he is. He should have loved Melinda when he had the chance. I'm never letting her go."

"When are you all going on your trip?"

"I telephoned Anita and asked her to arrange for Melinda and me to meet at the airport on Thursday evening. We're leaving for Mammoth on Friday morning."

"You did that already before talking to me?"

I laughed, "Yes, I know you would support me."

"You better be glad I like you, or I would have my shotgun waiting."

"I'll be good to her and respectful."

"I'm not concerned. I trust my daughter. Just have a good time."

Tanya attempted to call me again several more times. I just let the phone go to voice mail. I did listen to one message. She apologized and said she wanted to get back together.

Before I got on the plane, I saw a missed call from Anita. She informed me that Melinda's flight was coming in earlier than mine. I telephoned Sheila to pick her up and left Melinda a message since she was already in the air.

Once I got to LA, the driver picked me up and took me to my parent's house to get my car. I turned my phone on to call Melinda to let her know I had made it to LA. My phone indicated I had several messages. Two messages were from Tanya. I finished listening to the messages and noticed there was an incoming call. I answered, saying, "This is Anthony."

Tanya responded, "Hey, Babe."

"Hey, Babe? I thought that ship had already sailed."

"You know how I can be."

"Yeah, Tanya, I do. That's why we are where we are."

"Don't be that way. You know you miss me."

I asserted, "You ended things, remember? You said the children were deal breakers. We needed to move on with our lives. I've moved on."

"Anthony, give me twenty minutes of your time face to face. If you still want to leave things the way they are, we can."

"Fine, you have twenty minutes."

"Let me go home and slip into something red, then I'll come over to your place."

"No, I don't think so. Meet me at my parent's house at 7."

"Oh, I finally get to come to your parent's house. That sounds encouraging."

"For twenty minutes."

"Fine, I'll see you at 7 PM., Babe."

I got to my parent's house, and no one was home except Mom, sitting in the den. As I entered the room, she said, "Hey, Son, how was your trip?"

"Too short in Atlanta and too long in New York."

"Are you hungry?"

"A little, but Melinda is here in Los Angeles. I thought we might go out to dinner. Then I want to hold her. That's the only thing I could think of on the plane."

"Well, you two are really hitting it off."

"Yeah, it went well in Atlanta. She came this weekend so that we can go to the mountains." I sat down and continued, "Guess who has been blowing up my phone?"

"Tanya?"

"Yep, how did you know?"

"It's the nature of women. What does she want?" Mom asked.

"To get back together."

"I figured that would happen. What did you tell Tanya?"

I said, "I am going to meet with her tonight."

"What are you thinking? Isn't Melinda here?"

"Yeah, I got this, Mom. Melinda doesn't have anything to worry about. If you don't mind, I told Tanya to come by this evening."

"Why?"

"I have some things of hers in the trunk of my car, and I want to tie up loose ends."

"I thought that was done."

"So, did I. If I return her things and let her know I've moved on with Melinda, she'll get the picture."

"Well, you make sure you tell Melinda what's going on. You don't want that to blow up in your face. That's no way to start a relationship."

"Melinda will understand. I'll tell her tonight at dinner after I talk to Tanya." I stood up. Where is everyone?"

"Your dad and Howard went to the store. I don't know where Sheila is."

"I asked her to pick Melinda up from the airport for me. She's probably at the King's house."

After about thirty minutes, Dad and Howard came in. Howard was still acting a little salty, but I just ignored him and loved him anyway. Thirty minutes later, I heard Sheila come in the door. I went out into the vestibule to make sure Melinda got in okay. Unexpectedly, Melinda was with her.

Sheila smirked, "Oops, my bad, I didn't know you were here, Ant."

I looked at her sideways and said, "I just got here."

Then I went over to Melinda, hugged her around the waist, kissed her on the lips, and greeted, "Hey, Babe."

Sheila smiled, "Apparently, you two have finally come completely out of denial." Melinda and I laughed. Sheila went into the den.

Still embracing, she looked up at me, "How was your flight?"

"Long. I'm a little tired. All I want to do tonight is get a bite to eat and come over and hold you for a little while. I talked to the guys, and they said we could leave tomorrow afternoon. Do you mind if we go to the mall in the morning? I'm so tired I'm just going to sleep here tonight."

"Do you want me to fix you something?"

"You've had a long day yourself. Let's get pastrami from Samos."

"That sounds good."

"Would you mind picking up the food? I have some loose ends to tie up. Then I'll come right over."

"I came with Sheila. I'll ask her to take me after I say hello to your folks."

She and I entered the den, where Howard and Sheila sat on the couch. My parents were sitting on the loveseat. Melinda said hello to everyone.

Mom looked up from her word search, "How was your flight, Melinda?"

"It was fine."

Dad inquired, "What are you young people up to?"

I rubbed Melinda's shoulder and announced, "We are in a committed relationship now. She came out here because we are going to Mammoth." Melinda blushed and looked up at me.

Sheila said, "Yawl should have gotten together when you were here last time."

Melinda responded, "There she goes."

Mom gestured to the couch, "Have a seat." Melinda sat on the sofa beside Sheila as she moved closer to Howard. I sat on the arm of the sofa next to my lady.

Before we could get comfortable, the doorbell rang. I wasn't expecting Tanya for another thirty minutes. Howard got up. "Oh, that's for me." After a few minutes, he returned, "Melinda, it's Tanya. She's here to see your man. What are you going to do?"

Sheila looked at Melinda and said, "Ignore him."

"I'm not thinking about Howard. I know he's crazy," said Melinda.

I was praying, please don't let this be an issue. I wasn't expecting Tanya and Melinda to be in the same place simultaneously. I got up, "Excuse me, Melinda. I need to talk to Tanya."

When I entered the living room, Tanya looked as stunning as ever. I motioned for her to sit on the couch, and I sat on the chair, "You wanted to talk?"

"I thought a lot about what you said you wanted. I know I've been selfish."

"Tanya, we've been off and on for two years. Now you want to admit you've been selfish?"

"I don't want to lose you, Anthony."

"How can you say you don't want to lose me? You no longer have me. If I'm not mistaken, you acknowledged that we were no further than where we started and weren't in love. I need to be in love."

"Us being a part helped me see things clearer. I realized that I'm in love with you, Anthony. That's why it was so frustrating that you wouldn't say you loved me, nor would you come to

Chicago. You can have it all with me. Just tell me what you want."

"Why are you doing this now?"

"You know I always talk crazy about leaving, but I always come back, don't I?"

"Not this time. I'm done."

"Is there someone else?"

"At your suggestion, we mutually agreed to move on."

"Who is she?"

"That doesn't even matter. All you need to know is she's my Clair Huxtable."

She moved forward, "I know you're not serious about anyone. We've been through this before. You'll be back."

Shaking my head, I stressed, "Not this time."

She stood and suggested, "I'll tell you what. I'm going to give you some space for a few weeks. When it doesn't work out, I'll be here."

I stood up and said, "Tanya, I'm not seeing her to spite you or to compete with you."

"We'll see."

"I have some of your things in my trunk. Let me walk out with you."

We got her things, and I walked her to her car. She said, "Don't let me wait too long."

I approached her, "Don't wait, Tanya, please. I've moved on for real. I'm seeing someone else and in love with her."

"You're in love with her?"

"Yes, Tanya, I am."

"How long have you been seeing her?"

"What does it matter? We mutually agreed at your suggestion to end things."

"Are you telling me that we saw each other for almost two years, and you weren't in love with me? Now you're in love with someone else."

"Yes."

It was as though she had an epiphany, "You're serious. You really have moved on?"

"I'm very serious. I've moved on."

"Wow." I could tell she was hurt but was trying to be gracious when she looked up at me and said, "I wish you the best." Then she got in her car and sat looking out of the front window, "This really hurts."

"I'm sorry it came down to this."

With a forged smirk, she said, "Me too, and started her car."

All I wanted to do was spend the rest of the evening with Melinda. After Tanya drove off, I returned to the den. I looked down at her sitting on the couch, "Are you ready to go?"

She and I said our goodnights to everybody. Sheila got up, "Let me get those books," and trotted up the stairs. Melinda and I started strolling to the door.

We stood in the foyer, waiting for Sheila. I looked at Melinda, who was looking down at the ground. She gathered a suspicious smile on her face. I whispered, "I've missed you."

Sheila came down the stairs and handed her the books. When Melinda and I got on the porch, I hugged her from behind, "You were on my mind the whole time I was in New York. All I wanted to do was come home and be with you."

She didn't say a word. But her distance was speaking loudly. I probed, "What's wrong?"

She turned around and, with force, asserted, "All you wanted to do is come home and see me? That's not what it looked like. Looks like you wanted to see someone else. Is that why you were trying to get rid of me?"

My heart dropped to my stomach, "What are you talking about? I wasn't trying to get rid of you."

"Your display with Tanya." With much attitude, she turned and started walking. When she arrived, she stood looking inside the car, waiting for me to open the door.

I came and stood behind her, "Melinda, what's up? Talk to me."

She didn't say anything. I knew then she was hurt about Tanya. I had messed up. So, I opened the door and let her inside. Then I got in the car, leaned back on the seat, and looked at her. "Melinda, let me explain."

Man, she let me have it. "Go ahead. Explain what that was all about?"

The last thing I wanted was to argue with her. I pleaded, "Can we talk about this without fighting?"

"How could you disrespect me like that? Maybe we shouldn't date! God! All men are the same! Just take me home! You're tripping!"

All kinds of thoughts started going through my mind. Is this relationship going to be another rollercoaster? Did I blow it? Is she a jealous woman? I responded in a defensive tone. "Whoa, time out, Melinda! Are you going to let me get a word in?!"

"I don't have time for this. I'm not going through this again. I've been through so much with…." Melinda's voice trailed off.

Angrily, I surmised, "With who? Not me, Trevon, that's who. I'm not him!" I grew angrier and more resentful. "I care for you. I'm not going to be his clean-up man. Do you think you have been through so much with him? I don't know whether you want me for me or if I'm a standby. He gave you flowers when I was in Atlanta, but you're sweating me because I talked with Tanya. What kind of fool do you think I am? Why would I have her over to my mother's house if I were up to something? Today was the first time she ever came over here. I'm taking a chance just like you are. I know I can love you. I question your ability to trust me and receive my love. I know this is new to you, and we're not in the same place. My chest is big enough to handle that. I can take it. But I don't want you to be in a relationship you can't handle. We'll both be miserable. Since we met, I've never lied to or mistreated you, have I?"

"No, Anthony, you haven't." She quieted down, "Anthony, I'm sorry."

"You saw me talking to Tanya and didn't want to give me the benefit of the doubt. In my business, I will constantly be confronted with women. My woman has got to trust and know me. I thought you, of all people, would. I wouldn't just disrespect you like that. You already want to leave me, and we're barely getting started."

"I didn't know what was happening with you and Tanya."

"Think about it. Shouldn't you be asking yourself about what's going on with Anthony? Please get to know me. I think you got me confused with somebody else. I haven't given you a reason not to trust me. I told you I had some loose ends to tie up. Yes, she wanted to get back together again. She wants to pick me up and put me down like a sweater. She's been calling my cell phone and leaving messages for the last two weeks. Melinda, I didn't answer or return her calls. I'd planned to tell her she couldn't come in and out of my life. So, I wasn't going to get back with her. I wanted a clean break. I told her to meet me at my parent's house, not at a restaurant or my place. That would have been disrespecting you. I didn't think it was fair to us for her to be still calling me to try to get back together when I've moved on. I gave her everything I had that belonged to her, so there would be no reason for her to call me."

"I spoke out of turn, Anthony, and I'm sorry."

"It's funny you want to compare Trevon and me. Had he ever given you a reason to trust him?"

"That's not fair. Why did you have to say that?"

"I don't appreciate being compared to him."

"Where do we stand now?"

I quieted down, "Melinda, I love you. When I said I wanted to be with you, I meant it. But I don't want to be on another love rollercoaster. Maybe it is too soon."

"Anthony, I love you too, and I'm sorry."

I said, "All I was looking forward to on my trip was coming home. I knew you were going to be here for the weekend. I wanted to spend time with you." Then I sat for a minute and then started up the car. We didn't say anything on the way to her house. When we pulled in front. I was angry so I looked out into the night. I was exhausted from the trip. The conversation with Tanya weighed me down, and I was tired from arguing with Melinda. I knew I would say the wrong thing if I didn't get some rest. I just wanted to be alone. I looked at her and said, "Let me walk you to the door."

She probed, "I thought you were hungry."

I said, "If you want me to take you to pick up something, I will. I'm too tired to eat. I want to go to my house and get some rest."

Melinda concluded, "Or get away from me."

My voice grew softer with controlled frustration, "Please don't put words in my mouth. Let's just go."

I exited the car, opened the door to let Melinda out, and walked her to the porch. I said, "tell your father I said, hey." When I started walking to my car, I could tell she was still standing on the porch.

Once I got to my vehicle, I opened the door and looked back. Melinda was still standing there. Not wanting to leave things the way they were, I stood at the car's door for a minute, contemplating. I glanced in the back seat and remembered the gift I had purchased for her in New York. I summonsed her, "Come here."

I reached into the back seat, got the big olive-green gift bag with a handle, and met her halfway up the walkway. Then I stood there looking at her beautiful face for a minute. I couldn't help but kiss her on the forehead. I handed her the gift bag and said, "A little something I picked up when I was in New York."

She started to reply, "Anthony, I...."

Putting my finger to her lips, softly silencing her possible retort I said, "Enough has been said tonight. Think about what you want. Take all the time you need. I want you to be sure. I'm more tired than I realized. I'm going to go home and get some rest." She and I embraced for a few minutes before I said, "Good night."

Advice taken: Innocent.
Advice ignored: Betrayal.

Chapter 11

Why I Love You So Much

Most mornings, I roll over on my knees to pray. Afterward, I lay a while examining myself. The harshness I exhibited with Melinda the night before was way out of line. Anger rose inside me because she didn't give me a chance to explain. Madness roared because she had brought her past baggage with Trevon into the conversation.

Judgment showed me that while I was pointing the finger at Melinda, there were at least three pointing back at me. Pardon the excuse, but I was short with her because I was so used to Tanya always wanting to argue. To top it off, she compared me with Trevon. Nonetheless, she had the right to her feelings. Melinda had no idea why Tanya was there. I messed up and had the nerve to usurp her right to be upset. How was I going to make things right with my girl? God obviously heard my prayer. She telephoned and said King would drop her off on his way to work.

The woman really knew how to mix things up. I opened the door and found her in the jean outfit I'd purchased for her in New York. She looked good in everything, not just red. I complimented, "Wow, you look great."

"Can I come in?" She asked. "I have a peace offering. Here's a cappuccino."

Smiling inside, I took the cup and said, "Thanks, come on in." Then I gestured toward the couch. "Have a seat."

She placed her cup on the table and started taking off her jacket. I put my cup down and helped her. Before she sat down, I asked, "Are you sure you want to be here? We can go somewhere else and talk."

Looking me square in the eyes, she asserted, "I came over three thousand miles to be with you. You made those arrangements because you said you wanted to be with me. So yes, I want to be here, and no, I don't want to go anywhere else unless my man is there. Anthony, I thought about you a lot while you were in New York. I concluded our relationship was worth a chance, so I relaxed and welcomed you into my heart. Last night, I got scared you might hurt me. I guess I was trying to escape. I acted like a spoiled child, and I'm sorry."

"I owe you an apology too. I was responding to some past baggage myself. When I said I wanted you, I meant that. I'm prepared to do what it takes to make our relationship successful. I'll always be open and honest with you. I need you to trust me with your heart. You're a good thing, and I would never disrespect you. I'm not trying to hurt you. I'm trying to love you."

I sat down, and she followed. I took her hand, "Melinda, I have a lot of accomplishments. I started going to work with my dad when I was just a boy. When I was a teen, they put me on payroll, working part-time. I worked there full-time while I went to college. I own my own home. I'm established in my career. I have awards, a nice car, and I've traveled around the world. None of those things mean much when there is no one to share my life with. I'm twenty-nine years old, beyond the stage of playing games. I've met all kinds of beautiful women. I would never jeopardize my for sure good thing with a maybe thing. I'm ready to settle down with my woman. I was hoping that woman would be you."

"Anthony, I am that woman."

Looking dead into her eyes, I pulled my lady to me and confessed, "I love you. Don't you ever forget it."

"I won't, and I love you too."

I started rubbing her face and stroking her hair. Then, I took my time and kissed her lips, moved to her beautiful neck, and finally kissed her passionately. Afterward, I said, "I want you to trust me. If you want to know anything or feel insecure, tell me. I know you've been through a lot. Babe, I need you to give me a chance to show you something different".

"I'll give you a chance and won't bring Trevon up to you again."

"If you want to talk about anything, even Trevon, I'm here. I just felt hurt when you compared me to him. I would never treat women like he does. Brothers like that make it hard for men like me who are trying to be right. Women are precious and to be valued. A lot of females like roughneck men. I'm not a roughneck. I'll be good, and I'll be kind to you. Just don't take my kindness for weakness. If you ever say you're leaving me, mean it."

"I understand. I need to clarify something. Anthony, I'm committed to our relationship. Just as you don't want me to take your kindnesses for weakness, don't take me for granted."

"Baby, I don't."

"Babe, I am confident of who I am and who's I am. I am not the type of woman who will be checking up on you, trying to see what you are doing. My God sits high and looks low. That's his job. I will never be okay with any disrespect. Last night, you assumed I would be okay with seeing Tanya at your parent's house. If you had told me, you were meeting her beforehand, there would not have been a problem."

"I feel you, and you're right."

She ran her fingers through my hair and softly said, "One other thing, you don't get to raise your voice at me, ever."

"I'm sorry." Then I blushed and asked, "Didn't you raise your voice at me first?"

"Anthony, I'm serious. It makes me nervous. I'm no match for you."

"I feel like there are some double standards in this relationship."

"You don't have to worry about me raising my voice. I know how to get what I need."

"Indeed, you do."

She smiled, "As long as you love and treat me right. There is nothing I won't do for you."

"I feel you. Let me take you to breakfast. I don't want that outfit to go to waste. After that, we've got to go shopping to get the things we need for the trip." I kissed her on the lips. With our kiss came a promise of our commitment to a healthy relationship.

Later that afternoon, she and I met the others at Ricky's house. We listened to music, talked, and slept on the long ride to Mammoth. Once we got to the mountains, we went directly to Jack's two-bedroom condo.

Daniel hugged Sonya around her waist no sooner than we got in the door and said, "Sonya and I will take this room. Ricky, you and Anthony can decide who's getting the other room."

I didn't want to be tempted or be a bad example to the others, so I spoke up, "Melinda and I will take the sofa sleeper in the living room."

The others napped while Melinda and I put the groceries away and unpacked our things. It was a little chilly, so we cuddled on the sofa under a blanket, watching a movie. After a couple of hours, everyone came out of their rooms and assembled in the kitchen with hot chocolate. Then, the four of them went skiing.

I had lowkey bragged to the fellows about Melinda's cooking. So, at my suggestion, we stayed behind in preparing dinner.

We did everything in concert as if we had been together for years. That was the thing that made me love her most. Our relationship was easy and organic. Nothing was a struggle or forced.

When the others returned, we ate dinner, played games, and then roasted jumbo marshmallows in the fireplace. We also listened to oldies while reminiscing about back in the day.

I didn't realize Melinda could sing or dance as well as she did. My lady showed what she was working with when we formed a soul train line. Later, we were doing karaoke, and I started singing Teddy Pendergrass's part of "Feel the Fire." Melinda got up, grabbed the mic, and did Stephanie Mill's part effortlessly. After we were done, everyone cheered, gave Melinda a round of high-fives, and requested her to sing another song. Sonya and Melody sang backup while my girl murdered Monica's song, "Why I Love You So Much." She sang it directly to me. While she was singing Daniel, Ricky and I were looking at each other in awe at what we were hearing. Seldom do we hear artists sing this well. Here it is, my lady killing it, and had the facial expressions and performance presentation that was fire. I was left mesmerized.

When I regained my composure, Daniel, Ricky, and I became Jagged Edge. I returned her gesture singing to my girl, as I led, "I Gotta Be" while the fellows sang backup. We even had choreography. The women were throwing unworn panties and scarves and screaming like groupies. I appreciated that my girl had a sense of humor and knew how to have fun. It helped to balance my seemingly serious persona.

I invited Melinda to slow dance when "Always and Forever" came on. While we were dancing, I started singing to her. After the song ended, I looked into her eyes and asked, "Will you always and forever be with me?"

She answered with a question. "Will you always and forever love me?"

I said, "Forever and a day."

She agreed, "Then I will always love you."

Melinda and I pulled out the sleeper sofa when everyone went to their rooms. She put fresh linen on the bed, and I set more wood on the fire. We showered individually, and both wore appropriate bedclothes to avoid temptations. I got in bed beside Melinda and assured her, "You don't have anything to worry about. I'm a gentleman". To break the ice, I offered, "If you had gone out with Ricky, that might be you in there."

She giggled, "I know. Ricky never called me about lunch or a movie."

I smiled, "I know."

"Did you have anything to do with that?"

I deflected, "Do you wish you would have gone out with him?"

"If I had gone out with him, there may not have been us."

"I've been thinking about us and where our relationship is going. The night I first met you, I told you I was old-fashioned. At that time, you thought it was a good thing. How do you feel about it now that you're with me?"

"Specifically, what do you mean?"

"All of it, marriage, children, raising them..."

"If I had a man who loved me enough and was committed for life, I'd have one hundred of his children. Regarding staying home with my kids, my mom stayed with me until I went to kindergarten. She worked part-time while I was at school. My mom worked an entire shift when I started going all day. I was never left at daycare or home alone. Sometimes, I think she became a teacher to be close by in case Kenny or I needed her. My parents worked together. They genuinely love one another, and Dad loves and protects my mother. I've never seen my father disrespect her. Watching my mom, I've learned how to support a man. They have been married for thirty-three years. They've had problems, but they work them out together. They still kiss in front of me, and still date. I know they still sneak away for honeymoons. I want the same thing. Because of my dad, I know what kind of man I need. My father loves me good, Anthony. It still hurts when I think how I almost let Trevon ruin that."

"But you learned from it."

"I did. I thank God for the experience. Now I know I should listen when my dad says something."

"What does your dad say about me?"

"I don't think I have to tell you. I'm here with you, aren't I?"

"Do you think you can be subject to a man?"

"I can be subject to the true meaning of the word."

"What is the true meaning?"

"My parents taught me that submission is positive, not negative, not passive, but aggressive. A lot of people think that being submissive is being a doormat. As a woman, I have a voice. My opinions are valued. Submission is simply yielding the right of way to my man. If he makes the wrong decision, he has to answer to God. I can rest in that because I know he's responsible for relieving my stress. Love is demonstrated to me firsthand. I've seen my parents operate under those principles, which has worked for them. My father says he's the manager, and my mom is the assistant manager. They are an example of true love as God designed it."

I kissed her and said, "You become more beautiful every day. Your dad has taught you well. He's pretty deep. He and my father are cut from the same cloth. My father has always told me how to love a woman. I can still go to my father for advice. I really respect him. Times weren't always good between my parents either. My dad never ran out on us, though. He stands on Godly principles. He had a hand in raising us. He didn't just leave it all to my mom. Even though my dad is in the industry, we've always come first. My parent both came to our parent-teacher conferences."

"That's awesome."

"When I was in the band at school, my dad came to see me perform. Melinda, I don't take commitment lightly. I'll never leave my wife. And I'll be there for my children. That's why it's important to me who I marry. I'm glad we came this weekend. I got to know a side of you I've never seen."

She smiled, "And what side is that?"

"For starters, I didn't know you had pipes like that. Babe, you can really sing. Have you ever considered singing professionally?"

"Absolutely not. When Kenny and I were younger, my parents would put us on showcase. I hated it."

"So, Kenny can sing too?"

"Yes, Dad wanted both of us to sing professionally, but neither wanted to. Reluctantly, my dad respected our wishes. We obliged him every so often if he needs us in the studio, though."

The next day, we all went out on the slopes. Melinda had never skied, so I ensured she got some training from a ski instructor. After a few hours on the slopes, we strolled into the various shops and had lunch. Later that evening, we all went out for a walk. When we returned to the condo, she and I went out on the veranda. I sat on the brown chaise lounge chair, and she naturally sat in front of me, leaning back on my chest.

That night, I became vulnerable when Melinda probed, "I remember when you said we could talk about anything?"

"Yeah, what's on your mind?"

"Have you had any other girlfriends besides Tanya and Tangi?"

"Not that you can call girlfriends. Why do you ask?"

"I was just curious."

I sensed she wanted to know something else, but she wasn't comfortable asking, so I reassured her, "Sweetheart, I told you could ask me anything. What do you want to know?"

I surmised nervous energy caused her to start rubbing my leg. "I noticed that you don't talk much about Tangi. I know

138

you said she committed suicide, but were you two together then?"

I wasn't expecting her to go down that road. I leaned my head back to relieve the tightness in my chest the subject brought on. Next, I took a deep breath.

She said, "Baby, that is really sensitive for you. We don't have to talk about it."

"It is a sensitive subject, but we can talk. If I want you to know me, I must be vulnerable sometimes."

She leaned back and nestled into my chest. I stroked her hair and began, "I told you she used to use drugs, and she took an overdose. I didn't tell you that we had broken up earlier that day. She committed suicide in my apartment when I was at work."

Melinda sighed, "Oh my God! That must have been awful. Are you the one who found her?"

"Yes, my dad was with me, though."

"Oh, Baby, I'm sorry to hear that." She paused, "Was the breakup mutual, or is that why she killed herself?"

"I broke up with her because she refused drug treatment, and she was insanely jealous."

"That's deep."

I was out there, so I went all in, "It gets even deeper. Tangi was pregnant with my baby."

Shaking her head, "Wow, I don't know how to take that. I'm not trying to be insensitive, but last night, you said that you would not leave your children. Now you're saying you broke up with someone who was carrying your baby."

"Melinda, she sprung the baby up on me after I told her I didn't want to be with her anymore."

"Are you sure she was really pregnant?"

"I never really thought about it. Why would Tangi lie about something like that?"

"To keep you. Women do that all the time."

"After she told me she was pregnant, I begged her to get help. I promised I would take care of my kid. She threatened to abort the baby and left my office. That's the last time I talked to her."

"Honey, I'm not convinced that she was really pregnant."

"I guess we will never know." I took a deep breath, "That didn't make you want to leave me, did it?"

Melinda leaned back and looked at me, "Everyone has a past. We all have made mistakes."

"I did make a mistake, but I repented to God."

"He forgave you, but did you forgive yourself?" I got quiet. She sat up and turned around, "You haven't, have you? I want all of you, Anthony. If this situation still has you, there will be a piece of you that will always be missing. How are we going to be always and forever?"

"I feel you. That's why I love you so much."

That trip was a landmark for Melinda and me. We got to know each other on a more intimate level. Our conversation confirmed for us that we would always and forever be. However, the lingering question, "Was Tangi really pregnant?"

All the advice taken: Innocent.
The advice ignored: Betrayal.

Chapter 12

Tell Me What You Want Me to Do

Every moment that Melinda and I spent together confirmed she was to be my wife. When Melinda returned to Atlanta, we spoke on the phone every night for at least two hours and saw one other at least twice a month. Whenever I visited, I would bring her jewelry or outfits I had picked up from the various places I'd traveled. She would always wear them when I came to visit. While I was in town, she would cook and go to recording studios, live plays, and concerts with me. I'd meet her at work just about every day for lunch.

If I worked in a nearby state, I'd extend my stay, and she would come and spend time with me. We never slept together. I would always get a suite with two rooms. If there were only one room, I'd let her have the bedroom, and I would sleep on the sleeper sofa in the living area. I had reconciled in my spirit that Melinda was not a thorn in my flesh. She was the favor that is talked about in Proverbs. I also understood that God had extended new mercies, and I didn't want to tempt my flesh.

Her favorite meeting place was Chicago. Mine was when we met in Miami, Florida, for her birthday weekend. I usually stayed at the Legacy, but since she came to town, I upgraded to a suite at the Sagamore. I had arranged for her to come up on Friday for her birthday weekend. A car was supposed to be waiting for her at the airport because I was working. Frustration emerged when I got to the hotel and learned that she wasn't there. Embarrassment joined after I found out that somehow the arrangements got mixed up. Melinda ended up taking a rideshare to the hotel and paid for it. I had also made reservations at an exclusive restaurant.

By the time we got there, it was too late. We made the best of it and had an intimate late-night dinner on the mezzanine. Gazing across the table into my woman's beautiful eyes was priceless.

It made up for all the mishaps that day.

New challenges met us the following morning through a call from Anita. There were last-minute unscheduled meetings that were added to my itinerary. Before I left the hotel, I arranged for Melinda to be served breakfast on the mezzanine, followed by an appointment at the spa.

When work ran longer than expected, I made sure the salon came up and did her hair and nails. Nothing was too much for my woman's birthday. I returned to our suite at about 7 PM to find her sleeping peacefully across the bed. I sat beside her, kissed her forehead, and said, "Wake up, beautiful."

She opened her eyes, "Hey, Babe."

"I'm sorry I've been gone all day. After everything we went through yesterday, this is not turning out to be such a great birthday weekend, is it?"

She rested her head on her arms, "I appreciated the breakfast and all the pampering today. You didn't have to do all that."

"It's your birthday weekend, and I wanted to spoil you. I was hoping to do most of it myself."

"I was lonely without you, but you're here for work. Regrettably, though, we only have tonight and part of tomorrow.

I don't know when I will see you again after that."

I rubbed her face, "I'll come to see you in Atlanta in a couple of weeks."

"You promise?" She asked.

"You have my word. Remember the last time I made a promise we went on a ski trip? Now get up and put on something nice so I can show off my beautiful woman. Miami is waiting."

Melinda and I dressed and went to a high-end seafood spot called Ravoy's. Trevon Campbell was singing live that evening. As we entered, he sang, "Tell Me What You Want Me to Do." Sheila, Damien, Tracey, Reggie, and a few of her other friends from Atlanta surprised Melinda. They came to Florida to celebrate with her. After dinner, everyone came back to our suite. The next day, we hit the beaches of Miami.

As I had promised Melinda two weeks later, I visited her in Georgia. There was a little turbulence, but not on my behalf this time. Karen was driving drunk and had a car accident. That night, Melinda and Tracey found out she had an alcohol use disorder.

On the way back to the house from the hospital, Tracey and Reggie got into a heated dispute. The disagreement escalated when we returned to the house, and they parted ways for good.

Others said Melinda was Daddy's little girl and my trophy. It was an understatement. She was Daddy's little girl, my trophy, and much more.

My girl had so many layers. She became my best friend and knew how to be my woman. Listening came easy for her. Anytime I needed to talk, she would tilt her head to the side. Every so often, she'd glance down at my mouth as if hanging on my every word. My woman would gently rub my head when I was having a bad day.

Melinda was matchless compared to the thirsty, insecure women of my past. She wasn't constantly blowing up my phone, asking where I was and what I was doing. Most of the time, I would call her. I was the pursuer, and she knew how to be pursued. Melinda allowed me to do things any man would do for his lady. And she was secure in it.

Her confidence was so attractive. She knew how to play her position. At times, she would accompany me to my business events. She knew when to be at my side, in the spotlight, or when to give me space to do business. Melinda was even un-moved on the occasions I had to work with beautiful women.

The day my spirit overruled my flesh let me know I was a changed man. A scary ordeal happened to Melinda downtown when she had a flat tire. She was stranded and encountered some transients that scared her. I finally got to her, changed her tire, and followed her home.

I purchased her a new cell phone the next day and brought it to her parents' house. She and I were alone in the house, sweet-talking and getting cozy. The passion became very sensual. In the midst, she whispered, "Anthony, I don't trust myself right now. I want you to make love to me."

Melinda was desired in my loins. But she had previously talked about how special she wanted her first time to be. Nonetheless, I loved her too much to take a chance to disappoint her or God. I also wanted to avoid crossing any boundaries. I remember the heartache she conveyed to me when sleeping with her was always at the top of Trevon's agenda.

I wanted all of Melinda, her love, trust, and respect. Knowing all I knew about her; I could lose if I made love to her prematurely. My love for her ran deep. That love helped me not to act on my desires. I gathered all my spiritual strength and said, "Trust me. I can handle myself. Love will let me wait." Lust, indeed, was a thing of the past.

However, lust was not a thing of the past for my baby brother. Sheila called me one day upset, saying, "I am sick of your brother."

I said, "He and I talked last week, and he assured me he was back on track. What is he doing now?"

"He's trying to be a player. I found condoms in his pants pocket the other day while I was doing the laundry. He has the nerve to be using the ones with assorted flavors."

I laughed, "Sheila, I'm not celebrating him indulging in sex. But at least he has enough sense to use a condom and not trust his little girlfriends."

"He may not be being reckless that way, but he is being emotionally irresponsible. He is fooling around with an array of silly little girls."

"Sheila! Silly?"

"What? That's what Timothy 3:6 says they are, and I quote, "For of this sort are they which creep into houses, and lead captive silly women laden with sins, led away with diver's lusts." I hear him on the phone with these girls. The sad part is they believe his hype and come running."

"I'm a little surprised. That doesn't sound like Howard. It seems like he's different. Is he still dealing with dude?"

"I don't know."

"Is Dad aware of what he's doing?"

"He is clueless. He and mom would have an aneurism if they knew what he was doing."

"It sounds like he's out of control."

"He is completely out of control. You had better talk to him. He even has the silly girls visiting him at the house while Mom and Dad are not there."

"In his room?"

"Please, he's not that crazy. I thought he and one of those girls were up to something in the den. I came in, and they jumped up quickly. If they weren't doing anything, why did they jump?

I don't want to tell Mom and Dad, but he is taking advantage of the brother-sister privilege."

"I agree. But don't tell yet. Let me talk to Howard. I'm over Melinda's now. He'll be out of school in a bit. I will go over to the house when I leave here."

"Okay. That will work. Sidebar."

"What's up?"

"Damien and I are going to get some sushi and then karaoke at Shakeels tonight. Would you and Melinda like to come?"

"Sounds good. What time?"

"I get off at 6. We could meet you all at Melinda's at about 7:30."

"Okay, I will talk to her and get back to you."

When I hung up the phone, Melinda inquired," What's going on, Babe?

"Howard, again?"

"Yes, I don't know what has gotten into him."

"He's seventeen."

"...and smelling himself; trying to be a player."

"Howard is handsome, Anthony. I know those girls are probably all throwing themselves at him." She smiled, "Like they do, his big brother."

I returned the smile, "Yeah, but he's an athlete and a lot more charismatic."

"That indeed. Howard has charisma and charm. He was trying to charm me out of my car. I would have given it to him if I didn't need it. So those little girl's panties don't have a chance."

"He has plenty of time to deal with thirsty females. He needs to keep his head in school and on his sports. He's entering his senior year and has an opportunity to get a full ride."

"Listen at you. Thirsty females?"

"You know I'm right."

"I hate to admit it, but you are." She pondered momentarily.

"What," I asked.

She grinned and asked, "Can you quench my thirst?" Then she busted out laughing.

I joined her contagious laughter, "You know you're not thirsty."

She said, "You better know it."

"You are something else. Hey, do you feel like going out tonight for sushi and karaoke with Damien and Sheila?"

"Yeah, Babe, sounds great."

I will go to my parent's house, nap, and talk to Howard when he comes home. Can you call Sheila for me and let her know we're in?"

When I got to my parent's house. From the vestibule where I was standing, it appeared to be no one home. Suddenly, out walks this young lady from Howard's bedroom and travels down the stairs. She was surprised when she saw me, so she covered her mouth and said, "I'm sorry. I didn't know anyone was here. Howard asked me to get him some water."

I countered sarcastically, "Really?" Then I called out to Howard before redirecting to her, "Aren't you supposed to be at school?"

"Yes, but…"

Howard came out of his room and came down the stairs. As he approached, I asked, "Why aren't you at school?"

"I'm dropping my seventh period."

"Does Dad know?"

"I haven't told him yet."

"Isn't that your calculus class?"

"Yes."

"You two get your stuff. We have somewhere to go."

I dropped the young lady off at Melinda's house so that she could take her home. Then Howard and I went up to the school. I found out that he had missed his seventh-period class thirteen times.

When we returned to the car, I looked at Howard, "Man, what's going on? This is not like you. You're running around with dudes that don't have anything going on. You're missing school. You're acting promiscuous. When I saw the young lady come out of your room, it tripped me out. That's not even the same one you were with three weeks ago. Do you even like this girl?"

"She's alright."

"Yeah, I know what that means. She's the flavor of the day. Man, that's dangerous."

"I've got protection."

"You're sleeping with more than one young lady. Those are somebody's daughters. Are you ready to deal with their emotions, big brothers, or daddies? And what if they find out about each other?"

"I've got it under control."

"Howard, Man, you think you do but you don't. You are out of control. And what about you not going to play ball this year?"

"I don't want to play anymore."

"Why? You only have one more year.

"I'm probably failing calculus. So, I probably won't be eligible."

"Isn't Coach Randle your calculus teacher and the basketball coach?"

"Yes."

"It's to Coach Randle's benefit for you to pass the class. Have Dad talk to him. I'm sure he will give you some make-up work. You are smart as a whip. I know you can do it."

"I'm too far behind."

"I'll make you a deal. I will pay for a tutor and get you a car when you pass the class."

He sat looking out of the window for a moment. Then asked, "Are you going to tell Dad?"

"Howard, we have to tell Dad about the grades. He's going to find out. It would be better for him to hear it from you."

"What about the girl at the house? Are you going to tell that?"

"No, but what are we going to do about it? You are too young to be sleeping around. Are you wrapping it up every time?"

"Yes."

"Dial it back, Man. It's not going to end well. This sleeping around ain't good. Someone is going to get hurt."

"Alright. I'll dial it back."

"Are you telling me the truth? You told me you would get it together a few weeks ago, and here we are."

"You have my word. I am going to do something different."

"Alright."

He gave me his word that he would talk to my parents that night. I dropped him off at home and proclaimed, "I love you, man. There is nothing I won't do for my little brother."

While the four of us were at Shakeels, Howard became a point of conversation when Sheila received a text. She said, "Ant, Dad just texted and asked if I'd seen Howard. "Did you talk to him today?"

"Yes. I dropped Howard off at home at about 4:30. He promised to talk to Mom and Dad about his grades."

"Well, he didn't because they are clueless about where he is."

I picked up my cell, called his phone, and reported, "He did not answer."

Sheila said, "Text him, Ant. Maybe he will answer a text."

I looked at my phone, "It's a text from Dad asking if he's with me." I returned the text to Dad, letting him know Howard wasn't. Then I texted Howard, enquiring about where he was. There was no immediate response.

Sheila asked, "How did it go when you talked to him?"

"I caught him at the house with some little girl while he was supposed to be at school. Melinda took her home, and he and I went to the school."

"What, he had a girl in the house? Melinda, what was her name? Did she say anything?"

"Her name was Taylor.

She appeared to be a sweet little girl and very respectful. I think she just got caught up in Howard's charm. She expressed how much she liked him. Truthfully, I think you were her way of escape.

Taylor said she had never cut class before and that they had not done anything but were going to. I told her that was not how to get Howard to like her."

"I hope you educated her on how. You know we have to look out."

"I sure did. Taylor thanked me for the conversation and took my number." Suddenly, Melinda got an epiphany. "You know what, her number is in my phone. She didn't have anything to write with, so I dialed her number so she could save mine in her phone."

I said, "Call her."

Melinda got her on the phone. When Taylor started giving her pertinent information, Melinda said, "Hold up, let me give the phone to Anthony."

Taylor told me that she and Howard had spoken. He was afraid to have a conversation with my parents. Something had happened to him at school to make him not want to be there. My brother didn't say what. Howard had also told her the guy Montel was terrible news. Montel was trying to get him to sell weed and join a gang. My brother didn't want to. He was going somewhere with them this evening because he didn't want to go home.

While I was talking to Taylor, Melinda motioned for me to look at my phone. There was a text from Howard. In the text, he expressed that he was in trouble. Please don't call his phone. He offered an address where to pick him up. We recognized that the address was Montel's house.

When we arrived, Montel's car was in the driveway. Damien and I went to the door. His mom answered, and I asked for Howard. She invited us in and led us to their garage, which had been converted into a man cave. When we entered, Howard addressed Howard, "Hey Man, I need you to make a run with me."

He said, "I already have plans."

I knew what he was doing and said, "Man, it's an emergency with Grandpa. You have to come.

He stood up, "Is he okay?"

Since Grandpa was already deceased, I knew my brother was telling me to get him out of there. There was a danger to him and us. So, I continued the act, "No, Man. The doctors say he may not make it. We have to go now."

The three of us left with Howard sandwiched between us. When we got to the car and pulled off, I said, "Damien, take us to Melinda's so I can get my car and meet me at my parent's house."

Howard pleaded while shaking his head, "Please."

"What's up, Man? You told me you would talk to them, and now the mess has gotten bigger."

Howard put his head in his lap and started weeping. I knew it had to be something serious. My little brother needed me.

When we got to Melinda's house, Damien said, "Can I have a word with you, Anthony?" He and I exited his utility vehicle while the others stayed inside.

Damien said, "Howard is crying out. Something deep is going on. If he's saying he doesn't want to go home, maybe you should take him to your place and see what's up."

"Yeah, I was feeling the same thing."

I returned to the truck and said, "Howard, I'm going to take you home with me tonight. You've got to come clean, though." He nodded his head yes.

On the way, I asked, "What did I walk into back there?"

"They were going to commit armed robbery tonight. They wanted me to come with them. I knew if I tried to leave, they would come after me. They would have shot you if you had come in there blazing."

"I knew something was up. Were you told who they are robbing?"

"No."

"That's good. The less you know, the better."

When we got to my house, I sat in the music room. I didn't want to come down too hard on him. I knew he was nearing the bottom of his issues. He needed comfort, compassion, and a hand-up. I immediately gave him the floor by saying, "Talk to me, Man."

Shaking his head, he said, "I messed everything up. I'm in too deep. Those dudes are going to kill me."

"I'm not going to let anything happen to you."

With intense apprehension, he wondered, "What are you going to do?"

"Help you figure this out."

"You don't know anything about this. You are Anthony, the man. You have it all. You don't have to fight."

"I have it all? What does that mean?"

"A good job, nice car, graduated top of your class. I can't compete. It all came easy for you. You didn't have to go through anything."

"Where did you get your information?"

"Growing up in your shadow." He grew louder and more emotional with every word, to the point of angry tears. "I can't do it anymore. I am tired of trying to prove I am something. I even have to prove I am a man."

"You think sleeping with everything that has a skirt on makes you a man? It makes you needy and weak."

Howard lost his head and started screaming at the top of his lungs, "I'm not weak! I'm a man! I'm a man!"

I thought he was having a breakdown. I knew there was something deeper going on. Something dark had to have happened. My heart went out to him. I hugged my brother, "I love you, man. You can tell me."

"That pervert tried to get at me." Then he started crying violently. Realizing he needed to release all the pressure he had bottled up, I let him cry until he was finished. I understood then that all of his antics were just a symptom of his dark secret. I was angered inside and wanted to hurt the person who had scarred my baby brother. But I knew I had to remain calm, supportive, and not judgmental.

Once I felt the atmosphere shift, I shared, "I know it seems like my life is flawless, and perhaps I appear to be this perfect person, but I'm not. I will not glorify my past issues or failures, but you need me to be transparent and share some of my truths. Do you remember when you were about ten, and the corporate attorney, Jack, and Dad were at the house?"

"Yeah, I do. Something was going on with you, and nobody would tell me what."

"Yes. Howard, most of my issues or mess was acted out when you were too young to remember. That situation was so bad that no one ever talked about it. My girlfriend committed suicide in my apartment, and I ended up in jail for having drugs in my house."

"You?"

"Yes. There was a time when I was using drugs. I messed up at school, my job, and with Mom and Dad. Thank God they found out the drugs weren't mine, or I would still be in jail.

Howard, don't try to measure up to me or anyone else. You don't have to. You are an awesome dude. I might be good at my job, but I can't play ball nearly as well as you. That's your thing. It will take you a long way. You are a good student too. We have to get you past calculus."

Howard put his head down, "Calculus is easy. Coach Randle is the pervert who tried to get at me."

"What do you mean, get at you?"

"He gave me a ride home from a summer league game. He put his hand on my leg. I didn't think much of it until we returned to school. We were in the office, and he tried to kiss me. I fought him and ran. I have not been to his class or practice since."

"Then why do you only have thirteen absences?"

"He just started marking me absent. I haven't been there all semester."

"Howard, you know we will have to tell Dad."

"He's going to make a scene, and everyone will think I'm gay."

"Is that what all the sleeping around was about?"

"What made him come after me? It had to be something."

"It was something wrong with him, not you."

The next day, Howard and I talked to Dad together. Our father took it from there. Howard went back to calculus and basketball without fear. The coach was expelled immediately without Dad making a scene or Howard's dark secret exposed to the student body. Taylor, who became Howard's only girlfriend, was the only residual left from that particular situation.

Montel and his crew thought they got away with an armed robbery that night. Imagine the coincidence: my frat brother's sports bar was robbed that night. There was an anonymous tip to the police indicating Montel may be a person of interest. Now, you can find Montel and his crew doing time in Chino Prison.

With my brother's issues under control, it was time for me to move forward with my plans. The final confirmation came by way of additional income. Melinda had landed a job in Los Angeles. The same week, I got a promotion that significantly boosted my revenue.

Unannounced to my girl, I had previously sat down with her parents and asked permission to have her hand in marriage. They were staggered by the time frame but gave me their blessings.

I wasn't sure if the excitement displayed on King's face was because Melinda would be marrying me or because she wasn't marrying Trevon.

That particular moment had to be perfect. I didn't want to risk mishaps, so I spent the day planning, shopping, and plotting.

We had a lovely, intimate table at Crestations and an evening of Jazz. Earl Pugh was performing live, and there was a surprise appearance with Jeffery Osborne. Melinda and I ended the evening at my place.

After telling her the news about my promotion, I bent down on one knee and asked her to be my wife and the mother of my children. After she accepted, I sealed the deal by placing a two-karat platinum ring on her finger. The two-month time frame was unexpected by her as well, but she agreed on the date.

Sheila and I accompanied Melinda back to Georgia for her graduation. On the day of the commencement ceremony, the entire King family came in, including Grandpa King and Mrs. Bradford's sister, Aunt Louise.

A couple of days later, when Melinda returned to California, her dad and mom gave a dinner party in her honor at The Mining Company. Ricky, Sonya, Daniel, and Melody were there, as well as Lisa, a Puerto Rican girl from Melinda's job. She started at the accounting firm around the same time as Melinda did.

In front of everyone, I gave her a black velvet box. She opened it, and there was a beautiful gold locket with a heart of diamonds on one side. King got her a gold Infiniti hat and jacket. Infiniti was embroidered on the front of the cap and the back of the jacket in black. Melinda's parents also gave her a model-sized Infiniti and a check for two thousand dollars. She was disappointed that she didn't get the car. Admittedly, I was a little surprised, too. Melinda was Daddy's little girl. King would do anything for her.

The following month, our relationship went in a different direction. I spent long days at the studio. When I was home, I spent a lot of time in my music room. Occasionally, Melinda would sleep over because her new job was close to my place. She would sleep upstairs in my bed, and I would sleep downstairs on the sofa. I loved it when I came home, and Melinda was there. Most of the time, she would cook me dinner. If my fiancée' wasn't going to be there, she'd cook days in advance. Sometimes, my lady would leave love letters and then go home before I got there. Surprisingly, King never said a word.

Our parents were like an enigma at times. One day, the Kings, my parents, Melinda, and I had dinner at the King's house. Though they tried to disguise it, it was a let's teach the kids how to be married session. They offered very sound advice and invited us to come to them if we ever needed it.

The nuggets they shared were essential. My dad shared, "Son, be the man in your home. Protect your wife. Love your wife, as Christ loves the church." Mrs. King offered, "Be honest with one another no matter the cost." King rounded out with the Bible, saying, "This is the solution to all your problems. With this, there is nothing you can't work out. All the answers are here." He laughed and said, "Besides, she can't come back once she moves out."

I said, "She won't be back. My wife will never leave me, and I'm never leaving her.

I did not realize how much those words and that night meant at the time. That night would be the definition of beginnings and endings, the beginning of us, and the last night with him.

The advice taken: It would make me wiser and better.
Advice ignored: There would be inevitable Betrayal.

Chapter 13

Love Won't Let Me Wait

About three weeks before the wedding, Kenny needed to use Melinda's car, so she rode in to work with King. She'd planned on coming to my place when she got off. We just bought a new aquarium, and she wanted to prepare it for the fish we were buying on the weekend.

King and I were working on a project. He had not arrived yet, and I was waiting. I had already spoken to Melinda and knew he had dropped her off. I called his cell and the house. There was no answer. Concern began to set in. I didn't want to worry Melinda or her mom, so I called Kenny's cell to see if he had heard from King. He answered with anxiety, "Man, I'm glad you called."

"What's going on?" I asked.

Kenny said, "Dad was in an accident on his way to work."

"Oh my God. Is King, okay?"

"No, my mom and yours are at the hospital."

"Kenny, what are they saying?" I asked.

"They haven't got a chance to see him yet. They are saying they are working on him and will let us know. Hold on, Mom is on the other line." When he got back on the phone, he said, "Man, let me call you back. The doctor just came out."

About five minutes later, my mom called and put Mrs. King on the phone. She explained what had happened, told me what the doctor had said, and asked if I would bring Melinda to the hospital.

Saddened and concerned about what could happen to King, I stared out of the large plate glass window, waiting for Sandra to let Melinda know I was there. My woman came into the lobby behind me and asked, "What's wrong?"

In shock, I didn't move but pondered how to tell her about her dad. I turned and looked at her, but I was still speechless.

She repeated, "Baby, what's wrong?"

I knew I had to be strong for Melinda. I cleared my throat and said, "Your dad has been in an accident."

"What kind of an accident?"

"A car accident."

"Where is he now?"

"He's at the hospital. We've got to go. I'll tell you the rest on the way."

I continued when we got in the car, "Your mother told me your dad was on his way to work when someone slammed into him. Honey, it's pretty serious. My mom is at the hospital with her, and Kenny is on his way. She wanted me to bring you."

"When did this happen?"

"This morning on his way to work."

"He dropped me off this morning." She dropped her head. Sensing she needed encouragement, I put my hand on her knee and asked, "How are you feeling?"

"I'm numb."

As we stepped off the elevator, we turned right. The doctor, Kenny, Mom King, and my mom were about fifteen yards ahead.

Mom King took a step back and shook her head no. I knew it wasn't good news. Kenny started hugging her mom, King. Melinda approached them, "Mom? Kenny? Say something."

Melinda looked at the doctor with a look of confusion on her face. He exclaimed, "I'm sorry."

"Sorry for what? Where is my daddy?"

With his voice choked up, Kenny responded, "Sis, he's gone."

Melinda went into a distraught rant asking, "Just like that? What do you mean? I just got here. I want to see my daddy! Where is he?"

The doctor pointed down the hall, "He's still in the room."

Melinda ran down the hall, door to door until she got to where King was. I went in after her. He was lying there lifeless. There was a bandage wrapped around King's head, and the I.V. was still in his hand. He had a sheet covered up to his neck.

I came behind Melinda and held my baby tight as she stood over King weeping. I needed to give her space to grieve, and I allowed her to. I cared for Tangi, and it was hard to see her body lying lifeless. I could only imagine how hard it was for Melinda to see her dad lying there, whom she loved much more.

Soon, her mother came into the room. She and her mom embraced and cried together as Kenny comforted them until the orderlies rolled King's body out of the room.

Shortly after, my dad showed up. I had only seen him cry once before, and it was when my grandma died. Tears flowed from his eyes as he comforted Mom.

We left the hospital together, and both families assembled at the King's house as one big family. Later that evening, my family went home. Kenny and I stayed to look over Melinda and Mrs. King.

The next evening, my parents returned to the King's house. Melinda's Aunt Louise and Grandpa King had also come over by this time. Together as a family, we planned King's funeral services.

Later that night, Kenny, Lisa, and Melinda came to my place. We all sat in the living room. That's when I first observed a connection between Lisa and Kenny. He even went home with her.

Melinda and I had not been alone since King's accident. I felt this was an excellent time to see where Melinda's head was concerning the wedding. I suggested perhaps postponing it. That made her a little insecure. She even asked, "Have you changed your mind?"

I looked into my lady's face, "Where did that come from? Why would you ask me that?" She put her head on my chest. I held her tight and kissed her on her forehead and said. "Don't start getting insecure about me. I love you."

"I know."

I stroked her hair until we both fell asleep cuddling on the couch. Luther Vandross singing, "Dance with My Father," in a heavenly choir full of angels graced my dream. King appeared in a black tux and held his hand out. Melinda stepped into his arms dressed in a white wedding gown, and father and daughter danced.

I woke up at about 4 AM and noticed Melinda was gone. My concern led me upstairs to check on her. When I saw she was safe and lying in my bed, I went into the bathroom and showered. I'd gotten out and was shaving when I heard Melinda call out, "Anthony."

I said, "I'll be there in a minute." Then, I quickly finished shaving, grabbed a T-shirt, and went into my room. She was awake, so I sat on the bed. While stroking her hair, I asked, "What's wrong? I thought you were asleep."

She whined, "I can't."

"Do you want to talk?" I asked.

She sat up and said, "I need a kiss."

I kissed her quickly on the lips. Before I could pull back, she looked into my eyes sensually and softly ran her fingers through my hair and down my neck. Miss Lady kissed me with a come hither as she'd never done before. I answered by kissing her neck and caressing her soft body, promising I would not go all the way. She trumped my advances by stroking my bare chest and kissing my body.

My spirit told me through my manhood to bail because I was getting to the point of no return. I stopped and looked into her eyes with a slightly serious snicker, "Baby, I'd better go downstairs before this gets out of hand." I got up and started walking away.

I could hear her getting out of bed. She called out, "Wait."

I turned around, and wow! Her top was open, revealing her black laced bra and panties. Trouble notified me that I would be its owner if I did not turn away immediately.

Resistance was voided. I and my eyes had to get a glimpse. From her hips to her eyes, I traveled. Now, I was perplexed in my body, mind, and spirit. I wandered over to her and rubbed her face with the back of my finger and the ounce of spiritual strength I had left and asked. "What's going on? Where is this going?"

She looked up into my eyes, "Don't leave me tonight. Make love to me. I'm ready, Anthony."

"I know, Bae, but I thought we agreed to wait two more weeks."

She demanded, "Kiss me."

This was against my better judgment. I was already overextended. Shaking my head with apprehension, I yearned, "Melinda, Baby."

She looked at me with pouting eyes, "Anthony, I need you."

That was all the invitation my flesh needed. It was now in complete control of my spirit. I extended my arms, and she naturally stepped inside. Slipping my arms underneath her shirt, I held her body tight. She felt so good. We met each other halfway, lips to lips and then tongue. She exhaled and looked into my eyes, "I need you to make love to me tonight."

In the recesses of my mind, "Love Won't Let Me Wait" sang by Major Harris played loudly. She lay back on the bed, and her body invited me to take residence. My loins were already there. I let my eyes follow as my lady pulled her nightshirt to her shoulders and then let it drop to the floor. Now, she was standing with just her lace bra and panties. I whispered, "Oh, Baby," and then I started kissing her on her lips. Then I moved down to her neck. Running my fingers through her hair while still kissing, I looked into her eyes and said, "I love you."

"I love you too." With those words, my spirit took control of my flesh and reminded me that love would wait.

Tears started rolling down my lady's face, allowing me to escape. I wiped a tear and asked, "Why are you crying?"

"I'm not," she whispered as the tears intensified.

"Why do I see tears?" I felt terrible, so I pulled back and confessed, "I'm sorry." At that moment, I sat up on the edge of the bed and put my face in my hands. I felt like I had failed her.

She sat up and touched my arm, "Don't go. I'm ready and don't want to be alone tonight."

As revelation kicked in, I turned and held her tight, "Baby, you're not alone. I'm here for you." While wiping her tears, I admitted, "I know you're hurting, grieving, scared, and vulnerable. If we made love tonight, it would be wrong. I'm sorry. You needed me to be stronger."

She begged, "Please don't leave me alone."

"You don't know how bad I want to make love to you. You look so good to me." I digressed, "But I think you need me to hold you in my arms. I'm going to go and take another shower and try really hard to get the vision of you in that black lace set off my mind."

"Do you think I'm a tease?"

I blushed, "Yes, but it's sexy as long as you're only teasing me. I'd be in trouble if we weren't getting married soon. I will not be able to get this close to you before then. Now, I don't trust myself. In fact, while I'm in the shower, why don't you look in my drawer and put on the ugliest, bulkiest sweats you can find, and I will hold you all night long."

Melinda's sense of humor again added balance to my mostly serious persona. Her antics that night were definitely needed to redirect our focus. I came back into the room. Melinda's back was turned with her head covered. She appeared to be asleep. Candles were lit on the nightstands. "The Closer I Get to You," by Luther and Beyoncé, played softly. I stood there momentarily, a little confused since we had agreed not to make love. I pondered what I would do if I pulled the covers back and she still had on that black lace two-piece. As soon as I pulled the covers back, she sat up and turned around. Bae had painted her face with makeup so bad that she looked like a clown.

It was funny, and I laughed. After I hollered, "You scared me, seriously, Melinda?"

She laughed and said, "You hollered like a..."

"Don't even say it." I playfully demanded. Then I started moving towards her.

She rolled over on the bed, away from me to the floor, "That was the guts." I noted she had on the worst possible unsexy sweats I'd seen.

Smiling, I said, "I'm glad you got a kick out of it."

She ran around the room until I caught her and pulled her onto the bed. She was laughing and hollering, "Stop, Anthony!"

We lay there next to each other, laughing. I turned over towards Melinda, "You do know you look ridiculous, right?"

"I knew that was the only way you could get past my hotness."

I sat on the bed, pulled her to me, and looked deep into her eyes. "You're something else. You're hot even if you wear oversized sweats and that ridiculous makeup." We really did need that laugh, Babe.

She said, "Well, get one last look because I will wash my face."

When she came back, I held her until we fell fast asleep. I loved and desired her more now than ever. She would have lost respect for me if I had made love to her.

It was my job to protect and watch over her. Denying myself and being sensitive to her feelings was important. We were thankful later that we had not made love that night.

Advice Taken: Innocence is kept.

Advice ignored: Betrayal because the wage of sin is death.

Chapter 14

Have You Seen Her

Melinda was disappointed when she learned Karen did not fly in with Tracey for the funeral. Family and friends came out to pay their respects. Jack and my dad were amongst those who said kind words about King.

I had planned on being strong for Melinda. It was the weirdest thing. As much as Melinda loved her dad, she did not get very emotional. In fact, she was like an unusual blank canvas for most of the service. Tracey, on the other hand, took it hard. We both ended up consoling Tracey.

Death and mortality snowballed on me in the privacy of my home. I didn't share it with Melinda, nor did I share it with anyone else, but I was struggling. At Mammoth, Melinda asked me if I had forgiven myself for Tangi's death.

Melinda said, "She could never completely have my heart if I didn't release Tangi by forgiving myself." The truth of the matter is I wasn't sure. From the day I found Tangi lying on my bed unresponsive, intermittent nightmares interrupted my nights. A continuous recording of her twin sister citing, "You used my sister and threw her away," often invaded my spirit. I knew it was like Melinda said, "She could never completely have my heart if I didn't release Tangi by forgiving myself."

King's death intensified my stance on mortality. Tears flooded my eyelids as I lay on my sofa, thinking about him. He was such a remarkable man. If the relationship, we started was a precursor to what he would have been like as a father-in-law. Man, it would have been fantastic. King was team Anthony.

My mind drifted to Tangi and my unborn child. In the twilight, I could hear the Chi-Lites singing, "Have You Seen Her?" as I drifted to sleep. My dreams had me travel to a grassy area. Tangi was pregnant and running. I ran behind her, hollering, "Tangi, please come back."

She ran and ran. Finally, I caught up to her and held her arm. Tussling, she said, "let me go!"

"I can't. You have my son."

"If I let you have him, will you let me go?"

I said, "Yes."

She suddenly passed out and started hemorrhaging. Instantly, she was lying in a pool of blood. I lifted her head and put it on my lap. The music got louder as the Chi-Lites sang, "Why oh why did you have to leave and go away."

A little boy who was about two years old from the blood formed. He took off running. Drenched in blood, I ran after him, hollering, "Son, don't go! I need you." I woke up panting, as I often did. Then, I lay drowning in my tears for at least an hour. Afterward, I rolled on the floor onto my knees and solicited God to help me.

The next day, I believed I needed to face my fears and Tangi's sister Angie. I didn't know where she lived, but I did remember she worked at Lorna Jacques Ad Agency.

At about 10 AM, I telephoned Angie's job. She came on the line. "This is Angie. How can I help you?"

"Angie, this is Anthony. The one that used to date your sister."

"I know who you are. What's going on?"

"Please don't hang up the phone."

She snickered, "I'm not, although I see why you might think I would."

I took a deep breath, "The last time we saw each other...."

"Yeah, about that... I'm ashamed of the way I acted. I had just lost my sister and was looking to blame anyone. Please understand. You were my target."

"I understand."

"Listen, Anthony. I'm happy you called. I'm on my way into a meeting. Can we speak later? We need to talk. Let me have your number, and I'll text you."

After I gave her the number, she hung up the phone. Inside, I said, "Wow. That could not have gone better." I looked towards heaven and said, "Thank you, Lord."

Coincidentally, the day Melinda and Kenny moved her things to my place was when I met with Angie for dinner. I wasn't trying to keep anything from Melinda and had planned to tell her what was happening.

I helped bring her boxes and things in when she and Kenny got to my place. Melinda noticed I was a little distant. She and I were in my room when she enquired, "Honey, what's the matter? You seem like you are distracted."

"I have a meeting tonight, and I'm a little nervous."

She came over to me and rubbed my face. You do this all the time. Why would you be nervous today?"

"I'm meeting with Tangi's sister, Angie."

"That's surprising after the way you say she treated you the last time you saw her. How did that happen?"

"I called her at work the other day. She apologized and said she came for me because she was grieving."

"The meeting was your idea?" Melinda asked.

"Yeah, Babe."

"Is everything okay?"

I said, "I need some closure."

"I understand. I'm proud of you for reaching out to her. Are you going to ask her about the baby?"

"I don't know."

She rubbed my chest, "What do you need from me?"

"Your love, trust, support, and understanding."

My lady said, "You have all that."

"Do you want to go?"

"No. I think this is something you need to do alone."

I took her hand and put it on my chest. "This is why I love you so much."

She asked, "Do you want me to stay here until you get back?"

I smiled, shaking my head, "No."

She smiled, "What...?" and then inquired.

"You know why. I still have visions of that black lace. I'll just come by your mom's when I'm done. It's safer that way."

Blushing, "Go think about that lace in the shower. You're sweaty from pretending like you were moving boxes. Kenny and I are going to go on to the house. I'll see you later."

I whispered a word of prayer before I went into TGIF. Angie was already there in the lobby texting. It's eerie how she looked just like Tangi, only sober and dressed professionally. We took our seats, and our order was taken. While waiting for our food, she led by asking, "How are you doing, Anthony?"

"I'm okay."

"I thought the least I could do was buy you dinner and apologize again for blaming you. You know Tangi was my twin. There is a special bond. I was so hurt when she passed, Anthony. I always thought someday she would get it together."

I said, "I had just found out she was using cocaine."

"She had been using it off and on since she was 17. Most of the time, she was on."

"I had no idea."

"She was a functioning alcoholic and addict. When my husband and I cleaned her place, I discovered she had started using Crystal Myth."

"Yeah, I found that out too. While I was in jail."

"Why were you in jail?"

"She had been at my place for two days without me. They found her drugs there, assumed they were mine, and arrested me."

"That's wrong. How did you get out?"

"They couldn't find my prints on anything."

"Thank God."

I dropped my head, "I wish there was something I could have done. I tried to get her to go to rehab."

"Don't blame yourself. There was nothing you could have done. Tangi needed to want it for herself. She was an attic, and she was manic."

"Bipolar?" I asked.

"Yes, you didn't know."

I said, "This is all news to me."

"I guess you didn't know she had attempted suicide at least twice before, either."

"No."

"God, I miss her." Said Angie

"I feel you. I have my own struggles getting it off my mind."

"That had to be difficult, finding her and all."

I shared, "More than you know. I still have nightmares."

"That's awful. I am so sorry you went through that. Did you love Tangi?"

"I can't say I was in love, but I did love her, Angie."

"That's real." She paused, "Thank you for being there for Tangi when you were. I can tell you cared for her. Even though I didn't say it, the money you sent for the funeral was kind and greatly appreciated. Only someone who loved her would have done that. I could sense in your voice when you called that you were in a bad place."

"I'm getting married next weekend. I just needed some closure."

"You're getting married? Congrats. She's a lucky young lady."

"I'm blessed to have her."

She touched my wrist, "You have to let it go. None of it was your fault. Move on with your life."

The courage to ask about the baby was halted by Angie putting her head down, concealing the tears starting to flow. She said, "I guess I'm preaching to the choir." I got up and sat next to her. She leaned her head on my shoulders and said, "It's been five years since she's been gone, but it still hurts."

I walked Angie to her car, and we said our goodbyes. Afterward, I saw my lady and told her what had happened. Although I was able to gain some relief after meeting with Angie, Melinda and I still wondered if Tangi was pregnant and what the dreams were trying to tell me.

The week before the wedding, Tracey came back. Melinda was so excited because Karen was with her this time. They all went to church together on Sunday and then to Melinda's house. I didn't see Melinda at church but briefly visited the King's house to see Karen and Tracey.

We only saw each other twice for wedding rehearsals the rest of the week. Melinda was busy working, entertaining, and getting things prepared for the ceremony.

However, I did get a thought-provoking phone call the afternoon of Melinda's bridal shower. Mom King telephoned me with her voice cracking. She said I needed to come by because she needed to show me something. She also told me she didn't want Melinda to know.

Aunt Louise answered the door and showed me into the kitchen. Mom King was sitting at the island, having a cup of coffee. She wasn't dressed as if she was going anywhere. I noticed the clock behind her head when I kissed her on the cheek.

I sat at the counter beside her, "How's it going, Mom? Aren't you going to the shower?"

"I don't want to upset Melinda, but I can't do it. I'm still overwhelmed with grief."

"I'm sure she'll understand. Is there anything I can do?"

"Yes, we have a situation."

I took a deep breath, "What's going on?"

She swallowed, "Do you remember at Melinda's graduation party when King made all the noise about the car?"

"Yes, Melinda was so disappointed that he teased her with the Infiniti gifts but didn't give her the car."

"There was a car."

"What? I should have known."

"He had it customized for her, and it wasn't ready. It's in the garage. He was going to give it to her the weekend he passed. I don't know when to give it to her."

"Do you mind if I see it?"

"Not at all. The keys are on top of the fridge."

I entered the garage and returned inside, "Mom, that car is clean. Melinda is going to lose her mind when she sees it. It must have cost a fortune. How much is the note? Please give me the bill. I'll take care of it. I can't let you pay the car note with everything you're going through."

"I know it's a lot, but her dad wanted her to have it." She pulled out some paperwork. King made sure we were covered. I paid the car off in full. The only thing that has to be paid is the insurance."

"I might as well get used to spoiling her. She's going to be my wife. Let me give you at least half of the money back for the car. You have to continue to live."

"That's okay, Baby. I need to do this in his honor. You know how he felt about his baby girl."

"Enough said. Can I at least pay the insurance?"

She rubbed my arm, "Yes, you can."

"Do you need money for anything?"

She pulled out an insurance policy. Does it look like I am going to be struggling?"

I saw the figures. All I could say was, "No, Ma'am." I pondered, "When will you give it to her?"

"Baby Girl has a lot on her right now trying to plan a wedding. My sister said I should wait until after it's over."

"Mom, I asked her if she wanted to postpone it. She wants to keep our date. I even discussed Kenny walking her down the aisle. She said she felt that would be taking her daddy's place."

"She is her father's child. I'm a little concerned about her, though."

"How so?"

"I have not seen Melinda cry or even acknowledge King's passing since the day at the hospital. At the funeral, she was blank. Have you seen her cry?"

"To be honest, I haven't."

"Watch my baby, Anthony. I feel like she's going to break."

"I got her, Mom. You don't have to worry."

She rubbed my face, "You really love her, don't you?"

"Yes, I do. With everything in me."

"Her father can rest in peace, knowing she's in good hands."

"And we're here for you too."

Advice taken: My girl will stay innocent.
Advice ignored: She could be betrayed.

Chapter 15

For You

Finally, the day I had been waiting so long for. Friends and family members gathered poolside at my parent's house. The woman of my dreams was going to be my wife.

When the ceremony was ready to begin, Damien, who was officiating, and I came in and took our position. The rest of the wedding party entered one by one. It was all blah, blah, blah to me. I just wanted to lay eyes on my girl.

The time came for Melinda to walk down the aisle. I couldn't see her because everyone had stood up and obscured my view. There was sighing, awing, and whispers, "She's beautiful."

Finally, I saw her at the top of the aisle. Wow! My bride's total package was not only stunning, but it was also labeled elegant and classy. The dress that graced her body was simple, fitted, and sexy. Her hair was done up in a way I'd never seen before.

She stood there for a moment. The minutes continued until it became silent and evident that something was happening within her. The look on her face was as if she had stage fright.

I remembered what her mom said about her breaking. I started to go and get my lady. Kenny gently grabbed my shoulder, "I got this." He went and whispered something to her. She nodded, clinched onto his arm, and the two strolled down the aisle. Inwardly, I was praising God for giving me another chance and answering my prayers. Outward tears of happiness, joy, and anticipation of our tomorrow ran down my face as she drew nearer to me.

The moment intensified even more when Damien, who was officiating, asked, "Who gives this woman to this man?"

She looked at Kenny, who was looking at her. He shifted his eyes towards Damien and loudly proclaimed, "Our father."

She mouthed to Kenny, "Thank you," as tears rolled down her face. Kenny kissed her on the forehead and joined her hand with mine.

Melinda and I embraced, and I held her. Teardrops fell sporadically throughout the audience as we paid silent tribute to King's memory at his daughter's wedding. Our friends and loved ones understood and honored the moment.

I whispered in her ear, "Are you alright?" Then, I wiped the tears from her face with my handkerchief. It was a very emotional moment. She nodded her head, "Yes." When she was ready to proceed, she and I turned to Damien to continue the ceremony. Everyone started clapping.

Damien prayed for God's blessings on our union. Then he signaled me to begin saying the vows I wrote for her. "Melinda, I stand before God and these people and say and mean these vows to you. As Christ loves the church and gave Himself, I will love and give myself to you. I will stand on Godly principles in our home. I won't lie or speak to you with guile. I will be your loving husband and a devoted father to our children. I will always speak to you in truth and love. I'm committed to loving, protecting, and comforting you. For the rest of my life, I will be with you. I'll never leave you. I will forsake all others and give my body only to you. I will hold you near and dear to my heart. You are my rib, Melinda."

She replied, "As rib of you, Anthony. I will hold you near and dear to my heart. According to the principles of God, I will submit myself to you. I will forsake all others and give my body only to you. For the rest of my life, I will be with you. I will never leave you. I will be your loving wife and the mother of your children. I will be truthful to you. I won't lie to you. I am committed to being your helper. Before God and before these people, I say these vows. These vows I don't take likely and say truthfully."

Then music came on and I surprised my lady by singing, "For You" originally sang by Kenny Lattimore. As I sang to my lady, I looked in her eyes. She would blush like a schoolgirl and shed tears intermittently. Then we exchanged our rings and ended with me kissing Mrs. Anthony Bradford.

Five events highlighted the reception and made it beyond exciting. We choreographed the best wedding party entrance. Melinda and I sang a remixed version of "Endless Love," originally sung by Diana Ross and Lionel Richie. My frat brothers did the traditional bride Serenade. Sheila stood over to the side, trying not to participate, when Melinda threw the bouquet. Tracey almost caught it but accidentally tipped it, and it landed right in front of Sheila's feet. The last thing is when I pulled the garter from Melinda's leg. The fellows at the studio and my frat brothers made a big to-do out of it. I didn't want them looking at my woman's thigh.

We spent our wedding night in the Presidential Suite at the Beverly Hills Estates. Before we arrived, I had arranged to have our suite decorated with white candles and vases of white roses. The bed had white satin sheets and a white goose-down comforter as she'd dreamt and desired.

Thoughts of her in the black lace panty and bra set were reintroduced to my memory as I showered. I closed my eyes and enjoyed the vision. It was okay because now she was all mine to hold, and our bedroom was undefiled.

While she was in the shower, I placed white rose petals leading from the bathroom to our bed and all over the white satin comforter. I also lit scented candles on both nightstands. Soft music by Eric Benet added to the atmosphere.

Melinda came out in a beautiful white see-through gown. Everything was in plain view. The black lace was not to be compared. I extended my hand to my wife. She put her hand in mine and slid into my arms.

After we slow danced, I sat on the edge of the bed and gently pulled her to me. I became intimately familiar with every inch of my woman. There was no better feeling in the world than making sweet, passionate love to my wife.

That night, we reached a level of intimacy that I'd never known. I woke up the following morning not only to new mercies but also with favor, now named, Mrs. Anthony Bradford.

The next evening, Melinda and I flew to the Pocono Islands. For the next seven days, she and I became one flesh. After our honeymoon, I was inspired to write new music. Only now, it came from an intimate place in my soul. A love ballad titled "Being Intimate with You" was the first baby we conceived.

Our first night home as a married couple brought exciting conversation. We called my frat brother Marcus to lease the condo and purchase a home in the valley.

Since we emerged in deep conversation, I probed, seeking how she felt about her dad. I needed to see if she could handle receiving her graduation present. We agreed to go over to her mom's house on the weekend.

That's not the only thing we agreed on. We decided not to use any birth control and let things happen naturally. While in bed, I kissed Melinda all over her body. I looked into her eyes and said, "Let's make a baby?"

She sighed, "I'm ready." Although we had just had eight days of climatic bliss, this experience was different. We reach yet another level of intimacy. Melinda and I experienced one-ness. Our souls and spirits connected when our flesh joined to-gether. We were on one accord to create a new life that would be us. After we reached that point of ecstasy together, she started crying.

Mom King prepared Sunday dinner for everyone. Kenny, Lisa, Aunt Louise, and all my family were there too. This would be our first dinner with the family as Mr. And Mrs. Anthony Bradford.

After we finished dining, Mom King handed Melinda the card her dad had given her for graduation. She opened it and read it silently. My wife looked at her mom. "What?"

"Mom handed Melinda the keys, "It's in the garage."

My lady exclaimed, "No way. I knew he would forget me."

Mom King said, "He didn't. It has been there since…"

"I know, Mom."

We entered the garage and were formally introduced to her gold-colored, brand-new, customized Infiniti. It even had per-sonalized plates. She said, "Mom, I can't expect you to pay for this."

Mom King stated, "Anthony, tell her it's taken care of."

"Melinda, your mother and I have discussed it. I wouldn't let you take the car if it caused her hardship. Trust me."

"Anthony said you guys would take care of the insurance. See, we worked it all out."

Melinda announced an additional surprise, "If it's okay with my husband and father-in-law, I would like to give my Mitsubishi to Howard."

Howard pitched, "Dad, Ant, please let me have it. I love that car. I'll do whatever it takes."

I said, "I don't have a problem with it. Dad?"

"I'm okay with it. There needs to be some stipulations." Said Dad.

"Tell me what you want, and I will do it."

Dad had a contract drawn up for Howard. To get and keep the car, he had to maintain good grades and provide a way to pay for gas, maintenance, and insurance.

Melinda and I found a house after about two months of house hunting. It had a spiral staircase, five bedrooms, three full bathrooms, an office, a family room upstairs and down, and a bonus room downstairs. We planned to convert that room into a music studio. There was a big kitchen and a formal dining room. The backyard was big, and it had a hot tub inside. We also had a three-car garage.

Melinda was a little apprehensive about buying the house at first. Her first obstacle was that she felt it was sinful for her and me to occupy that much of the house. I reminded her that we were filling it up with little Bradfords.

Next, unaware of our financial worth, she feared the house was too pricey. I put her mind at ease when I told her I'd been preparing for her and my children since I was twenty. Then I assured her everything that we had, or we would ever get, we would be able to do on her husband's income.

Melinda became weak emotionally when she spoke of King. Then she expressed being overwhelmed because things seemed to be moving so fast, the wedding, the house, and she announced that she missed her monthly. After we celebrated the possibility of Melinda being pregnant, I understood the real issue was grief.

I sat on the spiral staircase and invited her to sit beside me. My wife put her head on my shoulder. I held her and just let her cry. This was the first time I saw her have a good cry since the day King died.

I offered, "It's going to take some time."

"He had just dropped me off at work."

I said, "His death isn't about you. You're not responsible. Melinda, we don't know why it happened. God has a plan."

"I get so scared sometimes. I love you so much. I need you. Please don't ever leave me."

I kissed her on the lips, "I never will. Who would I share this big house with?"

That evening, I got all of our financial records together. I gave Melinda bankbooks, pay stubs, and bank statements. She spent the next two evenings setting up a ledger for our household. She learned that our income was six figures, three times what she imagined. We owned stocks and bonds and had three savings accounts. One account was for the Bradford children.

The following morning, Melinda was awakened by a nauseous stomach. That did not stop her from coming to the real estate office with me to sign the papers for our new house. Marcus let us know it would be no problem leasing our condo. We could also move into our new house in thirty days.

Melinda was to see her regular Physician, Doctor Burrows. They immediately took a urine test. I went into the examining room with my wife. While we were waiting, she was lying on the examining table. I sat nearby, reading a parenting magazine.

Dr. Burrows said, "Melinda, I hear you're not feeling too well."

"My stomach has been bothering me a great deal. I think I might be pregnant. I'm sorry.

How rude of me. This is my husband, Anthony."

"How are you, Anthony?"

"I'm okay. I'm a little concerned about my wife, though."

"Well, we'll see what's going on."

As she lay, I stood next to her, holding her hand. The nurse came in and gave Dr. Burrows the results of her test. She viewed them and reported, "You're not pregnant."

Wow! That hit like a ton of bricks. Dr. Burrows probed, "Melinda, did you want to be pregnant?"

"Very much so."

"How long have you two been trying?"

"I answered, "A couple of months."

"Don't worry; it hasn't been long. There's no reason to be alarmed. I need to get to the bottom of what's going on with your stomach and why you're missing your period. We can do some tests if you aren't pregnant in a couple of months. When you do get pregnant, we want a healthy mommy."

She started pressing on various areas on her stomach. My wife would react every time the doctor got to a tender spot. After Dr. Burrows finished examining Melinda, she said, "Get dressed and come to my office."

When the doctor left, I held Melinda close and offered, "As she said, we just started trying. It will happen. I want you to feel better." I was disappointed but knew I needed to stay strong for my wife.

We went to Dr. Burrow's office. She assured us that there was no reason to be alarmed. She attributed Melinda's missing cycle to stress and diagnosed Melinda with a spastic colon. After the doctor learned about King's death and all of Melinda's new life events, she suggested Melinda take a week off work. She teased about us going somewhere and working on the baby.

I took Melinda on a trip to Santa Barbara to relax and clear her head. The scenery was beautiful, and we had a fantastic suite with a view of the ocean. There were plenty of delectable cuisines. We fed the birds and went on romantic walks hand in hand.

Parts of the conversation resonated with me. On the last day we were there, I noted she still had not mentioned King. When I probed about her feelings concerning him, she became irritated, "I don't want to feel anything. Can't you see! It's just too complicated! Trevon, him, you, I don't want to think about it."

"Whoa! Hold up, you said a mouth full."

"Any man I ever loved hurt me. Trevon cheated and Daddy left me. He died on me, Anthony." She started crying, "I didn't even get a warning. He couldn't even wait until I got to the hospital. He dropped me off for work, Baby, and it was over. I love you so much. If I lost you, I would die." She stood there sobbing.

I comforted her, "You're not going to lose me."

"How do I know that? That's the same thing my dad said. He said he'd always be there for me."

"You think I'm going to die or leave you?"

"I don't know. I'm just scared."

"Baby, where is this coming from? Everything I've told or shown you has represented me spending my life with you. What have I done?"

"This is so good."

"It's supposed to be."

"Every time I get happy, something bad happens. Can't you see? That morning, I got out of that car so happy. I'd just graduated, I was marrying you, and Daddy and I were tight again. I miss him so much, Anthony." She lay on the bed, crying, "Daddy, I miss you so much. Why didn't you wait until I got there? Daddy, why?"

I lay beside her and held her, "I know it's been a bumpy road for you, honey. Trevon was a jerk. He didn't know how to treat a good woman. King's death wasn't your fault. You've got to give me a chance. I'm with you because I prayed to God for you. We're so connected. I know God put us together. Enjoy us, Honey. We have at least fifty or sixty good years." She lay there and kept crying. I continued to comfort her until she fell asleep.

When we left Santa Barbara, she felt better but knew she still had mountains to climb. When she was to start her cycle the following month, she did. We were glad because that meant she wasn't stressing. We were sad because our journey toward parenthood had not yielded positive results.

Advice taken: Innocent.
Advice ignored: Betrayal.

Chapter 16

Love and War

Melinda was happy because she and Karen were talking more regularly, and Karen had also met a guy named Michael. Tracey was still dating Gary and had gotten the building she wanted for her boutique.

One day, she called with exciting news. She and Gary were getting married and asked Melinda to be the matron of honor.

Tracey's mother's retirement party was going to be the following weekend. Melinda wanted to go to both events. I told her to put the dates on our calendar.

For the next couple of months, Melinda and I would continue to work on having a baby. Our attempts were unsuccessful. I was starting to get worried, and frustration was beginning to set in. It made it even more difficult for Melinda when we found out Lisa was four months pregnant by Kenny.

The following month, when she was to have started her cycle, she did not. One evening, I came home to Melinda lying on the bed. Her monthly hadn't started, and she was doing one of those home pregnancy tests. She didn't want to tell me, citing, "Just in case I'm not, I didn't want to disappoint you."

I said, "If we never have children, I'll still love you the same."

Melinda went into the bathroom to check the test. It was negative. She came back and lay next to me on the bed. I said, "Melinda, make an appointment to see Dr. Burrows. You can't keep going through this every month."

"Going through what?" She asked.

"Your cycle being late or not starting at all, thinking you're pregnant, and then you're not. You get depressed every single month."

My wife said, "I'll be okay."

I sat up and sternly stated, "Melinda, make the appointment." That was the first night it was cold in our marriage bed. I don't know if it was because we were tired of trying to conceive or we'd started giving up hope.

When I got ready to leave for work the following morning, Melinda confessed, "I feel so inadequate."

I encouraged, "There's no reason to feel like that. You're beautiful no matter what."

"Anthony, would you mind if I make the appointment after we return from Atlanta? I have a lot to do next week. Then it will be time to go."

"Okay, but first thing when we come back."

She agreed, "I will."

That was the same day I first became acquainted with Theresa. I rolled into the studio's parking lot and pulled into my parking space. Loud voices peeped my curiosity. I got out of the car and looked around. I couldn't tell where it came from, so I proceeded to my trunk to get my things.

At that point, I saw a young lady getting out of the passenger side two cars over. Sister girl slammed the door. As she hurried past me, our eyes briefly met. She was upset and had been in an altercation. It was confirmed when the car she was in pulled out, and the gentlemen stopped where she was and got out of the vehicle.

I stood watching as he called out her name. She went back to the car, said something, then hurried into the building. He sped off, apparently in a fury.

I spent a couple of hours in my office and then entertained a meeting with my artist. Barbara was a telling it like it is sister, who had been at the studio for at least seven years. She started as a background singer for Eric Benet. Now, she was a solo artist. We were releasing her second single on the heels of her first hit single that was blazing up the charts.

We'd received word that a massive press tour was on the horizon. While awaiting confirmation of the schedule, I joined her in rehearsal. Her dancers and backup singers were all waiting when I entered the rehearsal hall. As they got into formation, I took notice of one of the singers. She was the young lady I had seen in the parking lot earlier. Again, she and I briefly met eyes. This time, she nodded her head to acknowledge me. I returned the nod. When they finished the rehearsal, I returned to my office. I pulled up the tour schedule as Barbara was coming through the door. I expressed, "Aw, man."

"What's going on? Is there a problem with the schedule?"

"Melinda and I had planned to be out of town on some of these dates."

"I can handle it by myself."

"No. This is a major tour, and Jack wanted me to accompany you."

"Can you push your vacation with Melinda up or back?"

"We were going to her best friend's wedding. That date is etched in stone."

"Ouch, sounds like you have a dilemma."

"Major. We've been planning it for months. She's going to be disappointed. I'd better go home and give her the news."

"Hopefully, something will work out. I really like Melinda. You did good, knucklehead. You have an awesome wife. I thought you were going to end up with that, Tanya."

"That Tanya? Really, Barbara?"

"I'm just saying."

"Just saying what?"

"I wasn't feeling her for you. Melinda, she's the business. She's all about Anthony."

"Indeed, she is."

"And you better not mess it up."

"Speaking of mess-ups, what's the story with that backup singer you have with the curly hair?"

"See, there you go."

"I just want to know about her. I'm not going to step out on my wife."

"Theresa just started singing with me last week. I met her a few years ago. She's good."

"I noticed."

"She's going to go on the tour, and then we will take it from there."

"I thought I was the decision-maker around here."

"As long as I make you those coins, I know I get a say."

"I'll give you that, because we are about to make some major cheddar."

"Well, on your way home, buy my girl something nice. You might be sleeping on the sofa once you break the news."

I made it home before Melinda. When she got there, I was there sitting on the couch. She greeted me with a kiss and exclaimed, "Babe, you're home."

I said, "Yeah, I rapped up earlier and wanted to see you."

"That's sweet. I'm glad you're here. You will never guess what I got in the mail." She handed me a letter and sat down next to me.

It was from a high-end hotel in Atlanta with an offer to stay one week free. I inquired, "Why is the letter addressed to Melinda King?"

She expressed, "I don't know. It came to my parent's house. Maybe Karen or Tracey put me on a mailing list."

"As Melinda King?"

"Maybe it was before we got married. I don't know. What does it matter? We can stay a week free."

"We're not going to be able to go."

"What do you mean?"

"The song I wrote for Barbara Wilson is being released that week. The studio thinks it's going to be a big hit. She and I are going to be on the Inside Today Show. I have to fly to New York. Then we're going on a talk show tour. It's the same weekend as the wedding."

"Honey, I'm happy for you."

"Babe, this success is for us. I want you to go with me."

"What about the wedding?"

"I'm sure Tracey would understand."

"Understand? I don't understand."

"Melinda, this is the opportunity of a lifetime. I want you to be there."

"I understand, Anthony, but this is my best friend's wedding."

"I don't feel good about you going out there alone."

She raised her voice, "Why Anthony? I don't see the problem!"

"I don't want my wife staying in some hotel for two weeks alone."

"I'll stay with Tracey at the apartment for the first week. Then I'll see if Karen will stay with me at the hotel for the second week."

"That makes it better? I'm supposed to trust that?"

"That what? My friend?"

No, Melinda, I'm not calling your friend "that." I'm talking about the situation. You said she trips out on you."

"That's when she was drinking."

"No. I'm not feeling it."

"You're not feeling it? Anthony, you're talking like I'm your child or a piece of property."

"No, you're not. But I did promise to love, protect, and comfort you."

"And that means putting your foot on my head?"

I didn't appreciate the inference, so I forged, "Whoa, you're way out of line with this. You're taking this all wrong. I didn't mean it that way, and I'm not going down that road with you."

"How should I be taking it, Anthony? We're talking about my best friend's wedding."

"No, we're not. It's not about the wedding. It's about us."

By this time, she was clearly agitated because she popped off an insulting, "What about us?!"

I felt her comment defied the rule of fair fighting. Refusing to engage, I crossed my arms and looked at her while shaking my head." Then I calmly said, "It takes two to argue. I'm going upstairs to shower."

When I returned, I stated, "I'm going to go into the studio and work for a little while. If you feel like talking, let me know."

She said, "Okay."

After I finished working, I started watching videos. Tamar came on singing, "Love and War." It reminded me that Melinda had not come downstairs.

I went up and sat on the side of the bed and suggested, "We need to talk. Let's go downstairs." Melinda and I went into the den and sat on the couch. I was so angry, but I remembered what Melinda said about me raising my voice at her. Also, as the man of the house, I knew it was my responsibility to ensure the sun didn't go down on our wrath. I said, "I don't want us to go to bed like last night. Why are you fighting me?"

"I don't think it was right for you to ask me not to attend Tracey's wedding."

"Melinda, we could have talked about it. You got very defensive and started yelling. You didn't even give me a chance to understand your point of view. Saying, I'm trying to put my foot on your head hurts. Go on to the wedding. It seems that it means more to you than us."

She defended, "That's not fair."

"What's not fair?"

"For you to put me in that position."

I forged, "We have never argued like that."

"I'm sorry I talked to you that way." Said Melinda.

"So am I."

"I didn't mean to fight, but I meant what I said, Anthony."

"Melinda, you said it, and I heard you loud and clear."

"Are you concerned about Trevon and me?"

"I hadn't thought about it. Should I be?"

"No, Anthony, you shouldn't."

"Why did you bring him into the conversation?"

"I thought maybe that was part of your apprehension."

"No, I trust my wife. I just want you safe, Babe. God holds me accountable for your well-being. I also wanted you to be there for me in my special time."

"I know, Honey, but I'm always there for you."

"I don't feel good about you going. But I don't want my foot on your head."

"I told you I didn't mean that. Honey, I'm sorry. I was wrong."

I had opened up a can of upsetness, so I continued to rant. "When you said you'd submit to me, I know it wasn't an agreement to be my doormat. Your input is valuable. The way you give it is another story. I'm going to go upstairs and go to bed." I stood up.

She called out, "Anthony!"

I turned and looked at her. "What do you need?"

She walked over to me and asked, "Aren't you going to ask me to come with you? I need you to make love to me. "

I said, "You know I always want you in my bed."

By this point in life, our bodies were erotically familiar, so we peeked more than not. This was the first night my body was all in, but my mind wasn't. The distance that existed the night before carried through to the next day. I worked from home.

That evening, when Melinda came through the door, I was cooking. Upon her entering the kitchen, I greeted her and kissed her on the lips. She and I exchanged awkward small talk momentarily.

While I was turned towards the stove, Melinda hugged me from behind, laid her face on my back, and said, "I love you, Bae."

I turned around and returned affection while admitting, "Babe. Clearly, we disagree about this situation. I don't want to fight about it anymore."

She added, "Me neither."

So, I suggested, "Let's agree to disagree. I want to take full advantage of the time we have left. I have to give you something to think about when you're in Atlanta." Then, I kissed her on the forehead.

"You've already given me so much," Melinda added while looking into my eyes.

On the Tuesday morning Melinda was to leave, we lay in bed for a while. My wife claimed to be exhausted. I turned on my side towards her and said, "This will be the first time we've been apart."

She agreed, "I know; I'm going to miss you."

I offered, "Well, at least I'm going to be working."

"Do you know when you'll be back?"

I said, "I have no idea."

Melinda suggested, "Maybe if you get done soon, you can fly to Atlanta."

I added, "Or if I'm still traveling, you can join me."

She explained, "Sandra would have my head if I missed that much work. My accounts are all caught up. I'll get behind if I miss more than two weeks."

"You know you can quit? You are going to have to stop working anyway eventually."

"Why?"

"The children."

"What if I can't have any?"

"Then we can adopt, Babe. Either way it goes, we'll fill this house up with little Bradfords. We have enough love between us to love children no matter where they come from."

Melinda said, "I wouldn't mind adopting."

"First, you're going to go to the doctor as you promised Mrs. Bradford."

"It sounds like a plan."

I started rubbing Melinda's stomach. "Let's keep working on putting a baby right here first."

She said, "I could get with that."

"I thought you were exhausted?"

Wifey informed, "You've turned me on. My energy has been restored. Then we made love as if it would be our last time. She and I were both sated.

We had an early dinner before I took her to the airport. I walked with her as far as I could go. Then, she and I cuddled for a minute. She looked into my eyes, "Honey, I love you, and I will miss you."

I stroked her hair and suggested, "It's not too late to change your mind."

"I know, Baby, but I've come this far. I promise you I will never do this again. Please trust me."

"I'm not at ease with this, but I do trust you."

She said, "I'll call you as soon as I can."

I offered, "I love you."

"Please don't ever stop, Babe."

I confessed, "I'll love you for the rest of my life, Melinda."

"For the rest of my life, I'll love you, Anthony Bradford."

When she got on the escalator, I walked away. I didn't want to see her leave. Before I left the airport, I already missed my lady.

Advice taken: Innocent.

Advice ignored: Betrayal; Melinda's Story.

Chapter 17

I Apologize

I went home to an empty house and a bowl of red beans and rice that Melinda had prepared before she left. My appetite failed me, and I felt sick to my stomach. 7Up seemingly calmed it down a little. I lay in our bed, fell asleep, and dreamt I was standing in our bedroom doorway. There was a figure of a woman lying face down in the bed. It looked like that young lady Theresa that I saw at the studio. As I walked towards the bed, it moved further away. I finally caught up and pulled back the comforter. The bed was soaked with blood. I woke up from my sleep sweating and sick with an upset stomach. I went to the bathroom just in time to throw up everywhere.

I turned on the sports channel and watched a game. Then I put in a movie and fell back to sleep. When I woke, I realized Melinda should have landed but had not called me. I got up and dialed her cell number. It went straight to voice mail. After about an hour, I called Tracey's house, and she answered, "Hello."

"Hey Tracey, this is Anthony."

"Hey Anthony, how are you doing? I hate you couldn't make it."

I said, "Next time."

"I understand."

"I've been trying to call my wife's cell for about an hour, and it's going to voice mail."

"You know what? Come to think of it, I have not heard a peep out of her either. Let me check on her." There was a moment of silence, followed by a knock on the door in the background. Then I heard Tracey loudly say, "Melinda, telephone, it's Anthony."

Melinda picked up the receiver, "Hi, Honey."

I said, "Hey Baby, I called your phone, and it went straight to voice mail."

"I can't find my phone."

"Where did you leave it?"

"I don't know. I thought I had it in the car. Maybe it's under the seat. Will you look for it in the car or around the house and see if you can find it?"

"Yeah, I can do that. Why didn't you call when you got in?"

"I wanted to take a shower and get in bed. I was about to call."

"You sound like you're asleep."

"I laid my head down for a minute. The next thing I knew, the phone was ringing. I must be more tired than I realized."

"Maybe you're jet-lagged. How was your flight?"

"At first, it was long, then I started daydreaming and was thinking of you. Last night and this morning with you were so good."

"Don't even go there, Woman. That's the last thing I want to think about. I'm not going to see you for two weeks. I'm glad you made it safe. Why don't you get some rest? Call me tomorrow."

"Okay, Honey, I love you."

"I love you too."

The following morning, I got up early and went to the studio to take care of some last-minute tour business. It was 9 AM, which meant it was noon in Georgia. Melinda had not called, so I called her. The phone rang four times before she answered. She was stunned when I said, "Good afternoon."

She had been sleeping since I spoke to her the day before. I was wondering if it was jet lag or something else. My concerns became void when she called me two hours later. She told me she spent over nine hundred dollars of my money at Tracey's boutique. I thought, "...And she's back, LOL." I was calm, though. I knew she was feeling better, and the purchases were for the remarkable women in my life. She also told me she purchased a little nighty with me in mind.

The conversation went left for a moment when she rubbed me the wrong way. I said, "I didn't find your phone."

She responded, "Okay. I can't think of where it could be. Maybe I lost it on the plane. I'll call and get it turned off before someone else uses it." Then she transitioned, "What time are you leaving the house?"

"About ten. Our flight is leaving at 1 AM.

"Who's our?" She asked.

"Barbara and I."

"Is her manager going?"

"He's going to meet us on Saturday."

She probed, "And the hotel accommodations?"

"Why are you doing this, Melinda?" I asked.

"What?" She asked as if she didn't know what I was talking about.

I was upset with the inference, so I fired back, "You're trying to check up on me. You had the opportunity to come, and you didn't. You're where you wanted to be, aren't you?"

"That's not fair, Anthony."

"What's not fair Melinda, is before you left LA, you asked me to trust you to go to Atlanta without me. Then you turn around and give me the third degree. Don't you trust me?"

"Someone's still mad, aren't they?"

"That's not the point, Babe."

"Yes. I trust you, Anthony."

"How about if we just trust each other, Melinda?"

"Fine."

I said, "Babe, I don't want to keep you on the phone too long. I know you have things to do. I'll call you when I get to New York."

"Oh, you want to hurt my feelings and then hang up."

"I wasn't trying to hurt your feelings. You just upset me with your double standards. This trip is about business."

"I know."

"Then, don't be acting insecure. You know there's nothing between Barbara and me."

"Yeah, I know."

"Then let's just drop it."

"Okay."

"Although you are miles away, I hold you near my heart."

"And I'll hold you near mine."

I didn't want to hang up on a sour note, so I said, "I'd kiss you right now if I could."

"Hold that thought until I see you, Anthony."

"I'll hold that thought and the visions of you in that new nightgown until you come home."

"I love you, Baby."

"I love you too. I'll talk to you later."

I spent the next day traveling. Barbara's house was on the way to the airport, so I had my driver pick her up.

She was the tell it like it is, chatterbox I'd learned to love. When we got through the security checkpoint and were waiting to board, she enquired, "Has Melinda left yet?"

I said, "She left on Tuesday."

"Will this be the first time you two have been apart since you married?"

"Yep, and I'm not feeling it."

"Why? What's your trip?"

"I want her with me."

"Anthony, you're just spoiled. You are used to her serving you. It's her friend's wedding. She would be here if she could, and you know it. Quit being selfish."

"Oh, I'm being selfish because I want my wife with me."

"No, you're being selfish because you are thinking about what you want."

"It's not that I don't want her going. I don't want her going alone."

"Oh, that dude she used to date is there, and you think she might hook up. Stop being insecure; she's faithful."

"No, I trust my wife. I just have an uneasy feeling about this trip."

"Did you tell her your concerns?"

"I suggested she not go, and she went in. She was talking crazy, so I just let her go."

"You're so stubborn."

"And you talk too much."

"Hey," came from a voice behind us.

We turned around, and Barbara said, "Hey Theresa, how are you?"

Theresa said, "I'm good. I like those shoes, girl.".

"Thanks", said Barbara. Do you remember Anthony?"

As I stood up and extended my hand, she said, "Of course." and sat beside us.

We continued the conversation until it was time to board. First and business class was called. Barbara and I stood up, and Theresa just sat there. I looked back, "Are you coming?" I asked.

"Yes, but I'm in Coach."

I said, "Okay, we'll see you when we land."

When we got to our seats, I said, "Who is being selfish now? You booked yourself into First Class, and you put Theresa in Coach? Trifling."

Barbara said, "Don't blame me. Your cheap behind gave me my budget."

I teased, "Yet you're in First Class."

She said, "Be quiet."

I laughed, "I'm just saying it's not a good look. I would have upgraded Theresa."

"She'll be fine. I had to sit in Coach when I first started."

"That was way back when."

"Why are you so nice and concerned about her? You were asking about her the other day, too. What's really going on?"

"My gut is telling me something about her. I just haven't put my finger on it. I'm just trying to figure her out. I really am concerned."

"Anthony, she's not your concern. Leave it alone. Let's not go down that road again."

"What road?"

"The days when you were dealing with Tangi. I never want to see you like you were back then."

I hugged her, "That was a bad time for all of us. I won't ever go back to that life."

"I'm just saying. Flirting and playing around is how it started with Tangi. Theresa is feeling you, Anthony."

"She has a man. I saw her with him the other day. Even if she didn't have a man, I told you, I won't step out on my wife."

"Okay, but I'm going to be watching, and if she gets out of line, I will fire her."

"Can I remind you that I am the boss?"

"Need I remind you that I make hiring and firing decisions regarding my singers?"

"Indeed, but it's not going to be a problem. I'm in love with Melinda."

I settled into my hotel. Then I called my wife. She said she was still fatigued and was about to have dinner with Tracey, Karen, Michael, and Gary. Some parts of me felt like I should have been there. But when I told her to tell everyone hello, Melinda nagged, "It would have been nice if you were here to tell them yourself."

I said, "Melinda, let's not do this today."

"Fine, so how are you doing?"

"I'm okay."

"And Barbara?"

"I thought we weren't going to do this."

"I just asked how Barbara was doing."

I said, "She's a little nervous. We're going to be on New York Live tomorrow morning." Then we concluded the conversation with affectionate salutations.

The following day, Barbra and I appeared on New York Live, some radio shows, and other appearances. Theresa and I became friendlier one evening when we were the last to leave the restaurant. She initially seemed uneasy until she opened, "Anthony, I'm feeling a little embarrassed."

"Why?" I asked.

"The day I first saw you, I know you saw me in the parking lot acting a fool."

"I do recall, and I was a little concerned."

"Well, that was my husband. He and I have been going through a difficult time. He didn't want me to get back into the industry."

"Why? You're good. I could see you being a solo artist one day."

"Really! Thank you. He doesn't like me traveling."

"Yeah, that part of the business can strain a relationship." I transitioned, "Is he going to join you on any part of the tour?"

"No, we have two little girls, and he has to stay with them."

"What are their names, and how old are they?"

"Aleesa is two, and Emani is seven."

"How long have you been married?"

"Ten years."

"You've never traveled?"

"Not since I had Aleesa. He forbade me to go on the road anymore. He even made me stop singing for a while."

"That's a lot. I can't imagine not being able to do my craft."

"So, you feel me?"

"I understand."

Although I spoke to my wife on the phone several times daily, I still greatly missed her. There was nothing I wanted more than to see her. But I admit my arrogance felt like she should have come to where I was.

On Friday afternoon, we learned that our event for Saturday was postponed. Therefore, I was free until Monday morning. Out of the ten of us who were there, five people were leaving and coming back on Sunday evening. Barbara had some relatives who lived nearby so she would be with them.

Theresa and two others were staying behind at the hotel. Me, I was on the fence. Should I go to Atlanta and be with my wife, or should my egotism make me stay in New York?

On the Saturday morning of the wedding, I called Melinda. She missed me as much as I missed her. My wife had to take care of some business concerning their Georgia property for her mom. Then she was going to fly out to meet me on Monday night. Before I hung up, Tracey and I talked for a few minutes. I had to get off the phone abruptly without saying goodbye to Melinda because someone was at the door.

It was Barbara pulling up before she left to spend time with her relatives. When the door swung open, she stepped in and started talking, "See, it worked out. Now you can go and be with your wife at the wedding."

I said, "I'm not sure I'm going anywhere. I might stay here and relax. Melinda is coming Monday night."

"Like heck. You're wrong, Anthony. You need to get out of your feelings and go to Atlanta. Be by her side for the wedding. Besides, I'm not leaving you here with those boss groupies."

"Boss groupies?"

"Yes, I've been checking them. Those silly women, trying to give it up to the boss."

"I told you…"

198

"I know you're not going to cheat on Melinda."

"They all know I'm married."

"Those tricks don't care. Don't act brand new. You know how it is out here in these streets."

"Alright, already. You're right. I need to be with my wife. I need her lovin' anyway. I can't take it another day."

"See how selfish you are. You're not going to be there for Melinda. You want to get you some. Just trifling."

I went to the computer and found one flight leaving in four hours. I would have to fly on standby. I wouldn't make it to the wedding, but I would make it to the reception. I didn't tell Melinda because I didn't want to disappoint her if I could not get a seat. Once I finished making the arrangements to go to Atlanta, Barbara was satisfied and left.

Advice taken: Innocent.
Advice ignored: There will be major betrayals.

Chapter 18

Who's Making Love

I had about an hour to get dressed and leave the hotel to get to the airport in time. While in the shower, I heard the doorbell ringing. Banging on my door followed. I jumped out, grabbed my towel robe, put it on, and rushed to the door. It was Theresa crying violently. I probed, "What is going on?"

She just kept crying. So, I invited her in, closed the door, and asked, "Are you injured? Is your family okay?" She shook her head no. I gave her Kleenex and offered, "Let me get you some water." I got the water and came back. When I got close, I thought I smelt alcohol on her breath.

Giving her the water, I said, "Here, drink this, and give me a few minutes." I went into the room, put some clothes on, and returned. She had her head on the arm of the sofa, and she was still crying.

I sat beside her and asked, "Theresa, what's wrong?"

She sat up and collected herself but was softly panting, "My husband is going to leave me."

"Why?" I asked.

"He said if I don't come home right away, he will take the kids and go."

I asserted, "Theresa, it's not worth all this. Why don't you go home and work things out?"

"What about what I want?"

"You can have what you want, but don't jeopardize your kids or marriage."

"I don't care about him. I don't want to lose my kids again."

I sighed, "You lost them before? What happened?"

"I don't want to talk about it. My husband just wants to control me."

"Forget all that control stuff. Barbara and I would never forgive ourselves if you lost your children because you're with us."

"It's just not fair."

"Life is not fair sometimes. Go home to your husband and kids. If your husband is not in agreement with you traveling, we can work it out for you to do local jobs."

"I can't let Barbara down."

"She will understand."

I talked to her for another twenty minutes until she calmed down and she said, "Thank you, Anthony."

"No problem, this business can be hard on a relationship. But we prioritize what's important, and your family is first." Right then, I heard myself. Conviction hit me like a ton of bricks. I was wrong. Melinda has always had my back. If she could be with me, she would. My attitude needed to be checked at the door. I was being selfish. The Lord had worked the way out by postponing my event. I should be with my wife in Atlanta.

I needed Theresa to go so I could get to the airport on time. I stood and said, "Give me a minute." I went into the bathroom and got a warm cloth. When I came back, she was standing. I noticed her short black dress, and it was a little sheer. I could tell this female wasn't wearing panties or a bra. The man controlling my flesh said, "Oh my!" I thought, "Here we go." I'd encountered this scenario many times before, but I was a young, immature man. Now, I was at the age of putting away childish things. Righteous indignation spoke to my integrity loudly, "Don't insult me or disrespect my wife." I looked at the clock and realized I had to be on my way in about ten minutes to get to the airport.

I handed her the washcloth and said, "Here, wash your face."

She took the cloth, said, "Thank you," stepped close to me, and extended her arms as if she was going to hug me.

I said, "I don't think so. That's not a good idea."

Theresa countered, "Don't you want to? It's my way of saying thank you. I won't tell anyone."

"There is not going to be anything to tell. You are attractive, Theresa, but you're married, and I'm madly in love with my wife. I think you should go."

She held, "I'm so embarrassed. I thought."

"What did you think?"

"You're so nice. I'm not going to lie. You are so fine, and I'm very attracted to you."

"And so is my wife. Theresa, you say your husband doesn't want you on the road. Maybe this is why."

"I told him I would never do it again."

"Yet, you're standing in my hotel room trying to give it up. Cheating is why your husband doesn't want you to travel. You did this before."

"Everyone does this."

"Not me. You need to go. I'll let it slide because it smells like you've been drinking, but don't ever do this to my wife or me again."

"You're wife?"

"You disrespected her by trying to have an affair with her husband. Come to think of it, you are on her time now. I should be on my way to the airport to be with her. You've got to bounce."

I walked over to the door and opened it to Barbara standing there. She stepped inside. What is going on here?"

I asserted, "Nothing. Theresa is leaving."

Barbara stepped to the side. As Theresa moved past her, she offered a rhetorical, "What do you have on?"

Theresa didn't say anything. She just kept walking out. I closed the door, "It's not what you think."

"What do I think? I think you told me you were going to be with your wife. I think you lied, and you and that trick were up to something. You told me you weren't going down that road again."

"That's not it."

She started crying, "What is it, then? Melinda doesn't deserve this."

I hugged Barbara, "I'm sorry. It wasn't like that. You were right to a point. She came ringing my doorbell and banging on the door. I opened it to her in hysterics. I thought something serious was wrong with her. Apparently, she was having serious problems with her husband. He mentioned taking the kids if she didn't come home."

"She's having problems with her husband because she cheated on him about three years ago and got caught up using drugs."

"Oh, that's why you likened her to Tangi."

"I guess so. Nonetheless, Theresa's husband Chris had left. The condition for him to stay in the marriage was she couldn't travel for a while. He didn't want her to come, but I asked if she could do it this one time. Chris agreed as a favor to me. I just got off the phone with him. He said she hadn't called him or the kids since we'd been gone. Her husband was livid. I returned because I felt I owed it to him to ensure Theresa was doing what was right. She has a really good dude who loves his kids and her."

"Barbara, I never would have let her in if she wasn't banging on my door and crying like she was hurt. I told her to leave when I saw what she was up to."

"Fine. Are you going or what? I'll deal with that trick."

"I'm on my way out now."

"Tell Melinda, Hey."

I realized that my dream was telling me that Theresa was a distraction. I desperately wanted to get to my wife now. I learned I had missed my flight when I got to the airport. Heartbroken, I telephoned Melinda.

When she picked up, I was so glad to hear her voice. She said, "Hi Baby, I miss you. I can't wait to leave this place."

"What's going on?" I inquired.

She said, "Hold on, let me get my tea." She stepped away for a moment. Then I came back to the phone. "You there, Honey?"

"Yeah, Babe, I'm here. How do you feel?"

"I'm on edge. My stomach is in knots."

"Why? What happened?"

"Karen and I had it out."

My heart dropped to my feet. I felt so bad for not being there. "What do you mean?"

"She was about to take a drink. I said something to her, and she exploded. She pushed me and told me I made her sick."

"What? She physically pushed you?

"Yes, she did."

"Where is she now?"

"She got her things and left."

My voice dulled, "Honey, I'm sorry that happened with Karen. Are you okay?"

"I think the confrontation upset my nerves. I had some herbal tea delivered to the room."

I started feeling very anxious and uneasy, and I didn't want her alone, "What are you planning to do?"

"About what?"

"The agreement was that you wouldn't stay at the hotel alone."

She got abrupt, "Anthony, what can I do? Tracey is gone on her honeymoon."

"I don't want you staying there alone."

"Let's not do this tonight, Anthony."

I grew angry, "We're not. I want you to take a flight out tomorrow. It's not optional."

"Fine, Anthony, I get it."

There was an awkward moment of silence. Then I said, "I don't want to fight."

"You're mad, huh?"

"I'm upset with you because of all the attitude. I'm mad at myself because I shouldn't have let you go alone. I didn't feel good about it. Next time, I'm going to listen to my spirit."

"How are things there?"

"Barbara's doing great." I paused. "Was he there?"

"Who, Trevon?" She asked as if she didn't know who I was talking about. "No, but I saw him here in the hotel restaurant."

My stomach started turning, "He was there at the hotel? How did that happen?"

"He said he saw Karen at the club next door, and she told him where I was."

"Did the two you talk?"

"Yeah."

"What did you talk about?"

"The past. I think it ended on a good note."

"Is he out of your system?"

"You are the only man in my system."

"Did he try to get with you?"

"Is he a man? I put him in check, though. Baby, you sound a little insecure."

"I'd be lying if I said I wasn't bothered a little. I don't trust Trevon, but I trust my wife."

"You have every reason, too. You're the only man I'll ever be with."

"What do you have on?"

"I have on that royal blue silk robe."

"What do you have underneath it?" "You naughty boy. I don't have anything underneath."

"Mrs. Bradford, I want to make love to you right now."

She suggested, "Keep your mind on that thought until I see you tomorrow, Mister."

I said, "Think about me in your dreams until you do."

"Why do you think I have nothing on except this robe? Good night, lover boy."

I grinned and said, "Call me when you wake up."

Melinda responded, "I will."

I was like a sick puppy on my way back to the hotel. When I stepped off the elevator and put my key card in the door, Barbara peeked out from her room across the hall and asked, "You missed the flight?"

"Yep."

"I'm sorry."

"I'll talk to you tomorrow."

I went inside and closed the door. Man, I felt so bad. Melinda had a hard time with Karen and wasn't feeling well. I should have been there with her. I lay down and fell asleep. I had the same dream when Theresa was lying face down like Tangi. I was trying to turn her over. The bed moved further and further away. When I reached her, I pulled the covers back and turned her over. It wasn't her. This time it was Melinda. She started crying out, "Help me, Anthony! I need you!" I tried to grab and hold her, but she kept slipping out of my hands. She was lying on the floor, bleeding from the waist down. In the background, I could hear Johnny Taylor singing, "Who's Making Love?" He got louder and louder, blaring, "Who's making love to your old lady while you were out making love," repeatedly until I woke up crying, panting, and sweating.

Once again, Melinda didn't call me as she said she would, so I called her and inquired, "Why didn't you call me when you woke up?"

She explained, "I'm sorry. You just woke me up when you called."

"Do you know what time it is?" I asked,

She paused, "I don't feel well, let me call you back."

"What's wrong?"

"I'm going to throw up." She hung up the phone. I got worried, so I called her right back.

She answered, "Hey."

"What's wrong?"

"It's my stomach again. It's never been this bad before."

"I hate you being out there sick. When you come home, I will never let you leave me like this again."

She asserted, "You promise. I never want too either." She started crying.

"Baby, what's going on?" I asked.

"I don't feel well, and I miss you so much. I should never have come."

"Well, we'll be together soon enough. What time does your flight leave?"

"Honey, I'm sorry I didn't make the arrangements. Can I go home?"

With a feeling of frustration, I said, "Melinda, come on!"

"I won't be any good to you there, sick, Anthony. Maybe I can get an appointment with Dr. Burrows."

I was feeling guilty, scared, and disappointed. My voice dulled, "That's fine, Melinda. Call my sister or Mom to pick you up from the airport when you get your reservations. See if Sheila will stay with you until I come home. I should be there in a few days."

My love said, "Okay," then started crying, "Honey, I'm so sorry I didn't listen to you."

"I'm sorry I didn't listen to my spirit. The important thing is that we both learned from the experience. I love you so much, Baby, and I wish I could hold you right now."

"I need you, Anthony. Don't ever leave me."

"Babe don't start feeling insecure again." I gently reminded, "You know I'm not going anywhere." Then I got reticent.

"What's wrong," She asked.

I said, "I feel helpless. I miss you so much and want to come and get you right now. But go on home and I'll get there as soon as I can."

We had a rehearsal that day to prepare for the venues that week. We were short one singer because Barbara had fired Theresa. All day, I thought about my wife and how stupid I had acted. I should have been there. I called back around 6 PM and asked, "How are you feeling?"

Melinda offered, "I'm sure I'll be all right tomorrow."

"Did you throw up again?" I asked.

"All I ate was a little toast and juice."

"Did you make your reservations?"

She said, "No, honey, I'm sorry. I went back to sleep. I'll do it now."

I asserted, "Don't worry about it. I'll call you before I go to bed. Order some dinner and get some rest. After room service comes, be sure to put the night latch on the door."

"Why did you say that?"

"I hate you being there alone. I'll call you later. I will never let you spend another night away from me. I couldn't concentrate all day."

She said, "Baby, I love you." But it didn't sound as it normally would.

I asked, "What's going on, Melinda?"

She whined, "You're the best thing that ever happened to me. I appreciate you. You're good to me."

"You're acting insecure again."

I telephoned Melinda again at ten. When she answered the phone, I said, "Hey, Babe. How are you feeling?"

She responded with a melancholy tone, "Okay."

I replied, "It doesn't sound like it. Well anyway. I made reservations for you. Tomorrow, Tamika and her boyfriend

Chasen will pick you up at noon. They are going to take you by the house, then drive you to the airport. Your flight leaves at 5 PM. When you get to LA, Sheila will pick you up and stay with you until I come home."

She said, "Thanks, Honey."

I expressed, "This is hurting me. You sound so depressed."

"I don't ever want to hurt you."

"I'll be okay. I want you to be alright. We just won't let this happen again. Get some rest. I'll call you in the morning. Good night."

I had a conference call with Jack and some other executives that afternoon. They extended the tour since Barbara's single was climbing the charts quickly. It was bittersweet. I was happy about the song's success, but this meant I wouldn't see my love for a couple more weeks.

I recalled all my dreams about Tangi, Theresa, and Melinda. Perhaps they didn't play out exactly how I dreamt, but they were foretelling. This prompted worry concerning my wife, recalling my dream about her bleeding. I called my mom and told her Melinda wasn't feeling well.

When Melinda got to my parent's house, she called. When I picked up the phone, she said, "Hi, Honey. Your mom told me you wanted me to call."

"Yeah, Babe, I wanted to ensure you got in okay. How was your flight?"

"Long."

"How are you feeling?"

She said, "My stomach is still upset."

I forged, "You need to go to the doctor."

Melinda countered, "She's only going to fill my prescription."

"Well, if that's what it takes to make you feel better."

"Alright."

I asked, "What happened to you getting an appointment?"

"I will."

"Why do you keep putting it off? Don't you want to have a baby?"

"Of course I do. But, I don't want to go alone. Can I wait until you come home?"

"Get the prescription filled and make the appointment."

"When are you coming?"

"That's the other thing. I won't be home for two weeks." She whined, "Honey…"

I affirmed, "I asked you to join me, and you wouldn't."

"I didn't know you would be gone two more weeks."

I suggested, "Fly out and meet me tomorrow."

"Honey, what about my job? I'll have to return to Los Angeles by the time I get there."

There were a few moments of silence, then I admitted, "I miss you, and I want you with me."

"This upsets me, Anthony."

"Honey, I don't want to fight. You started this by insisting I was trying to put my foot on your head. All I wanted was for us to be together. You would still be here with me. Now you're trying to put a guilt trip on me."

She got reticent. Then mumbled, "I know."

Then I expressed, "I want to hold you right now. When this is over, I want you in my bed every night, no matter where my bed is."

She didn't say a word.

I sighed, "What's wrong?"

"I just miss you."

"Are you spending the night over there?"

"No, Sheila's coming home with me."

"I love you. I'll call you to say good night."

"I love you too. Bye."

When I called Sheila to stay with Melinda, I planned for a card and a vase holding twelve white roses to be placed on her nightstand. The card read: "If I could marry you again, I would."

210

Melinda and I talked on the phone daily, but something seemed off. I assumed it was her challenges in Atlanta and our differences. I believed she and I could resolve them together when I got home. Barbara and I continued the talk show tour. "Being Intimate with You" had reached number three on the music charts and was still climbing. Three days before coming home, I learned I had been nominated for an award for writing and producing her hit singles.

Advice taken: We would have both been Innocent.
Advice ignored: There was Betrayal.

Chapter 19

Wildflower

It was Friday, and I was anticipating going home to my wife. She didn't have to pick me up because I used the car service. I stepped into the house and took a deep breath, inhaling the kitchen smell. There was no place like our home, and I was so glad to be there. I put down my bags in the foyer. When I stood up, I saw the most beautiful woman in the world standing before me. My wife was as stunning as the first time I saw her. I loved this woman with everything inside of me.

I blushed and said, "I've missed you. Get over here, woman." She moved towards me. I slipped my hand down her backside, pulled her closer, and brushed a kiss across her lips. She looked into my eyes and ran her fingers through my hair and down to the small of my neck. I brushed another kiss across her lips. Then we kissed one another with the passion that defined the trial we had been through.

I pulled back and suggested, "Take the phone off the hook, and let's go upstairs and shower together. I want you to model that sexy nightgown you purchased. Then I will spend the rest of the night making love to you."

Seducing me with her eyes, my wife suggested, "We have all day and all night. Why don't you eat lunch? Then we need to unpack your things."

I kissed her on the neck, "I haven't seen you for a month. We can unpack later, but something does smell good in the kitchen."

"I knew you'd be hungry, so I fried you some chicken, made some French cut string beans with smoked turkey and potatoes, and homemade macaroni and cheese."

"That's why I married you. You're smart, fine, faithful, spiritual, and can cook. On top of all that, you take good care of me."

She said, "And I married you because you are smart enough to know that. Go wash your hands, and I'll fix your plate."

As I was walking away, I turned around, "Babe?"

She said, "Yes, there is sweet tea." We both laughed.

After we had lunch, we went upstairs. Melinda suggested, "Why don't you get in the shower? I'll join you in a minute."

I came behind her, gently grabbed her shoulders, and kissed her back, "Don't be long."

I got in the shower. After a few minutes, I noticed my wife wasn't there yet. So, I called out, "I'm waiting." She finally got in. I washed her body, and she washed mine.

When I got out, she lingered behind doing lady things. I put in my oldies song by New Birth and sat on the edge of the bed, anticipating my wife's arrival. She entered the room in her new nightgown. By that time, "Wildflower" was playing. My eyes followed until she approached me, propositioning her into our bed. I stood up, ran my hands softly up the back of her legs to her hips, and kissed her on the neck, "You were right. That nightgown is so inviting."

She laid back on the bed, and I followed, thirsty for what was coming. We kissed until we became sensually heated, and the moment—was passionate and intense. Suddenly, she pushed me off her and quickly sat up. That completely confused me. With my forehead wrinkled, I asked, "Are you mad at me? What's the problem?"

"Nothing," she replied.

I said, "You pushed me like I was a stranger."

"I'm sorry." She responded.

Melinda appeared to be angry. So, I held her and offered, "I know it's been hard on the two of us the last month. We've never fought so much. Baby, I'm sorry."

"Me too."

I started kissing her again. She returned my affections. Softly, I whispered, "You know you're a tease, don't you?"

"Why do you say that?" She asked.

"I haven't made love to you in a month, and you're making me work for it. Lay back and let me relax you." I went down and got reacquainted with that which was mine. Afterward, I made passionate love to my wife. Together, time after time, we reached climactic ecstasy. Then, I held her safely in my arms. I loved her so much.

In the morning, I made breakfast and brought it to her in bed. As soon as I got there, she smelled the food, ran to the bathroom, and threw up. I wondered, "Is she pregnant?" I had heard of stories where the woman would exhibit signs of morning sickness as soon as the baby was conceived.

After she returned to bed, I asked, "Are you having morning sickness? Maybe we made a baby last night."

"I'm sure it's my nerves."

"After last night, I thought you would be relaxed. When is your appointment?"

"Monday."

"You get some rest. I'm going to take my tux to the cleaners."

She said, "Are you kidding? This is your big night. I've got to get my hair done and find a dress."

"Didn't you get new clothes? If you look as good in those as you did last night, I'm in trouble."

"Yes. But I still don't know what to wear."

"Try them on. I want to see what you've got."

She modeled all the clothes she had purchased from Tracey's shop. I picked out a red spaghetti-strapped dress with a red chiffon scarf to throw around her neck. Then I announced, "I've got something to go with your dress."

"What?" She asked.

"Did you think I would be away from you for so long and not bring you anything?"

I went to my suitcase, took out a black velvet jewelry box, and handed it to her. She opened it and discovered a beautiful pearl and diamond necklace with matching earrings. I pulled another box out of my suitcase. Melinda opened the box, which was wrapped in baby shower gift paper. It was a beautiful blue baby layette with a small musical note on the front.

"How cute, a little boy's set. The first Bradford is going to be a boy, huh?"

"A little girl can wear blue. I saw this set when I was in New York. I had to get it. Look at the music note."

"That's the first thing I noticed."

We lay in bed for a bit longer. Until I said, "I've got to get going so my tux will be ready in time. Pamper yourself today. Tonight is our night."

"The party is about you and Barbara."

I could tell she was feeling a little insecure, so I kissed her, looked into her eyes, and firmly said, "I would never do anything to jeopardize our marriage."

After I returned from running errands, Melinda wasn't home. I was in the den when she arrived. I'd just answered the phone, and someone hung up on me. I mentioned it to my wife but suggested perhaps it was someone who called the wrong number. I kissed my wife while pondering if that was Theresa on the phone.

A limousine picked Melinda and me up for the party. We arrived to the media, being all over the place. Barbara greeted me with a hug, and to Melinda, she said, "Hey, Melinda, isn't this exciting?"

My family, including Mom King, Kenny, and Lisa, joined us at our table. After they announced my nomination, I was asked to make a speech. I got to the podium and looked in Melinda's direction, "Honey, come up here." Holding her hand, I began, "I don't know if you all realized, but my love for my beautiful wife inspired this song." I kissed her and continued, "So I celebrate the song's conception with her. God gave me the melody and the lyrics. I thank Him for that. Barbara is the instrument that God used to bellow my emotions in the right key. Much love to you, Barbara. To all my friends and family who supported me tonight, thank you from the bottom of my heart."

The next evening, I went to the studio. When I got home, I called out for Melinda, "Babe, I'm home." Then I ran upstairs. She jumped up from the bed when I entered the room. I assumed I'd woken her. I said, "Hey, Babe, get dressed. I want to take you out to dinner."

She exclaimed, "Anthony, we need to talk."

"Baby, what's wrong? Look, let me use the bathroom and get comfortable. Then you can have all the time you need."

I started towards the bathroom. Melinda called out, "Anthony!"

"Just a minute," I replied.

While washing my hands, I saw a pregnancy test on the counter. At first, I didn't want to look. I was used to the disappointment my baby faced every time the test was negative. Then I decided to peek so I could know how to comfort her. That would not be necessary because it was positive. At last! I ran back into the room, "You're pregnant!" Is this what you wanted to tell me?"

She sat on the side of the bed. I kneeled in front of her and looked up into her eyes. "I love you. This is one of the happiest days of my life. The other is the day you became my wife."

She mumbled, "I love you too. "Then, she laid back and put her forearm over her face. That confused me. I got up and lay next to my love on the bed and asked, "What's the matter?"

My wife got up and walked over to the window. I followed behind her. With her back turned to me, she started crying. Her tears started flowing as if her eyes were endless faucets. Her head was bowed down towards the floor.

I hugged my wife from behind and softly inquired, "Melinda, what's wrong? Don't you want a baby? We've been trying for months. Was it us wanting this baby or just me?"

"Us."

"Those don't look like tears of joy."

"Anthony, please!"

"What? Babe, talk to me. I need to know what's going on."

She put her head back down. I gently turned her around and lifted her head, "Haven't we always been able to talk about everything?"

"Yes."

"Then, why won't you talk to me?"

"Baby, please."

"What, Melinda, talk to me."

"Don't leave me."

"I told you I'd always be here for you when I met you."

I wondered if someone had told Melinda about what happened in New York, especially when she blurted out, "No, you haven't! You told me you weren't going to keep traveling like you were. Every time I turn around, you're flying somewhere. You love your job more than me." Then she sat on the edge of the bed and put her head down.

I stood in front of Melinda. "That's not true. I love you more than anything. I have to work to make sure you have everything."

She stood up, "How much money do we need? When is enough, enough? I need you!"

"You have me."

"When? You're always traveling."

"Melinda, I cut down on traveling, and most of the time, I take you with me."

"I'm always with you. What about what I want? What about what I need?"

I put both of my hands on her hips. "What do you need?"

"You told me you would be there when I needed you. I needed you! Where were you when I was in Atlanta? You weren't there."

I realized this wasn't about what happened in New York but about me not being in Atlanta. I felt even worse now. I asked, "You're still hurt about that?"

"I needed you." She kept crying. "I needed you. Now I am going to have a baby. How do I know you'll be there? I'm scared."

I felt like such a jerk. I pulled my lady to me and held her tight. She kept crying. "I needed you. I needed you."

"I'm sorry, Babe. Please forgive me. I will never let that happen again. I promise you things will be different."

"When, Anthony, When?"

"Starting now." Running my fingers through her hair and looking into her eyes, I shared, "I love you so much. I didn't know you were so unhappy. You have me all weekend. I promise you there will be no work. We'll work this out."

"What happens after the weekend?"

"Monday morning, I take my wife to work. I go in and talk with Jack and see what we can do. At three, I go and pick my wife up from work. I take her to the doctor to see how she and my baby are doing." I rubbed her stomach. At that moment, I made a vow. I will never spend that much time away from my wife again."

She looked at me, "I love you, and I never want to be without you."

"You never will. How about I take you to dinner so we can celebrate?"

Melinda and I stayed out late on Friday night, so the following day she slept in. This made time for her husband to serve her breakfast in bed. I was so proud of myself when I came into the room carrying a tray with a cheese and mushroom omelet garnished with parsley, wheat toast, two pieces of turkey bacon, and a glass of orange juice. I went to her side of the bed and said, "Good morning."

"Wow! Good morning to you too. All of this?" She asked.

"Yes, "You're eating for two."

"If this is how it's going to be, by the time I have this baby, I will be as big as a house."

I offered, "There will just be that much more of you to love."

"Yeah, you say that now."

"I was just wondering…"

"Wondering what?" She asked.

"If I could have a little of your time today. I want to share a piece of my world with you."

"How intriguing? I think that can be arranged."

I drove Melinda to San Pedro to a place called the Korean Friendship Bell. A big, beautiful bell tower was in the middle of a grassy area. There was no one there but us. I pulled a picnic basket and a blanket from the trunk. Then I took her by the hand and walked her over to a cliff. Melinda joked that I had brought her there to push her off. After we laughed about it, she learned that at the bottom, there was a beautiful beach. I laid out a blanket. And then I pulled out a ceramic teapot and two white China teacups. We sat, sipping tea as we watched the water rushing against the rocks.

She leaned back on my chest and proclaimed, "There is no place I'd rather be than right here with you."

"There's nothing I'd rather do than hold my wife."

She turned her head and fell into my arms. I rubbed her face with my fingers and stared into her eyes, "I love you so much. I didn't know I could love you more than I already did.

Knowing that you are carrying my baby takes my love to a level I didn't even know existed. I want you to be happy. Just tell me what you want. I'll do whatever it takes."

She put her head down. "Just be there like you said you would."

"I will. But I need you to do something for me."

"What?"

"I know you, Melinda. Something is going on. Ever since I came home, you've been acting distant and insecure. Can I tell you something?"

"What?"

"I can only imagine how you must have felt with us fighting and me being gone from home so long, not to mention spending time with other women. If you think something happened while I was gone, don't. Like I told you the other day, I would never do anything to jeopardize our marriage. I committed to God before we met. If he sent you, I would value and never misuse you. Melinda, God blessed me, and I have to honor Him by giving you my complete loyalty." I hugged her, "You could have told me how mad you were and that you felt I wasn't there for you. I would have understood. We are going to be together for a lifetime. I need you to communicate what you feel, are going through, and need. I love you more than you will ever know. What's important to you is important to me."

"You're right. I have been acting insecure."

"I hope I have put your insecurities at ease. Now tell me, what does Melinda want to do about her career?"

"I know we said we don't want the kids to be raised by daycare. It makes sense that I would be the one to put my career on the back burner. But I want to keep working until I have the baby. Tax season is right around the corner, and I have clients that are depending on me."

"I see someone else loves her career too."

"Yeah, I guess the key is balancing. Eventually, I want to return to school for my master's degree."

"You're not in this marriage alone, nor do you have to make all the sacrifices. We'll work something out. Melinda, you take good care of me. You go to work and keep our home immaculate every day. I don't know the last time I went to a fast-food restaurant. You're there when I come home. When I need to talk, you listen. Baby, you even rub my head."

She looked into my eyes and blushed, "Is that all I do for you?"

I kissed her lips and said, "No, you give me plenty of lovin, too.'"

She surmised, "When we get home, I'll cook your favorite meal. I'll run you a bath, oil you all over, and then do everything that turns you on."

I forged, "I want to pamper you. Woman, this is your weekend. You don't have to worry about dinner. I will run your bath, get in, and wash your back. We can oil each other down and do everything that turns each other on,"

"You know what I think?" She asked

"What?"

"I think we should go home."

I said, "Well, I'm going to be the tease tonight. I'm holding out. The night is still young, and I'm not finished dating you."

After we left the Friendship Bell, we continued down the coast to Redondo Beach. We walked along the shoreline, holding hands as we watched the sunset. Then we went onto the pier and had dinner at the Seafood Tavern. We watched the seagulls from our table near the large paned window while waiting for our seafood platter. When we got home, as I promised, it was one of the most romantic evenings ever.

Melinda and I ate dinner at my parent's house Sunday after church. Mom, Dad and Mom Bradford, Sheila, Damien, Howard, Melinda, and me, were all at the dinner table when Dad announced, "Anthony, Jack said he's been trying to call you for the last two days. You haven't been answering the phone at home, and your cell phone is going straight to voicemail."

"I haven't turned that phone on all weekend. I needed to spend some quality time with my wife. We had some things we needed to work through."

"I understand. Jack said he wanted to meet with you Monday morning."

"Is everything okay?"

"Nothing that can't wait until Monday. You did the right thing. Sometimes, you have to take the phone off the hook and turn that cell off."

"I had planned on meeting with him Monday anyway."

When we were finishing dinner, Kenny and Lisa entered the house. Melinda got sick as they entered the door and ran to the bathroom. Mom and Mom King went behind her.

The moms put two and two together and added that Melinda was pregnant. I made the announcement to those who hadn't figured it out. Everyone expressed their congratulations and love.

Advice taken: Innocent.
Advice ignored: My wife's body could betray her.

Chapter 20

I Do Love You

On Monday, I was prepared to meet with Jack. I had plans to tell him I couldn't travel anymore. Before I could say anything, he offered me a new position. He stated that he had looked at me for months and felt I was ready.

Later that afternoon, I took Melinda to her doctor's appointment. Dr. Burrows confirmed that Melinda was indeed pregnant. Reality set in for us when we heard the baby's heartbeat. I held Melinda's hand and kissed her on the forehead. I thanked God for my baby.

We left the doctor's office and ran some errands before going home. As we pulled into the driveway, Melinda noticed the aroma from the kitchen. She looked at me, "Anthony, what's going on? Are you cooking?'

"No, it's a surprise."

"A surprise?"

Once we entered the house, I introduced Melinda to Lewis. He was her new personal chef, and I informed her she would also have a housekeeper. She said, "Anthony, what is all this for?"

"You don't have time to be in the kitchen and cleaning the house. Do you know who you are?"

"Mrs. Anthony Bradford?"

"You are Mrs. Anthony Bradford, the mother to my baby and the wife of the newest music executive at the studio."

"Bae. I am so Godly proud of you."

"Jack was looking for me this weekend to set an appointment for us to talk this morning. He gave me the rest of the week off. I start my new position on Monday."

"How is the pay?"

"More than I imagined."

"Honey, you deserve it. You've worked so hard."

"The money is great, but the best part is that there is very little travel, and I will be home most evenings. Do you know what that means?"

"I can have my husband home?"

"That means after you have the baby, your husband will be home in the evenings so you can return to school."

"I love you so much. You are so good to me."

By the time Melinda was five months pregnant, the nursery was decorated, and we were waiting for the arrival of our new baby. Martha, the housekeeper, was there three days a week, and our chef Lewis was there four. I was glad we had extra help. Melinda wanted to keep working, and when she got home, she was always tired. The music studio we had built in our house was finished, and I was typically home from work by six. I only went on one business trip.

Melinda was about six months pregnant, and an opportunity came up for some business in Atlanta. She could use the trip, which was an excellent time to connect with Gary for male bonding. He and Tracey had purchased the house Melinda had grown up in. They invited us to stay with them while we were there.

One morning, Michael, Karen's guy, came over. He'd scored box seats for a Hawks basketball game for himself, Gary, and me. We decided to make a day out of it.

We started early with breakfast, then went for a round of golf. Michael confessed when Gary asked, "So Mike, when will you and Karen tie the knot?"

"I don't know if that's ever going to happen. I love Karen, but I can't figure her out. She and I have been together for a minute. It seems like we start getting close, and then she pulls back."

Gary asked, "What do you mean?"

"When we first got together, she was all in. We saw each other every evening after work and went out every weekend. She was so much fun. Gary, remember when we would double date?"

"Yeah, I know she was feeling you. She'd be raving about you even when you weren't there."

"I don't know what happened."

"Do you think she started back drinking?"

"The only time I know about her falling off is your wedding day. Melinda called me from the hotel and told me she was tripping."

I interjected, "I remember that. Melinda was upset about it."

Michael replied, "I know, Man. I'm sorry about that."

"It wasn't your fault."

"I know, but I should have been on top of things. There was some drama at the reception between her and this dude she used to mess with. It sent her off the deep end. She was in a bad head space when I dropped them off at the hotel. It was against my judgment for her to go."

"Yeah, I feel you on that. I felt like I should have been there for Melinda too."

"I did appreciate Melinda calling me. I went up there and got Karen. She went back in recovery for a little while."

"My hats off to you, Brother. Not all men will hang in and give that kind of support."

"I love her, Anthony. I just don't know how to get her to marry me."

"Have you asked her?"

"About three times."

"What does she say?"

"I'll think about it."

"Man, I don't know…"

"A part of me thinks she might be cheating."

"Why is that?"

"She's not giving it up."

Gary said, "Man, if you're not sleeping with her, she won't marry you, and you think she might be cheating; why are you still with her?"

"Not too many people know it, but we split up for about six months. But I love her, so we got back together."

I added, "Michael, it sounds like you need some answers."

"That's real. I'm at a crossroads. Karen constantly tells me she loves me but will only let me get so close. I need her to marry me or let me move on for good."

Gary cosigned, saying, "And that's real."

After we golfed, we went by Michael's spot for a minute. On the way, Gary turned to the oldies station, and "I Do Love You" by GQ coincidently came on the radio. Michael was cool with it until the part came on that said, "Remembering the things we used to do. The places we used to go, and everything was so mellow."

I was thinking, "This sounds like him and Karen."

He finally said, "Dude, can you change the station? GQ is all up in my house."

We had some of the best seats at the game. The conversation was rich, and we fellows bonded. Before we dropped Mike off, we decided all three couples would get together the next day.

Melinda was already in bed when we got back to the house. Gary told Tracey, "We had a good time. The three of us guys want to get together tomorrow over here and grill with the ladies."

"I don't think that would be a good idea. Karen is not coming over here."

"Why?" Gary asked.

She looked at Gary, "I don't want her here."

"What happened?"

"I don't want to talk about it right now."

That was a good time to retire to my room. I said good night, showered and slept beside my wife. I sensed there was more drama between the three of them. Melinda was crying in the middle of the night. When I inquired, Melinda didn't want to talk about it either.

When my wife was a little more than seven and a half months pregnant, she woke up on a Sunday morning and wasn't feeling very well. She'd been tossing and turning all night from the pain in her lower back. I had gotten up earlier, showered, dressed for church, and come downstairs.

Melinda came downstairs to me, sitting at the kitchen table, having breakfast, and checking my social media. She kissed me and sat down. While eating, my wife complained that her lower back started hurting again. She kept placing her hand on her back. I looked up and asked, "What's wrong?"

"My back hurts. It's been hurting all night."

"Do you think you should stay home today?"

"No, Baby, I'll be fine. I'll take Tylenol. I'm looking forward to attending church and seeing the family at dinner."

"Okay, but you take it easy. That's my boy you're carrying."

She smiled, "I will, Babe."

After church, we went to my parent's house. The whole family was there, including Kenny, Lisa, and Damien. Melinda wasn't feeling well, so she excused herself from the table and went into the guest room to nap.

After a while, I heard Melinda calling for me. I entered the room and said, "Babe, what's going on?"

"I don't feel well and need to go to the restroom. Can you help me?"

I extended my hand to help her. She stood up, and water gushed out. She panicked, "Oh my God, Anthony. I think my water broke. Get Mom!"

I called out, "Mom!" They both came running.

My mom said, "Anthony, get the doctor on the phone. Her water shouldn't break this early."

Mom King asked, "Melinda, sit down. Let me get some towels. Have you been having pain?"

"In my lower back."

"How long?"

"All last night and today."

"You might be in labor."

I hung up the phone. "The doctor told me to get her to the hospital immediately."

On the way, I was so afraid thinking about the dream I'd had. Melinda was bleeding from the waist down. I prayed, "God, please don't let anything happen to my wife and son." After we got to the hospital, they took her to a birthing room. Sheila, Mom, Mom King, and I came into the room. The rest of the family stayed in the waiting room. I held her hand as the nurse took her vitals. She put the heart monitor on for the baby and said, "His heartbeat is strong. The doctor is going to be here in a couple of minutes." I was relieved to hear that the baby was okay.

Shortly after, Dr. Burrows came in. "Melinda, I'm going to examine you. It seems like you are in premature labor. You're five weeks early, so we will need to give you some medication to stop your contractions."

I asked, "Why?"

"If he comes this soon, there could be complications."

I started rubbing Melinda's forehead. "It will be okay."

She cried, "Dr. Burrows, please don't let anything happen to my baby."

"Melinda, relax. We're going to do everything we can. Lay back. Let's see if you're dilated."

She examined her and said, "We're not going to be able to stop the labor. We must let nature take its course. The baby has decided to be born today. He's crowning."

I asked, "What does that mean?"

"Come here. Look." I looked and could see the top of his head.

Dr. Burrows ordered, "Nurse, help Mr. Bradford get dressed. He's about to deliver his son." She went up to the head of the bed and said, "Melinda, you're fully dilated. When I say push, I need you to bare down and push. He's coming whether we like it or not."

When I returned, I kissed my wife on the forehead and held her hand. Dr. Burrows said, "Okay, Melinda, push!" She started pushing. She must have pushed about eight times. Less than one hour after arriving at the hospital, Joshua Alexander came out crying. Dr. Burrows let me cut the umbilical cord. Our moms and I crowded around the nurse as she cleaned the baby.

Melinda yelled out, "What's wrong?!"

The nurse handed me my beautiful son. I brought him to his mother. "Is he okay?" She asked.

The nurse smiled, "You have a completely healthy six-pound, three-ounce baby boy."

My wife held our son. He was so beautiful and high-yellow, like my great-grandfather. Melinda kissed our son and said, "Joshua Alexander, Mommy loves you so much."

The rest of the family came in to see Joshua. Afterward, they left. I stayed all night with my wife and son. As Melinda slept, I watched over our baby.

The following morning, I had dozens of red roses delivered to Melinda's room. The day we came home from the hospital, the whole family was there to greet us. There was food, balloons, and gifts. Mom King stayed over for two days. She'd planned to stay for a week to help. It wasn't necessary because Joshua's daddy wouldn't let anyone near him.

Advice taken: Innocent.
Advice ignored: Betrayal.

Chapter 21

Listen

Joshua was indeed daddy's boy. Melinda didn't have to do anything for him except when I was at work. When I came home, I wanted to care for Joshua. I would even get up with him in the middle of the night. I'd change Joshua's diaper and let Melinda rest. I brought the baby to her so she could nurse him, and then I'd rock him back to sleep.

I did not miss any of his doctor's appointments. When we took him for his first shot, you would have thought my wife was getting the shot instead of Joshua. Dr. Allen Joshua's pediatrician stuck our baby's leg with the needle. Our baby's bottom lip curled down, and he let out the most hurtful cry. Melinda cried right along with him.

I either filmed or took pictures of just about everything Joshua. I took photos of his first Sunday at church, his first time at each of his grandparents' houses, his first time at the grocery store, and all his first holidays. I got a picture of him sitting on the keyboard for the first time. I had him sitting in his carrier on the piano bench.

Joshua's first birthday was unbelievable. I insisted on hiring Mink, a world-renowned party planner. We decided on a circus theme, and Mink was able to reserve an ample space at Logan's amusement park. There was a live petting zoo, acrobats, clowns, jugglers, face painters, a piñata, and a bouncing house shaped like a big top.

There were about 55 kids in attendance, ranging from infants to 6 years old. The cake had three tiers. The top tier was a working merry-go-round that played Happy Birthday. It was all very exciting, but Joshua slept through most of the event.

The two of us were inseparable. I loved my son with everything in me. Melinda wasn't to be excluded, though. By this time, she'd put her career on hold and was a stay-at-home mom. I came home every day by 6 PM. We would have dinner together as a family. Then, one or both of us would give Joshua his bath and read him a story. After his story, we would gather around his crib and pray together as a family. Once Joshua was asleep, Melinda and I would have some time alone.

Besides taking care of Joshua, she spent a lot of time being the wife of a music executive. We attended dinner parties, industry events, and banquets. We entertained potential artists and out-of-town executives at our home for dinner or at exclusive restaurants.

One Friday, we sat down for dinner around 6:30 when I came home from work. Lewis had prepared Fettuccini Alfredo. Joshua was in his usual spot in his highchair next to me. After he finished his favorite meal, chicken nuggets and cut string beans, Melinda fixed him a bowl of applesauce. She placed the bowl on his tray, and he flipped it onto the floor. She got upset and yelled, "Joshua Alexander!" His little feelings were so hurt. He tightened his bottom lip, looked at me, and started crying.

Melinda was agitated, so I attempted to calm her down. I said, "Honey…"

"I know, Babe." She picked Joshua up out of his highchair and started comforting him. "Mommy's so sorry, Baby. I didn't mean to yell." She looked at me, "Daddy, can you get the applesauce off the floor? Joshua and I are going upstairs to run his bath."

I rubbed her shoulder and kissed Joshua on the forehead. "Yeah, Babe, I'll be up there in a minute."

Melinda bathed Joshua as we did nightly. I joined them in his room afterward. After putting on his pajamas, she laid him on his back in his crib. I hugged her from behind. "Why don't I play with Joshua for a few minutes and read him his story? I ran you a bubble bath with that aromatherapy you like."

"Gosh, a bubble bath sounds so good."

"I thought we might have some special alone time when you got out."

"I should have known you were up to something," she said as she left the room.

When I entered our master bath, Melinda was still in the tub. I started lighting the candles we always kept around it and said, "This isn't a relaxing bath unless you light candles and turn on the jets."

"What are you up to?"

I took off my clothes, switched to soft music, and dimmed the lights. Melinda moved forward and let me get in behind her. Then laid back on me and relaxed, "This is just what the doctor ordered."

"I thought a soothing bath would help. You were so short with Joshua."

"I know. I felt bad. Did you see Joshua's face?"

"Yeah, his feelings were hurt."

"I just had a rough day. He's been so cranky."

"Is he cranky, or are you frustrated?"

"He's cranky and whiney. I haven't had five minutes alone today, so I'm frustrated."

"How are you coming along with your book?"

"I haven't been in my office at all this week."

"That's not good."

"You're telling me."

"What do you need from me, Babe? How can I make it easier?"

"I love my baby, but I need a break. What I wouldn't give to put on some clothes and go out."

I held her tight. "I think I can handle that. Why don't we go on a date tomorrow night?"

"What about Joshua?"

"We have no shortage of sitters. Auntie Sheila could do it, or better yet, call your mom. I'm sure she would love to have him over all night."

"He's never spent the night away from us."

"I know, but he's a big boy now."

"He's one year old."

"Yeah, but he's my son."

"Oh, and that makes a difference?"

"His name is Joshua Alexander Bradford. The operative word is Bradford, who is to be interpreted as smart, intelligent, and genius."

"Oh, and my genes have nothing to do with his brilliance?"

I put my fingers together, "About this much."

She laughed, "He got beauty and brains from his mommy."

"Just tell me where I can take his beautifully smart mommy, and we'll make it happen."

"I want to go to dinner at one of my favorite restaurants, and then I want to go to a live play."

"I'll tell you what; call your mom and make the arrangements with her. Tomorrow morning, after breakfast, I'll take Joshua to the store so he can get a toy. Then I'll take him to your mom's. You go and do that thing you do with your fingernails and your feet."

"A Mani-Pedi?"

"Yeah, that thing."

"Not only am I going to get a Mani-Pedi, but I'm also going to get my hair done, and it's all on you."

"I think I can handle that, Miss Lady. What are you going to do for me?"

While running her fingers through my hair, she offered, "I'm going to let you keep a little of your money so you can do something with this."

"Okay, Babe. I'll get a haircut after I drop Joshua off. Then, we'll check into the presidential suite at a luxurious hotel of your choice. I'll take you to a play and your favorite restaurant."

The following day, when I woke up, Melinda was sleeping peacefully. I wanted her to rest, so I got up with Joshua. He and I went downstairs to the kitchen. I put him in his highchair with a cup of juice and started cooking breakfast. Before I finished, Melinda walked up behind me, hugged me around my waist, and said, "Good morning, sexy."

I turned my head and kissed her on the lips. "Good morning, sleepy. When I put Joshua back to sleep, I returned to the room, and you were knocked out."

"Why didn't you wake me?"

"I could tell you were tired by how hard you snored."

"I don't snore, and you know it."

"I know, Babe. I just wanted you to get some rest. I can't wait to go on our date tonight. It's good that Joshua is spending the night at his grandma's. We need to finish what we started last night."

"Bad, Daddy."

Melinda turned and started walking toward Joshua, "Your daddy is being naughty."

He started laughing.

I looked at him, "That's my boy." Joshua kept laughing, looking at me. "Daddy's going to take his boy and get him some toys today."

"Sounds like Daddy is feeling guilty about taking someone to Grandma's overnight. First, it was a toy. Now it's toys."

I blushed, "Yeah, but he's going to have to spend the night without us at the grandparents' sooner or later." I handed

Melinda the spatula, "Can you take the bacon out and fix the eggs? My son needs me." I picked Joshua up and started tossing him in the air. Joshua started laughing.

"Okay, Daddy, he's going to throw that orange juice up on you." Said Melinda.

After breakfast, the three of us dressed for the day. When we entered the garage, Melinda stood outside the car while I strapped Joshua into his car seat. She kissed Joshua and explained, "Mommy and Daddy will see you in the morning."

I walked Melinda around to the driver's side of her car and opened the door for her. I kissed my wife and said, "I'll see you in a little bit."

She offered, "Don't get stuck in the toy store."

I chuckled, "Nothing is too much for my firstborn." I hugged her and admitted, "I love you, woman. Now go. I'm looking forward to taking my beautiful wife out on the town."

Upon entering the store, my attention was immediately diverted to a Laker's bed. Joshua didn't have one at my mother-in-law's house, so I had to buy it. I was even able to get it delivered that day. My boy also had this thing for airplanes. They had two great planes my son had to have. After we left the baby store, I dropped him off at my mother-in-law's. I thought he would be anxious when I left him. He was so focused on his new airplanes that he didn't notice me when I left.

After getting my hair cut, I headed home. As I pulled into the garage, the mail lady, Miss Pam, was coming up the walkway. Once I emerged from the car, she greeted me, "Good afternoon. How's that baby?"

"That baby is a big boy now. He is at his first sleepover with Grandma tonight, so Mommy and Daddy can have a date night."

"Oh… Lucky grandma. He is so adorable." She handed me the mail, "Say hello to your wife for me, and you two have a wonderful evening."

I replied, "Will do," and flipped through the mail. There were a couple of bills, sales ads, and an illuminated envelope. The return address was from Phillips, Baker, and Taylor, a law firm in Atlanta. It was addressed to Anthony and Melinda Bradford.

I stood in my driveway, contemplating, "Why would Melinda and I be getting a letter from a law firm in Atlanta?" All of the reasoning I could come up with did not add up because any dealings with Atlanta would be pre-Melinda and Anthony. I momentarily reconciled, waiting for Melinda to come.

While unlocking the front door, I rationalized. "I'm being silly. This is addressed to Anthony and Melinda. It can't be anything serious. It's probably junk mail. I'm opening it."

My anxiety forwent a letter opener. Index finger did the deed. I quickly learned it wasn't junk mail as I unpeeled the pages. My heart dropped to the floor, and I was in disbelief at what I was reading. The devastation of the letter caused the airway in my throat to become obscured. Suddenly, the room seemed to be spinning. Making my way into our living room, I dropped my body on the sofa, completely shocked. There had to be some misunderstanding.

I am sitting with my head down and a letter in my hand. I vacillated between rereading the letter and thinking about when my wife was in Atlanta. I couldn't make sense of it. Melinda needed to come home and clear up this gross mistake, error, travesty, and impossibility.

The letter was from Trevon's attorney. He was claiming the paternity of Joshua. It even stated the date, time, and place where she and Trevon were together. He was also seeking visitation and offered to pay child support. I telephoned my wife. She answered, "Hey, Babe."

I solicited, "Where are you?"

"I'm just finishing at the nail salon. I'll be done in about fifteen."

"Hurry up."

"Babe, what's wrong?"

"I need you to get home."

"Is Joshua, okay?"

"Yes."

"You're scaring me."

"No one is hurt. I need you to come home right away."

"Okay, I'm leaving right now. I'll see you in ten."

Melinda came into the house and called out my name. Devastation from the news had me emotionally comatose. I couldn't move until she came in and cleared things up. In my mind, I thought, "There had to be a mistake. My wife would never do this to me. Why would Trevon do this?"

She moved throughout the house, calling out to me until she found me. Upon entering the room, she said, "Babe?"

Still unable to answer, I sat there with the letter in my hand and my head down. She got closer and ran her fingers through my hair, "Honey, what happened?

I kept my head down and handed her the letter. Her knees buckled as she read the letter, causing her to sit on the coffee table before me. She folded the letter and pleaded, "Let me explain."

I looked up in puzzlement. I couldn't believe what I was hearing. "What do you mean? Let you explain?" Anger replaced my shock. I stood up. "Are you telling me that letter is true? Is Joshua Trevon's son?" I stood looking at her for a second. My emotions were everywhere.

With her head and eyes slightly pointed to the ground, Melinda contemplated, "Give me a second."

"A second for what, Melinda? It's either true or not. Which is it?"

She sat and didn't say anything. Finally, she looked up at me. Her eyes answered in place of her mouth.

Brushing my hand down my forehead, I blurted, "It's true. Trevon, Melinda?" My voice grew louder. "I trusted you!" My anger was at ten, and I wanted to explode. I started pacing the room so I would not snatch her.

She cried, "Anthony, let me explain."

I came back and stood over her, "Explain what?! What can you tell me?!"

"I told you not to ever yell at me. You're making me nervous."

My voice grew even louder. "How do you think I feel?!"

She started crying harder, "Anthony, please."

I snatched the letter from her hands. "Is this what you did in Atlanta? How could you say you love me? How could you say you missed me when you were screwing around with him? You made a fool out of me."

"I only wanted you. Baby, please calm down and let me explain."

"Yeah, Melinda, explain how you came back with his baby and never told me."

"He raped me!"

"When did you decide that?"

"I swear he raped me."

"Melinda, you are a liar. I've got to go." I turned to walk away.

She grabbed the back of my shirt and pleaded, "Please don't leave me, Anthony. I need you. Let me explain."

I stopped and exhaled for a moment. Then I pried her hand from my shirt, "Let me go." I went over and leaned on the wall near the fireplace. My anger, hurt, and rage turned into tears. Like a waterfall, they fell from my eyes. I looked at her and calmed my voice, "I trusted you. When I committed to you, I gave you all of my heart. I kept nothing in reserve, and you betrayed me. I don't know if I can ever trust you again. Did you ever even love me?"

"How can you ask me that? You know I love you."

"I don't know anything. This whole marriage has been a lie."

"That's not true."

"Do you even know the truth?"

"I love you, Anthony."

"You're a liar, Melinda."

"I'm not. I swear."

"Were you with him?"

"Anthony, he raped me."

"Is he Joshua's father?" She didn't say anything. I continued, "Like I said, you are a liar, and this whole marriage is a lie."

She started crying hard, "Baby, please let me explain."

I held the letter up, "The letter is all the explanation I need."

I walked up very close to her. I wanted to put my hands on her like I'd never wanted to put my hands on a woman. I wanted to hurt her like she'd hurt me. At that moment, I hated her as much as I loved her. I lunged, "I was good to you. I guess I'm just not enough of a dog for you. I've got to get out of here. Where's my jacket?"

As I trotted up the stairs, she hollered, "Anthony, please... Don't do this!"

A family photo of my son, wife, and I stared at me from the top of the staircase. After busting through the French doors of our bedroom, I lay down on the bed and cried out to God. After a while, I washed my face and pulled myself together.

When I got to the edge of the stairs, I heard Melinda's voice from behind me whimpering. "Baby, wait."

I turned around and looked at her crotch down near the floor. It was so painfully pitiful. She pleaded, "Please let me explain."

"Melinda, I can't do this. I've got to go. I can't be here."

"You said you'd never leave me."

"You said you'd never be with another man."

"He raped me."

"So you say."

"He did."

"If that's true, why is it almost two years later, and you never told me?"

"I was afraid you wouldn't believe me and you'd leave me."

"I wouldn't leave someone who was raped, but I can never trust a liar."

"Please, believe me. I'm sorry I lied."

"I don't know what to believe. I've got to get out of here before I do or say something I will regret."

She stood crying, "Please, let me explain."

"You've had two years. You knew my son..." I stopped because, just then, I realized my son wasn't my son. I was starting to get choked up. I continued, "He meant the world to me. I've got to go." I turned and ran down the stairs.

The whirlwind of emotions in my mind had me all jacked up. First, I drove out to the Friendship Bell to clear my head. However, I quickly realized it was no longer my sanctuary or where I went to write music. It had become a place where my wife and I shared a precious memory. We celebrated there the weekend we found out she was pregnant with Joshua.

I got in my car and turned the radio to Beyoncé singing, "Listen." I quickly turned that off and put my head on the steering wheel.

Closing my eyes brought visions I didn't care to see. Trevon was sleeping with my wife. Once I shook that nightmare, I saw a vision of him picking my son up for a weekend visit. I laid my head back and tried to make sense of it all. But I glanced at the passenger seat where the love of my life sat every time we rode together. I started my car and drove until I somehow arrived at the studio. My dad was in his office. I came in and sat down and pleaded, "Dad, I need you."

"What's going on, Son? Why are you so upset? Are Melinda and my grandson, okay?"

"She betrayed me. Either she was lying, or she kept something important from me. Dad, she said, Trevon raped her.

Either she had an affair with him, or he violated my wife, and she didn't trust me enough to tell me."

"When did this happen?"

"When she went to Atlanta."

"A couple of years ago?"

"Yes, when she went to Tracey's wedding."

"That was two years ago. How did you find out?"

"A letter was sent to my house claiming Trevon slept with my wife. When I confronted Melinda about it, she said he raped her."

"You said she either lied to you or withheld some information."

"Yeah, she's lied about sleeping with him, or he raped her almost two years ago, and she didn't tell me."

"Had she ever been with him before?'

"No, she was untouched when I married her. She'd never been with anyone but me."

"She saved herself for marriage and then slept with another man? That doesn't make sense. Why do you think she didn't tell you he violated her?"

"She said she was afraid I would leave."

"Where did that come from?"

"She's been that way since King died."

"Have you given her a reason to cheat on you?"

"No, I've been good to her."

"Have you given her a reason to withhold information from you?"

"I don't understand."

"I'm trying to get you to understand your wife. It doesn't make sense that Melinda would lie. She loves you, and you treat her right. Think about it, Son. She wasn't with another man before. Why would she cheat now? Give her the benefit of the doubt."

"I know she loves me."

"Doesn't it make more sense that maybe she did withhold the information? As I recall, she was distraught the day she returned from Atlanta. I spoke to her briefly, and I'm sure I saw a scratch on her neck."

"I don't know what to believe."

"Sheila would know. She was with her that night."

"Sheila would have told me."

"You know your sister. Her mouth is like Fort Knots. She can keep a secret."

"I don't believe she would keep anything like that from me."

Dad sat on the desk in front of me, "When I think back about that night, she also said she wished she had not gone without you. Why would she say that?"

"I told her I didn't feel good about her going alone."

"Then why did you let her go?"

"She accused me of trying to put my foot on her head. It made me mad, and I didn't want her to think I was controlling, so I just let her go."

Dad contemplated, "You said she's afraid of you walking out on her? When did you find everything out?"

"This afternoon."

"What did you do?"

"I left the house."

"Does she feel like you're leaving her for good or for the night?"

"I didn't say."

"So basically, you validated her feelings. She felt you'd leave, and you did. Son, I'm not trying to take sides, but you didn't give her a fair chance. What's her story?"

"We didn't talk about it much. I confronted Melinda and didn't like her answer, so I left. I didn't know what to believe. Dad, she's the only woman I have ever been in love with. I gave her all my heart. I don't want her to take advantage of my love."

"Man, what's wrong with you? You're willing to throw your marriage away and haven't even heard all the facts. And now you're telling me you let pride get the best of you. You went against your spirit and let your wife on that plane. Why do you think your spirit warned you not to let her go alone?"

"I don't know."

"Pray about it and find out. You are responsible for your household. Sometimes, your decisions are not going to be popular. If God is tugging at your spirit, learn to listen and obey. God knew what would happen to her. Sounds like you need to be talking to your wife and not me. He grabbed my shoulder, "Go home and talk to your wife, Son. Stop being so arrogant and hot-headed. Give her a chance to explain."

"She hurt me, Dad."

"Put your feelings in your pocket until you hear her story. How do you think she feels? She got violated, and now her husband has just walked out on her."

"Devastated if what she told me is true."

"Air on the side of caution. Go talk to her."

"If what she said is true, I didn't protect my wife."

"Son, go home and deal with it. I didn't raise you to be a weak man. Marriage is a lifetime commitment. It takes work. Handle your business. You might bear some of the responsibility."

Advice taken: Innocent.
Advice ignored: Definite betrayal.

Chapter 22

Dream Merchant

On the way home, I was convinced I needed to listen to my wife. I pulled my car into the garage and entered the dark house. I went upstairs into our room and found Melinda lying in bed with her back to the door.

While I tried to find the words, she turned around and looked at me. Like a deer in headlights, I just stood there speechless. I wasn't ready. I just wasn't prepared for the conversation, not yet. I went downstairs, got myself a Coke, entered the studio, and sat at my keyboard. I put my fingers on the keys. There was no inspiration to be found. No melody or verse could convey my fractured emotions. I became a blank page of a song without a lyrics.

After a while, Melinda came into the room. She walked towards me with tears lightly flowing from her eyes, "I know you don't want me anymore."

I didn't know how I felt. I looked at Melinda, "Is that so?" I sighed.

She said, "Joshua and I are going to move out tomorrow. Maybe I can get my job back."

My heart hit the floor. I never thought I would hear those words from my wife's mouth in a million years. I looked down at the keys on the piano. She walked closer, and her tears flowed more rapidly, "I know you don't believe me, but he raped me. I'll get out of your life, and you won't ever have to see me again. I understand how you feel about me."

Softly, I asked, "What am I supposed to believe?"

"You obviously believe I had an affair."

I stood up and slammed the piano closed. Angrily, I asserted, "What would you believe?!"

"The same thing you chose to, I suppose. That's why I didn't tell you. I wanted it to just go away."

"This allegedly happened two years ago, Melinda. You told me he raped you today after I got the letter. What else were you supposed to say?" I sat and put my head down on the piano.

"It didn't allegedly happen, Anthony. It did happen. You don't have to believe me. I know the truth, and God knows the truth." She sat beside me on the piano bench and continued, "I can't believe you're treating me this way."

I turned to her, "I got a letter today that said Joshua isn't my son. It spelled out the date, the time, and the place my wife was with another man. My wife didn't tell me anything. What am I supposed to do, Melinda? All I ever asked of you is to be my wife, have my babies, and be honest with me. That's all gone. I don't have any of it. It was taken from me in one day. It's all a lie. We are a lie, Melinda."

"Anthony, I swear to you he raped me. If you want to break up, I'll go tonight. I can't change what happened. I love you more than anything in this life. I would never intentionally do anything to hurt you. I was wrong for not telling you. I'll give you that, and for that, I'm sorry. But I can't live here with you hating me."

I was so overwhelmed by what I read in the letter. Now my wife was talking about leaving me. That just made me angry. So, I went all in. "I never said I hated you, and I never said I wanted you to go. You brought up leaving. I've told you before. If you ever say you're leaving me, mean it."

At this point, she was completely overwhelmed with tears, "Fine, I'll go. I don't know what to do. I can't handle seeing you look at me the way you do. I already feel dirty and cheap. I don't need you to reinforce those feelings. I'm sorry your perfect trophy wife and world have a blemish. I can't change what happened. I feel horrible. I can't stand Trevon for violating me. Joshua is innocent. For his sake, I'll be better off by myself."

My emotions were everywhere. I hated seeing Melinda cry, but I was confused. I didn't want to see her leave, but I was too angry to ask her to stay. I didn't want to lose my son. I just wanted it all to stop. It was suffocating me. I got up and walked to the sliding glass door. With my back turned towards her, I admitted, "This really hurts." Tears were coming from my eyes. I had never been so hurt in my life.

She approached behind me, "Baby, please don't let Trevon do this to us. I never wanted anyone to touch me but my husband. Why would I do this now? Babe, he raped me. I didn't tell you because I couldn't make sense of what happened that night. I was scared I would lose you. Please, I won't withhold anything from you ever again. I love you."

I didn't want to lose my wife, but pain would not let me respond. My mouth struggled to open, but words would not form. So, I just kept looking out of the glass door.

Melinda stood momentarily and then said the worst words in the world, "I'll go. I just wanted you to know the truth."

At that moment, my world broke and shattered into pieces. What was I hearing? I was a fragmented man.

She left the room. I could hear her upstairs. Then I heard the entry closet open. I knew she was getting her coat. My wife was leaving me. I couldn't watch her walk out the door. I was still looking out the window when she returned to the room.

She was crying softly, "I'm leaving now. I'll arrange to have Kenny get my things, or I'll come while you're at work."

With my back still turned, I swallowed, "You're leaving me?"

"Isn't this what you want?"

"None of this is what I want, but I didn't have a say."

"Tell me what you want me to do. I'll do it because I don't know. We were supposed to always and forever be. I wasn't ever supposed to go back to my daddy's house. That's what you told my father, Anthony. There was no breaking up. Divorce wasn't an option. You weren't ever going to leave me. There was no contingency plan. Baby, I don't have a plan B. But I don't want to be here anymore, not like this. It hurts too bad. I can't stand the way you look at me."

She started towards me, bawling, "What do you see when you look at me? A tramp? What? Tell me. Get it off your chest. You can't even look at me, can you?"

I didn't want to look at her because I felt I would break down and she would see me as weak. I didn't like her putting words in my mouth. I was so confused. I loved her so much. I hated her. I was angry at her. I turned around quickly and yelled, "Stop, Melinda! I can't do this right now." Then I walked away and went into the kitchen. The next sound I heard was the door closing behind her.

That night, I cried like a baby. My wife's scent permeated the room. Yet, she did not wake up in bed next to me.

Morning time was not introduced by Joshua hollering "Daddy" from his crib. I had no reason to get up, get my son, put him into our bed, and we all lay together. There was no need for Lewis to cook breakfast. My family was not there to eat together, and I wasn't hungry for food. The hunger and thirst I was experiencing were being quenched with hurt, pain, and self-pity.

The house's silence got too loud and was too much for me to bear. The only thing I could hear in the echoes of my mind was a song I loved to listen to when I was little. "Dream Merchant" by New Birth. Our house was not a home without the residents who were my family. Arrogance and pride would not let me humble myself or forgive. It would not let me go and get my wife and the son I thought shared my blood. With each passing moment, it became harder, and so did my heart.

I got up and went into the office. Anita and Tyra were in the lobby. I walked past without making eye contact. Anita said, "What's going on?" I kept walking until I got to my office.

Anita came in behind me and asked, "What happened? Are you okay?"

"I don't want to talk about it. I need to get away for a couple of days. Can you get the keys to the company condo? Tell Jack I need about a week."

"What should I do with your calls?"

"I won't be taking any."

"Will Melinda be going with you?"

"No, I'm going alone. I won't be taking Melinda's calls either."

"Anthony, what's going on? Is everything okay?"

I snapped, "Anita, I said I don't want to talk about it!"

She raised her hands, "I'm sorry. Enough said," and walked out.

About 20 minutes later, Tyra came in and put the keys to the condo on my desk, "Miss Anita told me to give these to you. She also said all the arrangements have been made."

Still trying to make sense of things and searching for answers, I placed a phone call. Angie answered, "Hey, Anthony. I haven't heard from you in a while. The last time we talked, you were about to get married."

"Yeah, you're right."

"How is the lucky lady?"

"She's good."

"What's on your mind? I sense something in your voice."

"There is one other thing I needed to know."

"What is that?"

"The last conversation I had with Tangi, she said she was pregnant."

Angie sighed, "Did she really?"

"I have had difficulties getting past that."

"I'm so sorry. Anthony, that was just Tangi playing games and trying to manipulate you. She couldn't have any children. She had a cancerous tumor in her ovaries when she was sixteen."

This hurt me even more. I had to realize that not only was Joshua Trevon's son but there was also a strong possibility that I could not father children. My hope was shattered, and I had nothing left.

Still needing to make sense of things, I left work and headed to my parent's house. Sheila was the only one there. That was fine because it was her I wanted to see. She was in her room, lying across the bed. She turned over when I came in, "What is going on? Everyone is looking for you. You weren't at dinner yesterday, and Melinda is at her mom's. What happened, Ant?"

I sat on the bed, and I kept my head down. "Sheila, I need to know what happened in Atlanta."

"What do you mean?"

I'm going to ask you again, Sheila. I know, you know. What happened with my wife in Atlanta?"

"What is your problem, Ant? I don't appreciate you rolling up in here interrogating me. Acting like I'm hiding something."

"You are. Something happened to my wife, and you knew all about it, and you didn't tell me."

"It wasn't my responsibility. It was your wife's."

"So, you do know about it?"

"All I know is she said that fool raped her when she was in Atlanta."

"Why didn't you tell me?"

"She said she was going to."

"You're my sister. You should have had my back and told me."

"She is my sister and my friend. She asked me not to. She said she was going to tell you when you came off tour. Why is this coming up now?"

"None of your business."

"Just like when she told me. It was none of my business then, and it's none of my business now. Like I said, that was between you and your wife. Leave me alone."

Sheila and I went all in, yelling back and forth. She went over to the desk and pulled out a USB drive. Do you want to know the truth? You can see it in the lights. Everything is on here." She threw the USB at me and said, "Now get out of my room!"

I picked it up and put it in my pocket. Before I left, Sheila had sat on the bed and was crying. I asked, "How could you keep something like this from me?" Then I walked out.

From there, I took a drive to the company cabin. A couple of days were spent not sleeping, feeling sorry for myself, reflecting, and then I prayed.

When I finally fell asleep, I had another dream. Melinda was sitting on the bed crying. Upon my entering the room, she started screaming, help me, Anthony! I need your help! He's hurting me! She stood up, started hemorrhaging, and passed out. I woke up panting, sweating, and crying as I usually did when I had these dreams.

After rolling on my knees and praying, I was moved to pull out my laptop and put in the USB. I no longer needed to feel sorry for myself when I held the images before me. My love, the woman I adored, my wife, was pictured all battered, bruised, and scratched up.

The proof that my wife had gotten raped was right in front of my face, and it was undeniable. Conviction grabbed me by the throat and yelled in my face loudly, "YOU ARE WRONG!" I wept like a baby, realizing my selfishness, arrogance, and stubbornness aided in my wife being violated.

Next, I viewed pictures of Joshua. I thought about the bond he and I had. At that moment, I was motivated to get home quickly.

Suddenly, there was a knock on the door. I opened it. Behold, it was Tanya. I said, "What are you doing here?"

"I thought you could use some company."

"How did you know I was here?"

"A girl has her ways. Are you going to invite me in?"

"No, I'm not."

She stepped close to me, "Are you serious, Anthony?"

"I'm dead serious. This isn't happening. I'm about to go home to my wife and son."

"You mean I drove up here for nothing?"

I walked up close to her, "What did you think was going to happen?"

"I know things aren't working out for you at home."

"Are you serious right now, Tanya?"

"What?"

"I told you I was in love with Melinda when you and I broke up. I didn't get with her to spite you. But I just realized you are so self-centered and narcissistic that you can't see it. I don't know how you found out I was here, but... never mind."

"Never mind, what?"

"At the end of the day, I liked you. I thought you were beautiful, intelligent, and classy. We didn't work out. This stunt was a blatant disrespect to me, my wife, and my marriage."

I acted like she wasn't even there. She watched as I proceeded to get my things together and put them in the car. I pulled off and left her standing on the porch.

On the way home, I wanted to make some calls. I didn't bring my cell, so I used the phone in my car to check my messages. There were a couple from my wife, one from my dad scolding me, and another from Tanya, which I deleted immediately.

The ride home to get to my family was much farther than the ride away from them. Anticipation permeated my spirit as I longed to get to my wife and sort things out. When I arrived, Melinda's car wasn't at her mom's, but my mother-in-law was pulling into the driveway. Surprisingly, my little man was in the backseat. His face lit up, and he uttered, "Daddy," when he saw me. I noticed he was warm when I got him out of his car seat.

I kissed and hugged my mother-in-law, "Hey, Mom."

"How are you doing?" She asked.

I said, "As well as to be expected."

"I understand."

Holding Joshua, I forged, "Mom...."

She intervened, "You don't have to say anything. I love you..."

"I love my wife and son. This is just hard."

"I know it is. But you two can work this out."

"I want to. I don't want to lose my family, Mom."

She touched my face, "And she doesn't want to lose you either. As for our little man here, I have been trying to reach mommy."

"I noticed he had a fever when I picked him up."

"I just got him from school."

"School?"

"Yes, he's in school. They said they had been calling Melinda, but she's not answering, so I picked him up."

"I will take him to the doctor. I'll call Melinda and let her know. Tell her she can find us at home if you talk to her before me."

She stood smiling. I inquired, "What, Mom?"

"That's right, Son. Get your family." I hugged her and left.

A couple of hours later, Melinda came into the house and called out to me. I didn't answer because I didn't want to hurt Joshua's ears. My wife finally found us in the bathroom, where I was bathing him. She sat on the side of the tub opposite from me and said, "I'm sorry. I was at an appointment. I couldn't have my cell on. What did the doctor say is wrong with him?"

Still feeling a little awkward, I didn't look at her. "Joshua has an ear infection. He doesn't need to go back out in the night air. Can you get his pajamas ready?"

"Yeah, sure."

I took him out of the tub and brought him into his room. We followed the nightly routine. I sat in the rocker and started reading Joshua a story. Melinda went into our bathroom. I exhaled when I heard her in the shower. I went into our bathroom, thinking we could talk. She was putting on her pajamas. I said, "What's going on?"

"I need to spend the night. I'd be worried sick if I left without Joshua. I'll sleep in his room if it's okay. When he gets better, we'll go."

I thought, "We're still here." I sighed with frustration, leaned on the wall, and covered my eyes. Melinda walked past me and went into Joshua's room. I went and sat on our bed. She came back into the room. I opened, "I thought we agreed Joshua wasn't going to daycare?"

She walked in front of me, "He was at daycare because I had a couple of appointments. I'm trying to get my job back. I didn't know what else to do."

"He can stay here with me. I don't have to go back to work until Monday."

She stepped closer. I was melting. I looked into her eyes as she pleaded, "If I could take all this back, I would. I know I hurt you. I'm so sorry. I don't know how to fix this. What do you want from me?"

I melted, "I want my son to stay home and my wife in my bed. I rubbed her face, "Baby, we can work this out."

Tears fell from her eyes, "I thought you didn't want me anymore."

I pulled my wife to me by her waist, "I will always want you. I love you so much."

She fell into my arms, "I love you, too."

Stroking her hair, I said, "I think it's time we talk."

I got up, took her by the hand, and led her downstairs to the den. We sat on the couch side by side. She leaned her head back and looked at me. "Where have you been, and why is Tanya calling again?"

"I have no idea why Tanya is calling. I haven't spoken to her in over a year. I saw the missed calls but didn't call her back." I looked at Melinda. "I went to the company's condo. I needed to clear my head. It hurt to the core to find out Joshua was Trevon's son. Then, to think of him touching you in any way made me so angry. When you left me, Baby, it sent me there."

"Why did you let me leave?"

"I didn't want you to leave, but I was hurting too bad to ask you to stay."

"I didn't want to leave. But I didn't want to stay here feeling like you hated me."

I kissed her on the forehead and said, "I was angry, but I could never hate you."

"I'm sorry I didn't tell you."

"Was I so unapproachable that you felt you couldn't?"

"No, for weeks, I just felt cheap and dirty. I just wanted to forget it happened."

"The other night, I was only thinking about myself. How bad I was hurting and what I lost. Deep down, I believed you when you told me he violated you. Reality set in while I was at the lake house this morning. When I saw the pictures Sheila took, I forgot all about me. It hurt me to the core when I saw what Trevon did to you. All I wanted to do was get to you and hold you. I got in my car and went to your mom's house to get you and my son and bring you home. Then I found out he was sick. I felt like I didn't protect my family. Melinda, I love you and Joshua so much. I don't care what DNA says. He is my son. Trevon can't have him. I'm so angry. This man violates my wife and thinks he will be rewarded with my son. I want to hurt him so badly."

"I know how you feel, Anthony, but Trevon isn't worth it. We'll get through this."

"I spoke with Craig Hawthorne, one of my frat brothers, today. He is an attorney. We're going to meet with him on Monday evening. I'm not saying it will be easy, but we will fight this. He can't have my family."

"We can't let him or anybody come between us."

I slipped my arms around her and, with tears in my eyes, "I'm sorry I hurt you with the things I said the other night about you being with him. I should have known better. I was hurt, angry, and feeling guilty. The way I acted was inexcusable."

"Why were you feeling guilty?"

"I didn't feel good about you going to Atlanta alone. I knew God was telling me not to. You talked about me putting my foot on your head. My ego said, let her go. I should have stood for what I knew was right. It was my responsibility to protect you. I could have come to Atlanta and at least spent a few days. Because of my ego, my wife was violated."

"Anthony, I didn't have to go. I made that decision alone, without your blessing. I want to forget about Atlanta. We'll get through this if we have each other."

"The other night when you referred to yourself as my trophy."

She snickered, "Oh yeah, that."

"You are my trophy. Not in the way you said it. I planned and worked hard for the perfect wife and the mother for my children. I believe God rewarded me with you and my son. I could not have asked for a better wife. God knew just what I needed. I'm crazy about you, Lady. I've accepted the fact that I may not be able to get you pregnant. I'm blessed to have Joshua, even if he's not my flesh and blood. He's a part of you, and that's enough."

My wife offered, "You can get me pregnant."

"Melinda, we've tried for months and nothing."

"Anthony, there is something."

"What?" She placed my hand on her stomach. I turned to her, "What are you saying?"

"That appointment I told you about was with Dr. Burrows. I found out today. I'm eight weeks pregnant, and there is no question about who the father is this time.

I was so happy! This news could not have come at a better time.

Advice taken: Innocent.
Advice ignored: Betrayal.

Chapter 22

Back Stabbers

This chapter played out like The Ojay's "Back Stabbers." Monday morning, I went to work. I was looking for Anita, but she had not arrived. Tyra was there, though. I said, "Tyra when Anita comes in, can you have her come immediately to my office?"

"Is everything okay?" She asked.

Shaking my head, I said, "Can you just have her come into my office, please?"

I hadn't planned to stay for the day, so I was gathering some things to take home when Anita arrived. She opened, "Hey boss, nice to have you back. How are things?"

I said, "Have a seat."

I sat down, "Can you tell me why Tanya showed up at the lake house?"

"What?"

I reiterated, "Tanya showed up at the lake house. Can you tell me how she knew I was there?"

"I don't know how she found out, but I didn't tell her."

"I thought back. Since I have been with Melinda, things have gone wild. The See's Candy and the flowers were wrong.

My flights messed up when they involved her. My girl was stuck on the side of the road and broke down. She was told I wasn't here, and I was. The list goes on. I realize you have been sabotaging my relationship from the beginning."

She defended, "I know what it looks like, but you're wrong."

"You wanted me to be with Tanya."

"I did, but it was evident that you two wouldn't work out. Nonetheless, I would not jeopardize my professional career by telling your personal business. I have not and would not. Besides that, I have come to love your wife. I have never seen you happier, and I would not come between the two of you."

"Well, I just think we need to end things here."

"What are you saying?"

"I'm saying clear your desk. I can't have an assistant I can't trust."

"Anthony, please. You're making a mistake."

"The only mistake here was hiring you as my assistant."

She said, "All due respect, you didn't hire me. I was hired to support you and keep the mess from you. Why would I betray you? We have had a great working relationship. I promise I will get to the bottom of what happened."

"Anita, I may not be the one who hired you, but I do have the power to fire you. I'm done. I'm going home to my family. It's been real."

"After all these years, that's it?"

"Yep. I'm leaving, but you have the rest of the day to clear out. I will give you a few months' severance. Come by and get your package on Thursday. It will be ready."

When I got home, Melinda greeted me asking, "You fired Anita? Why?"

"She's been doing some trifling stuff. I had to let her go. How did you know?"

"She called me, sobbing and apologizing. Why didn't you tell me Tanya came to the lake house?"

"I didn't want any more complications amid what we were already going through. I handled it."

"So, you think telling me a half-truth isn't going to complicate things? Anthony, you told me you had not talked to her in a year."

"I hadn't. I only said a couple of words to Tanya at the lake. I didn't even let her in."

"What did she want?"

"What do you think she wanted?"

"Okay, I got something for her. Nonetheless, Anita wants to meet with you and Tanya on Thursday. She said if you still want her to go, she will."

I said, "She's going."

Melinda countered, "No, she's not."

"Excuse you?"

"Babe, you are being team too much right now. Anita has been with you and us through thick and thin. Stop being a hothead. You need to hear her side and see what Tanya's trifling behind has been up to."

On Thursday morning, Melinda and I got up and had breakfast. When I started getting dressed, so did she. I inquired, "Where are you going?"

"We have a meeting this morning, right?"

"We?"

"That's right. Did you not tell me you told Ms. Tanya to step off?"

"Yes."

"Yet she showed up at the cabin. I'm going to fix this once and for all."

"Melinda…"

"What?"

"Don't cause a scene."

"I'm not, Anthony. You know me better than that. But I am going to put an end to this mess. Miss Anita isn't going anywhere."

All I could say is, "Wow!" I actually found her strength very attractive. Melinda put on a very professional suit. She looked so good and conducted herself with class.

When we got to the office, Melinda walked past Tyra, sitting in front, and said, "Sweetie, can you join us?" She followed behind. Anita and Tanya were already in the conference room.

Melinda hugged Anita and said, "How are you?"

"As well as to be expected." Said Anita.

She looked at Tanya, "Ms. Cartwright, so glad you could join us. I was checking my girl out and loved every bit of it.

We all sat, and Anita started, "I just wanted this opportunity to clear things up about the lake. Tanya agreed to come. Well, I'll let her speak."

Tanya held, "Anita didn't tell me you were at the lake. I know you, Anthony. I knew where you were when you didn't return my calls."

I said, "So you're saying in the two years we dealt off and on, that one time you knew I went up there? I'm not buying that."

She roared back, "I don't have to lie, nor do I have to be here. You're trifling, Anthony."

Melinda chimed in, "Hold up! Hold up! Hold up!"

Tanya said, "Hold up. What? Little Girl."

Melinda facetiously grinned, "All due respect, Ms. Cartwright, let this little girl clear something up for you. My husband is mine to build up and we are one. Therefore, you will not now or ever disrespect or try to tear me or my husband down again with your derogatory retorts. Anthony Bradford is a handsome, intelligent, charismatic man. So, I could see how any woman would want him. Granted, you do have history, and you think you know him. However, your "knowing him" is limited to what a jump-off chick would know. However, you don't know me. So, Tanya, get and understand, if you step to my husband again, we will have a problem."

"Oh, Anthony, your little wifey is speaking for you now?"

I attempted to answer. Melinda touched my arm and lunged, "His little wifey will most certainly speak for him as it relates to you. Your days of calling my husband are over. Now, do you need my number?"

"No, I don't need your number."

"Well, make sure you lose his. Now, I'm going to let your past transgressions slide. We have a pressing issue today. It's one thing for you to set Anita up, but how could you use this baby to do your dirt."

I said, "Babe, what are you talking about?"

"Anita is not the one Tanya's been using to get to you. It's been Tyra. Most of the time, arrangements were made by her, not Miss Anita. When I was stranded, Tyra was the one who said you weren't here."

"Is that true, Tyra?"

Anita said, "Tyra, why would you do that?"

"I let Tanya get in my head."

"I didn't even know you knew, Tanya."

"I'm sorry, Ms. Anita."

"I'm sorry, too. You came in between my boss and me." Then she looked at Tanya and said, "We were supposed to be friends. And how dare you. Tanya, that was low. You would jeopardize my job?"

"I never said it was you."

"You didn't have to. There were implications. Now you're sacrificing this baby, who is trying to pay her way through college. I don't know what to think of you anymore, Tanya."

Tyra spoke up, "I'm sorry, Mr. Anthony."

I said, "I am too. Do you see the mess this caused? You messed up your career, and it almost cost Anita her job. You also inconvenienced my wife and me on more than one occasion. There are times you even put my wife in danger. That was foul. And for what?"

Melinda stood and walked over to Tanya. "Let me reiterate, Anthony Bradford and I are one. Don't ever try him or me again.

By the way, you can call me Clair." She kissed me and said, "Baby, I'll see you at home." Then she glanced at Tanya. "Our son is waiting." My girl put on her sunglasses and walked out. It was classic.

After Melinda left, Tanya tried to apologize to Anita and me. We both ignored her. After her failed attempts to get our attention, Tanya left shamelessly. A couple of hours later, I allowed Anita to terminate Tyra. To show our love and appreciation for Miss Anita, my wife and I sent her on an all-expense paid trip to Paris a couple of weeks later.

On Monday evening, Sheila came to the house to sit with Joshua, so my wife and I could meet with the attorney. When Sheila got there, Melinda hollered for me. I came down the stairs with Joshua and handed him to his mommy. There was an awkward silence between my sister and me. She wouldn't even look at me. Finally, I opened my arms, "So, can your brother get a hug?"

Sheila sighed and fell into my arms. I hugged her and kissed her on the forehead. "I'm sorry. I was in a terrible head space, and I took it out on you. Will you forgive me?"

While pouting, my sister said, "I don't know. It's going to cost you."

"What's it going to cost me this time, Sheila?"

"A dinner date with my brother and another hug."

I said, "I could do that."

There were no long-term issues between my sister and me. The sibling bond Sheila and I had built over the years sustained the temporary turbulence that the situation caused. It only served to make us stronger.

As Melinda lies on my bare chest, I lay in bed staring at the swirled patterns on the ceiling, not sleeping. I had been awake most of the night tossing and turning.

It was only interrupted by me getting up intermittently, looking in on Joshua as he slept. Wow, my boy was the joy of my life. It was hard to believe he was just past a year old. I also had gut-wrenching thoughts of Trevon slapping, drugging, and raping my wife. The man in me yearned to beat him senseless until he was bleeding profusely, and then I'd choke his neck until he was within inches of losing his life. He will be begging me to let him go like she must have been begging him to stop. Deep down, the blackening of my heart required Trevon to feel the aches, pains, and defenselessness my wife owned when he violated her. I also strongly desired him to wear the mantle of guilt and shame she wore for months after he dishonored and abused her virtue.

The man of God in me struggled to find answers. I throw out questions and grasp at straws as the answers disintegrate in my mind. Why has the God I love so much and served faithfully allowed this to happen? Is this karma for the many women I've hurt, Tangi, Tanya, and those who remain name-less? But you see, God, I cleaned up my life as promised. I've gone to church faithfully. I made financial provisions for my wife and kids before I knew them. I lived celibate for three years. Even when I fell off the wagon, I got back up and started over again.

When you gave me Melinda, I loved her as I told you I would. I respected her boundaries and obeyed her late father's wishes. I didn't make love to her until the time was right. I protected her as best as I could. Okay, God, I get it. I didn't protect her well enough. Is that it? You're punishing me because my pride and arrogance let her take that plane to Atlanta alone. Is it because when I had the opportunity to join her, my macho ego would not let me?

From day one, I was there at every prenatal appointment when I found out she was pregnant. After Joshua was born, I went to every one of his appointments. I stopped traveling with my work to be home every evening to have dinner with my family.

You know how much I wanted children and how long it took for Melinda to get pregnant. I love Joshua so much that I would lay down my life for him. Trevon now has the mitigated gall to claim he is my son's father. I should have known the bottom would fall out of our fantasy life. I have a job as a music executive. My wife is beautiful, intelligent, and an excellent homemaker. We live in a big, luxurious home on a hill, and I have a son to carry on my name. He raped my wife, and now I find out Joshua is his son. Let this bitter cup pass from me. Only you can curtail the tremendous anger I feel inside.

Melinda, Joshua, and I had taken a paternity test a few days prior. Afterward, She and I met with my attorney and frat brother, Craig Hawthorne. Together, we came up with a plan that we would present that afternoon. Melinda, Craig, and I met with Trevon and his attorney, Mr. Franklin, to develop a paternity agreement.

As I lay in bed thinking, I pull my wife close and hold her tight as I wished I had the night she was raped. While stroking her hair, I rubbed her face softly, kissed her forehead, and whispered, "I love you so much."

With her eyes closed, she grinned and said, "I love you too."

Looking into her face, I said, "Hey you. I didn't know you were awake."

While yawning she shared, "My eyes were just closed."

"How do you feel this morning?" I asked.

"I'm a little nervous about how things will turn out today." She exited the bed, pulled the covers back, and walked to the large window. I rose and followed behind her. She turned to me and said, "Anthony, what if they give him visitation with Joshua?"

I assured her, "They won't."

"How do you know?" Tears started rolling down her face. "I could never live with that. I don't know how I will handle being in the same room with him today. I haven't seen him since...." Her voice trails off, and she looks down.

I wrapped my arms around her waist, "Since he hurt you."

I sat on the baby blue and brown chair, gently beckoned her to sit on my lap, and offered, "Baby, Atlanta is three thousand miles away. Even if he lived here in California, I would never let him hurt you again."

"I didn't listen to my father. Trevon is a monster. I don't want my son anywhere near him."

"I would be lying if I said I'm not a little frustrated and concerned, but Craig thinks our plan will work."

"What if it doesn't?"

"No matter what DNA says, Joshua will always be my son." My wife offered, "I'm sorry for all this."

"This is not your fault. I don't want you worrying about Trevon or any of this." Switching the subject, I rubbed her stomach, and asked, "How is my baby girl doing?"

"She's not quite kicking yet, but I feel flutters."

"I'll get Joshua so we can pray. Then, if you feel like making some breakfast, I'll get him dressed so we can take him to your moms before the meeting."

She encouraged me when she asked, "Have I told you lately that you are the best husband and father ever?"

When we got to Craig's office, Trevon's attorney, Mr. Franklin, informed us that he was running late. Melinda dismissed herself to go to the ladies' room. My other frat brother Clarence, who worked with Craig, Craig, and me, was standing in front of the office when Melinda came around the corner from the ladies' room. She was winded, noticeably upset, and holding her stomach. My heart started racing, "What's wrong? Are you okay?"

She gasped, "I just saw Trevon."

"Did he say or do anything to you?"

"Yes. He tried to touch my stomach, and I slapped his hand away."

"Really, is that right? Okay. Where is he?" I inquired as my eyes cased the hallway.

"I think he went into the men's restroom."

I looked at Clarence and informed him. "Man, I've got to go to the restroom and get some water."

He responded, "I feel you. Why don't I come with you? I need to get some water, too."

Melinda grabbed my wrist and looked into my eyes, "Anthony, don't."

I grinned, "What are you talking about, Baby? It's all good. Trust me. I wouldn't do anything stupid." Then I opened the door to the office and said, "Go inside. We'll be right back."

Clarence and I went into the restroom. A man was in there with a navy-blue suit washing his hands. When he turned around, I knew it was Trevon because I had seen pictures of him. With my heart pumping double time, I approached him while Clarence stayed near the door. He looked in the mirror, turned around, and leaned on the sink, "You must be Anthony."

He was so smug. I wanted to hurt him so bad. I crossed my arms, offering self-restraint so that I would not punch him, and said, "That's right. I'm Anthony, Melinda's husband. We need to talk."

Trevon said, "I thought that's what we have lawyers for, but alright, Doc. Whatcha got?"

"Um, not Doc; I prefer Anthony. I'm good going through the lawyers regarding my son. My wife told me you upset her a few minutes ago. We need to draw some boundaries."

He looked over at Clarence and then back at me. I nodded at Clarence, signaling him to stand outside the door.

Trevon continued, "I don't know what she told you, but you know Melinda and I go way back. She was my girl right before you two hooked up. As a matter of fact, I think we were still together."

"No, Melinda and I didn't hook up when you were together. We started dating after you two broke up because you got Kristin pregnant. Isn't she your baby's mama?"

He stood up, "It appears your wife is my baby's mama too. How's my son?" Then, I believe he swung at me. Yeah, let's go with that. I'm pretty sure that's how it happened.

I grabbed his wrist, stopping him from hitting me. I hit him in the stomach, grabbed him by the collar, firmly posted him against the wall, and notified him, " I just wanted to talk. But you don't know how bad I want to put your head in the wall. I'm not going to do it because I promised my wife, I wouldn't get physical. So, don't make me hurt you. I'm about to let you go, but if you ever go near my wife again, you'll regret it. Consider this a warning."

I threw him towards the door. He came back towards me in a threatening manner. I kicked him in the stomach, and he hunched over. Then I grabbed him by his collar and took him to a stall, putting his head in the toilet and said, "You have a choice. I can walk away, or I can drown you. It will be our word against yours who started this."

"Alright, Man, it's cool."

By this time, Clarence had returned and stood behind us and warned, "Anthony, don't. I got this. I stood up, and Trevon stayed on his knees in front of the toilet. Clarence continued, "Get yourself together, Man, Melinda's waiting. Is there any blood?"

I shook my head "No" and fixed my clothes as I left the bathroom. Clarence caught up to me when I stopped at the water fountain. When I got to the office, I was still a little breathless. Melinda whispered, "Anthony, what did you do?"

I informed, "I used the bathroom and said hello to Tre-von."

Clarence looked at Craig and nodded. Craig and I shook hands and bumped shoulders. Then all entered the conference room. Trevon's attorney was already inside. Trevon came in and didn't say anything. He just sat across the table from Melinda and me, next to his attorney.

Mr. Hawthorne started, "This is a meeting to come to some decisions about Joshua Alexander Bradford."

Trevon exclaimed, "Let's start by giving him his father's last name."

Melinda looked at Trevon and shook her head with disbelief. Under her breath, she murmured, "Trifling."

Craig interjected, "Mr. Howard, my client does confirm that Mrs. Bradford was at the said place at the stated time and that there was intercourse. However, my client alleges you assaulted her. With that said, my clients are asking you to sign over your parental rights, and there will be no prosecution for the rape.

Mr. Franklin said, "I don't believe I know of any charges being filed."

Craig pulled out the photos of Melinda's bruises and put them on the table. "These photos were taken of my client the day after the assault. A bellhop at the Ambassador Hotel will testify that Mrs. Bradford never left her room. Another witness will testify that she picked Mrs. Bradford up from the Ambassador Hotel. She noted that my client was noticeably traumatized. Mr. Howard, is it my understanding that you are one of the managers at that hotel? This gave you access to the keys to my client's room. I also have a statement from the same bellman that you are the one who prepared my client's drink and had it delivered to her room. This would be how you drugged my client to rape her."

His attorney sat back, crossed his arms, and asked, "May I have a word with my client?"

After about twenty minutes, Mr. Franklin and Trevon returned to the room. We all sat at the table. Mr. Franklin stated, "My client has agreed to give up all parental rights to the minor child Joshua Alexander Bradford."

Craig interrupted, "We take our offer off the table." Melinda and I looked at Craig. He nodded at me. I'm sorry, Mr. Franklin, but your client has no rights to the minor child Joshua Alexander Bradford. I just reviewed the paternity results. As you will see," he passed the results to Mr. Franklin, "It has been determined, with 99.99% certainty, that Mr. Bradford is the father of the said minor. However, I will meet with my clients and let you know how we intend to proceed with criminal charges.

We decided not to press criminal charges against Trevon for several reasons. However, he was terminated from The Ambassador Hotel. They gave Melinda a sizable settlement out of court.

After Trevon got wind that I wrote a tell-all book, he decided to write a book from his perspective, Innocent Betrayal: Trevon's Story. There is nothing innocent about that dude, but then again God's grace is sufficient.

Karen and Melinda finally renewed their friendship. Karen also wrote a book. It helped her get past her issues and become a good wife to Michael and mother to Aaron and Michael Jr. It also clarified the struggles that led to her promiscuity and alcoholicity.

As you see, my life wasn't always easy, and I wasn't al-ways the man I am now. Looking back at my story, you will find my arrogance, short temper, and lust caused hurt and pain to me and others. You don't have to go down the same road. My brothers and sisters, every day, there are indeed new mercies. But who says you are going to have a tomorrow? I encourage you to get your life right today.

Advice taken: You will remain innocent.
Advice ignored: You will get betrayed.

About the Author

Cynthia Valentine is the owner and CEO of Destiny Publishings' LLC. She graduated Magna Cum Laude' from Georgia State University with two degrees, Journalism and Professional Writing, Journalism with a concentration on Broadcast, and she minored in speech. In addition, she studied for two years under renowned playwright Dr. Shirlene Holmes. Cynthia has over 20 years of acting, writing, and theatre experience.

On the film side, Cynthia produced segments of the talk show "Dropping Gems." She produced three media projects for the legendary Bill Duke, including an animated film, "The Journey." Under her company label, Valentine has two upcoming shows, "My Glory, My Story," "Cynthia Valentine Unleashed," and other film projects.

Her professional stage play "Nativity Unleashed" debuted in August of 2017 to a sold-out audience. The play did two runs in 2018 and a short tour in 2019. She is launching new "Unleashed" stage plays, "Calvary Unleashed; I'm Not Going to Nail Jesus to The Cross" and others.

Cynthia is the author of two poetic and dramatic reading books, "Inspired by Destiny" and "If I Could Rewrite the Poetry," and a biography, "My Glory, My Story." To her credit are three poetic, spoken word albums, "Role Model," "Messed Up to be Blessed Up," and "My Heart Said I Love You.

As a publisher, Ms. Valentine has produced over 20 media projects, including books and albums. Cynthia offers public speaking and acting coaching, both virtual and in person. She also teaches writing to those who want to improve their writing skills or write a book. "Learn how to Write a Book While Writing a Book." For more information, go to her coaching page. For her complete biography, visit: **cynthiavalentine.com**

About
The Innocent Betrayal Series

Cynthia's novels are cutting-edge. Noting that African-American men are often cast in a bad light in books and films, she wanted to change the narrative. Therefore, her novels are written from a patriarchal perspective. In most cases her stories highlight positive characteristics of men. Even if the character isn't favorable, she still brings out their positive qualities. Cynthia says when she writes, as an actor, she can embody the character and become one with them. Therefore, she can write in that character's voice.

Anthony's Story is the second of the Innocent Betrayal Series. The others are "Innocent Betrayal Melinda's Story" and "Innocent Betrayal Trevon's Story." Originally, Innocent Betrayal was going to be one book. The book's fans, men and women, were so intrigued about the characters that they wanted more. Cynthia is currently working on the fourth installment of the five-part Betrayal series. "Innocent Betrayal Karen's Story." Next up is "Innocent Betrayal Kristen's Story." Could there be more? We shall see.

www.ingramcontent.com/pod-product-compliance
Lightning Source LLC
Chambersburg PA
CBHW070727280626
47159CB00023B/2848